Like Vanessa

Tami Charles

Charlesbridge

First paperback edition 2019
Copyright © 2018 by Tami Charles
All rights reserved, including the right of reproduction in whole or in part in any form.
Charlesbridge and colophon are registered trademarks of Charlesbridge Publishing, Inc.

Published by Charlesbridge
85 Main Street
Watertown, MA 02472
(617) 926-0329
www.charlesbridge.com

Library of Congress Cataloging-in-Publication Data
Names: Charles, Tami, author.
Title: Like Vanessa / Tami Charles.
Description: Watertown, MA: Charlesbridge, [2018] | Summary: It is 1983 and
    Vanessa Martin, a thirteen-year-old African American girl in Newark's public housing,
    dreams of following in the footsteps of the first black Miss America, Vanessa Williams;
    but with a dysfunctional family (mother in jail, father withdrawn, drunken grandfather,
    secretly gay cousin) the odds are against her—until a new teacher at school organizes
    a beauty pageant and encourages Vanessa to enter.
Identifiers: LCCN 2016053961 (print) | LCCN 2017022713 (ebook) |
    ISBN 9781632896070 (ebook) |
    ISBN 9781580897778 (reinforced for library use) |
    ISBN 9781580898997 (softcover)
Subjects: LCSH: Williams, Vanessa—Juvenile fiction. | African American girls—
    New Jersey—Newark—Juvenile fiction. | Beauty contests—Juvenile fiction. |
    Dysfunctional families—New Jersey—Newark—Juvenile fiction. | Urban schools—
    New Jersey—Newark—Juvenile fiction. | Self-confidence—Juvenile fiction. |
    Nineteen eighties—Juvenile fiction. | Newark (N.J.)—History—20th century—
    Juvenile fiction. | CYAC: Williams, Vanessa—Fiction. | African Americans—
    Fiction. | Beauty contests—Fiction. | Family problems—Fiction. | Family life—
    New Jersey—Newark—Fiction. | Schools—Fiction. | Self-confidence—Fiction. |
    Newark (N.J.)—History—20th century—Fiction. | LCGFT: Historical fiction.
Classification: LCC PZ7.1.C4915 (ebook) | LCC PZ7.1.C4915 Li 2018 (print) |
    DDC 813.6 [Fic] —dc23
LC record available at https://lccn.loc.gov/2016053961

Printed in the United States of America
(hc) 10 9 8 7 6 5 4 3 2
(sc) 10 9 8 7 6 5 4 3 2 1

Display type set in Wanderlust Boho and Avaline Script Bold
Text type set in Adobe Caslon Pro
Printed by Berryville Graphics in Berryville, Virginia, USA
Production supervision by Brian G. Walker
Designed by Susan Mallory Sherman

"Closed mouths don't get fed."

—Marie "Nana" Carlisle (circa 1986)

Dearest Grandmother,

I didn't understand it then, but I get it now.

Rest easy,

Mik-Mik

September 17, 1983

America

All them lights, bathing her white, washing away
  the slightest trace.
Miss America they call her, smile so bright,
  eyes shut tight, brand-new day.
Everybody talking 'bout history'll be made;
  we'll win the race.
Really? I say, 'cause if it were me,
  would they feel the same way?
In the land of the free, home of the brave,
  we'll bust up that long-shut door.
Course it'll be a light-and-bright,
  two-shades-from-white,
least—America ain't the America we know from before . . .

Dear Darlene,

  Miss America's coming on tonight. You ready?

    —Nessy

Fifty Stinkin' Years

Pop Pop gave me my very first "Darlene" eight years ago and a brand-new one every year after that—custom-made of pressed, dried wildflowers spanning every color of the rainbow. Most kids my age would call Darlene a diary, but she's much more than a place to write stupid lists of the cutest guys in eighth grade. Darlene's my chill spot: a place to share the lyrics in my head, the words crawling through my bones, the latest gossip running through Grafton Hill. Today's hot topic? Miss America.

Pop Pop and I got a bet going for this year. Miss America's never crowned a black girl . . . *ever*. And that pageant's been going on every year since 1933! Way I see it, the powers that be have no plans whatsoever to pick a girl who looks like me. Let Pop Pop tell you: everything's gonna change this year.

Watching Miss America is our little tradition. Each of us eyeing the screen, clutching onto a memory long gone. His memory is of time with his daughter, my mother. Honey-eyed, vanilla-coated, lullaby-singing angel. Him pretending that on this very day, every year, he could have a piece of his little girl back through me. And me watching alongside Pop

Pop. My memory: pushing, hoping, forcing myself to remember her. To remember what having a mother feels like. To, even for a second, drown myself in her beauty even though I don't look a thing like her.

I pull out the hot comb, pomade, and all my favorite hair bows. Pop Pop lets me straighten and braid his hair while he nurses a coffee cup of whiskey. Me pretending I'm the one getting my hair done, and Mama's doing it. Pop Pop pretending the whiskey's a cure-all. A magic potion in all of its bittersweetness, helping him remember too.

The hot comb glides through with ease. My grandfather has some silky, long, curly hair. Says he gets it from his Cherokee side. That Cherokee blood must have skipped over me.

Halfway through the show, two black women make it to the top ten: Miss New York, Vanessa Williams, and Miss New Jersey, Suzette Charles. They're both so beautiful—black, the light-skinned and curly-haired type like Pop Pop and Mama. Maybe they got some Cherokee in them too.

"This is it, Nessy!" Pop Pop says before they start to announce the top five. "This is our year. Get on in here, TJ, we 'bout to make history!"

My cousin TJ comes running into the living room, feather boa in one hand, pen and sketch pad in the other. He wraps the boa around my neck, saying, "Here you go, Miss America!" Then he plops down on the couch and starts drawing pageant gowns like mad.

On the fuzzy black-and-white screen, Gary Collins starts announcing the runners-up. And just as Pop Pop predicts, this is the year black women make history at the Miss America pageant. Because not one but *two* of us are standing there, waiting to be announced as the new winner. My fists clench with the strength of an army ten thousand strong, hopes flying sky-high, anxiety drowning in my chest. Would the Miss America pageant even let a black girl win? Give girls like me the tiniest piece of hope that, yes, black is beautiful? Even if it means that they'd start with the light-and-bright, two-shades-from-white kind? Because if so, then that means that one day girls like me—the darkest of black—could be seen as pretty too.

Suzette Charles takes the first runner-up spot. And at this point, I'm thinking, *Okay, we came close enough. We ain't gonna see a day like this for probably another fifty years.*

"And your new Miss America is . . . Vanessa Williams!" Gary Collins shouts into the microphone.

And I swear I just about lose my mind!

The spotlights lower onto Vanessa's bad-to-the-bone, silver-and-white, one-shouldered gown. The audience thunders with applause. After the crown is placed on her head, she takes her ceremonial walk down the runway. And she's working it too. Hips swaying. Teeth all shining. And she's got that Miss America wave down pat. I stare at the screen. Stare real long and hard. Vanessa Williams's face fades away, and Mama's sets in. I mean, really, they could be twins.

It's like Mama can see me through that television. Right through me. And the way she's looking, it's like she's making a promise. She'll come back some day. When things are right.

When all the broken pieces are mended back together. We'll go back to the time when we were us—the Martins—minus the booze, minus the stares, minus the whispers.

These days, you might as well call us the left behinds. We're the ones that were left behind the day Mama walked out all those years ago. That was when everything changed: the rest of the family forgot about us, Pop Pop turned to booze, Daddy's spirit up and died, and we moved to the projects of Grafton Hill. Daddy walked into that empty bedroom of his, soul black as night, and locked his door. And I ain't seen the inside of that room or his heart ever since. Only comes out to go to work, which can be anytime, day or night.

Things will get better again. Mama's voice whispers through the television, sweet like honeydew in summer. A shiver courses through the arch of my back.

I'm soaking in Mama (well, Vanessa) through that screen, as if she sees me, the real me. It's like I know I gotta do something to make everything right. For everybody. All I gotta do is find Mama. But how?

I'm sitting on our brown shag carpet, boohooing like a dang fool, clutching onto Darlene, shoulders shaking worse than an earthquake. My prayers turn to words that I hold on to, fighting to remember, so me and Darlene can talk about it later.

Next thing I know, I'm up off that floor, wiping away my tears, jumping up and down and clapping my hands. I'm clapping for Vanessa, clapping for Mama, clapping for me. All the years I've watched this pageant and not once did I see a black girl win. Nobody ever did. Not before tonight. I know I'm never gonna forget this. I start prancing around the room, doing the Miss America wave. Close my eyes real tight-like. Picture that Miss America crown on Mama's head. Picture it on mine too. Picture Daddy smiling again, wrapping his big old earthy hands around Mama's tiny little waist, like he used to do.

Pop Pop pulls me close to his chest, his liquor-laden scent stinging my nose. "That's gonna be you one day, Nessy. Your singing is just as good as Vanessa Williams's. And Miss America's even got the same name as you. It's meant to be, baby girl!"

"Yeah, and when you do make it to Miss America, you already know who's doing all of your styling! I won't even charge you full price!" TJ jokes.

And in that moment I believe what they say could be true for me. That I could be like Vanessa Williams. Long as it doesn't take no fifty stinkin' years. 'Cause I'm not sure me and Mama got that kind of time on our hands.

September 19, 1983

Unpretty
The world ain't so pretty
if there are no flowers,
no seeds to bear,
no sun to cast out the darkness,
no soil to fill it with promises,
to remind us
that like wings,
hope can take flight,
even among all things unpretty.

Dear Darlene,

I love that part in *The Bluest Eye* that talks about the soil being bad for certain types of flowers. Pecola thinks that's why the seeds won't grow in her town, among the garbage. That maybe it's just too late. You think Toni Morrison's ever been to Newark? 'Cause there ain't nothing but garbage here too. Garbage on the streets. In those needles the dopeheads drop in the alleys. In the elevators that carry me to the eighth floor of my apartment in Grafton Hill. Except there ain't no flowers in my 'hood. Just that fake, plastic, general-store-looking sunflower Pop Pop puts on the windowsill. Trying to pretend like our crib is some penthouse out in Beverly Hills. But everybody knows you can cover up caca with perfume, but after a while it's still gonna stink.

    —Nessy

Not Even Daddy Calls Me That

It's ~~sixth-period chorus~~, and as usual I'm not the only one ignoring the teacher. The scattered noises of gossip and hip-hop rhymes battle it out against the melody Mrs. Walton's playing on the piano.

Eighth graders: 35; Mrs. Walton: 0.

My seat is in the back of our dungeon-like music room, behind the chaos, behind Tanisha, who's lost herself in her sketch pad. I sink into my chair, placing *The Bluest Eye* on top of Darlene, and reach for my next read, *I Know Why the Caged Bird Sings*. Pop Pop says he got it special for me because I'm his little songbird. I turn to the first page, ready to lose myself in the words. Ready to pretend I'm anywhere but here.

Mrs. Walton stops playing the piano, and suddenly I feel a pair of icy eyes hawking me. "Vanessa Martin, school's been in session for three weeks now. You think you want to join us sometime soon?"

Tension tiptoes up my spine. I sit up straight like I've been listening all along, which is a bald-faced lie. But of all the people in the room, she chooses to call on me?

Everyone turns and looks at me like, *What you gonna do*

now? Even Tanisha's staring me down, begging me to say something. Anything.

My lips turn to salt and start to quiver at the thought of being stared at. 'Cause even one second of attention is a second too long.

Everybody's got their rep in eighth grade. Mine? I'm like oxygen—you know I'm there, but you don't see me. I shut my mouth. I make good grades. And when the bell rings at the end of the day, I take my butt home, close my door, and dream of a place far, far away from here.

"Guidance made me take this class. Singing just ain't my thing." My voice is a loud whisper. It's enough to produce a few *oohs*. And once that starts, I know the teacher will have a point to prove.

Mrs. Walton slowly struts to my desk. The click-clacking of her heels echoes through the room. Her tiny frame grows larger as she walks toward me, looking like she's ready to start something. She's new to King Middle. Probably never taught a single black kid in her life. And like most white teachers they send here, she won't last the full school year. Especially once Junito Mendez orders the Latin Diablos to break into her car. That's tradition for every new teacher—black or white.

Mrs. Walton'll be here and gone within a season. Here to feed us with possibility. Blinded by her hope to make a difference. And before the school year ends, she'll bounce. But I'm used to that. I give her till Christmas.

"Tell me," she says, checking out the books that I've done a poor job of hiding. "What do you want to do with your life?"

My eyes rise up to the ceiling and stay there, glued to the dried-up wet-tissue bombs hanging on for dear life.

Lady, I don't feel like hearing one of those save-our-black-youth speeches. That's what I want to say to her, but I know that sass talk'll get me sent to the principal's office. And the last thing I need is Daddy coming up in here. Me and him got enough problems.

I hesitate before I speak, trying to think of what she'd want to hear come outta my mouth. Say I wanna end world hunger or find world peace. Teachers like that kind of talk. Plus, it seems like a safe enough answer to make her leave me alone until the bell rings. And then no one would have to know the real me I want to be.

"Nessy wants to be Miss America one day," spills out of Tanisha's mouth before I have a chance to lie. "And she can sing."

And suddenly I feel naked. Like straight-up covered in layers upon layers of fat and the whole class is looking at me like a tub of lard, naked.

Tanisha turns around and flashes me a cheesy smile, like she done said something good. My lips turn upward in a weak smile, but what I really want to do is smack her one good time upside the head.

Sometimes I think Tanisha ain't too bright upstairs. 'Cause if she were, she would remember that my Miss America dreams are private, for no one else to know about and make fun of . . . especially Curtis Dumont.

"Miss America? *Yeah, right!*" Curtis yells, with a toothy grin. Of course, all his homeboys laugh. I knew that was coming.

"Maaaan, please! *Real* black people don't win Miss America! That's for them high-yellow girls and white girls with light hair, light eyes, and little bodies," he shouts. "And last time I checked, yo' tar-baby self ain't got none of that!"

Curtis got a lot of nerve with his busted-behind teeth. The top row is doubled—yes, doubled, as in there are two complete rows of teeth. That probably solves the mystery of the missing ones on the bottom.

"Calm down now, everyone," Mrs. Walton squeals, but it falls on deaf ears.

Not stopping there, Curtis stands up with his fake-behind, wanna-be-gangster, rapper self and spits out a rhyme.

"Vanessa, Vanessa is wack, wack, 'cause Vanessa, Vanessa's too black, black!"

The whole class starts dying. Bust-a-gut, hunched-over, bladder-holding laughing. My skin grows too tight for my body. It wants to split open and empty everything inside out, but I ain't letting them see me like that. A knot the size of a baseball bulges in my throat, and here comes Tanisha, turning around, looking at me with those sad hazel eyes, mouthing, "I'm sorry."

Now would be a good time for the floor to open up and swallow me whole.

"I'm not playing with you guys. Settle down—now!" Mrs. Walton calls out, flailing her little arms like a helpless newborn bird. But her voice barely rises over the rumblings of the other students.

"She too dark!"

"Don't she know she too fat to be in a beauty pageant?"

"Man, that Miss America chick wasn't really black. She was mixed or something!"

"What talent would Vanessa do for a pageant? *Read?*"

It's like a dis-fest up in King Middle School today.

I sit at my desk, thinking about watching the pageant, anger boiling up inside me worse than a pot of collard greens on a Sunday afternoon. I might not ever make it to the Miss America stage, but it won't be because stupid Curtis says I can't.

I stand abruptly, my notebooks and pencils crashing to the floor. Curtis and his dumb friends laugh harder. Like a bolt of lightning slicing through the clouds, my words jolt them and leave them frozen in their seats.

"You can make fun of me all you want, but at least I got all my teeth. Looks like the top row ate the bottom row of yours!"

The class is singing, "*Daaaaaaang!*" as Curtis sits back in his chair all stupid-like, trying to come up with his next crack back. I'm standing there, towering over his scrawny little behind, wondering where this voice came from. Me, the girl who'd rather chew on her fingernails than talk in class. Me, the girl who just had her dreams put out there, only to be made fun of. Me, the girl who just shut down the class clown.

Tanisha slaps me a high five like I just won a championship basketball game. But I don't feel like a winner at all. Flames dart out of my cheeks. My all-too-small shirt has risen up yet again, and my stomachs are spilling out of my jeans.

"You gotta have talent to be in a Miss America pageant,

you idiot. And Nessy here got a voice straight from heaven. Believe that, boy!" Tanisha is up out of her seat now too, her long arms spread wide like eagle wings.

The class responds in true chorus fashion: "*Oooooooh!*" And someone hollers, "She served you, son!"

The bell rings, leaving Curtis no chance to crack back. The room empties, and Tanisha waits for me as I pick my things up off the floor. My whole body hovers there longer than it should. Truth is, ain't much left on the inside. Can't stand up if you ain't got no bones.

"You know, Vanessa, my daughter and I watched the pageant too. In fact, we watch it every year. A friend of mine volunteers for the Miss New Jersey pageant. She was able to get a few board members to help sponsor a pageant at King Middle this year. They're donating the crown, banner, the works! Flyers are going up tomorrow. Maybe you'll consider trying out?"

I rise up to see a much different face. The crunched folds around Mrs. Walton's eyebrows have softened.

Oh, now you want to be nice to me. Now that the circus act is over?

I could imagine Mrs. Walton glued to the television—for sure it's a colored one and probably big too.

"Humph." I shrug my shoulders, looking down at her. In this moment I'm painfully reminded of how big I am for my age.

"And I think you're right, Vanessa. You can absolutely go for Miss America in a few years, and why not? You're pretty and smart. Would be nice to actually hear you sing, instead of watching you hide behind a book. This is chorus, after all."

My cheeks grow warm again, and somewhere deep beneath the layers of black skin, I can feel them blush pink.

"Mrs. Walton," Tanisha interrupts, "Nessy sings in the church choir. You should come one—"

I poke her in the ribs. The last person I'd invite to church is Mrs. Walton. I could just see her sitting among all them black folks catching the Holy Ghost in the pews around her. That woman would stick out like a baby lamb in a field of lions.

"Don't listen to Tanisha." And with that, I grab my big-mouthed friend and drag her to next period.

I know Mrs. Walton's faking it anyway with all that talk. It's part of her job. To make girls like me feel like they could be somebody. To pretend like she's my friend when the truth is she'd probably dead-bolt her doors if I rang the bell to sell Girl Scout cookies. But still, she did ask me to be in the pageant. And she did call me pretty. As in lovely. As in gorgeous. Not even Daddy calls me that.

This Part of Town

The Sugarhill Gang is blasting on the corner as Tanisha and I walk home after school. Pop Pop says this rap stuff ain't nothing but the devil's music. But I kinda dig it. It's like the poetry Darlene and I share—like air and thunder rumbling and waves crashing, huddled together ready for combat, each one hoping to be the winner. Tanisha's dancing with the beat. She getting down too. Popping and gyrating her little body in ways that would get me slapped. Daddy would have my hide if he saw me dancing like that in public. I could hear him now: "That's how I lost yo' mama!" I still have no idea what he means. He never talks about her. Doesn't really let anybody else, for that matter, especially Pop Pop. And she's Pop Pop's own daughter.

Grafton Ave. turns into an open-air theater once the dismissal bell rings. To the left there's Raheem with his boom box balanced on his shoulder. He's rapping along with the Sugarhill Gang while his homeboys break-dance on pieces of cardboard. They're spinning on top of their heads and twisting their bodies in all kind of ways. To the right the *boricuas* are blasting that salsa music. Beats so fast, your hips would fall off if you even tried to move to it. But somehow they make it look so good. Héctor Lavoe's "Mi Gente" comes on the radio. And the *boricuas* go wild when the trumpet starts. "Ay, this brings me right back to Puerto Rico!" I hear Mrs. Mendez cry out. She owns the bodega on the corner and is the mother of the most popular girl at King Middle, Beatriz Mendez, and Grafton's number one gangbanger, Junito "El Diablo" Mendez. Mrs. Mendez is always dressed to the nines, and every guy in the neighborhood gets all spit-mouthed when they see her.

The two drastically different music styles fight to the last note. And in the mix of it all, the people of my 'hood are hustling. Hustling to catch the bus downtown to pick up a fresh new pair of Adidas. Hustling to get to their jobs. Seems like everybody who does have a job works at the auto-parts factory on the corner of Broad and Market. That's where Daddy makes cars for other people while he can't even afford one for himself. And some folks just plain hustle. Hustle anything. Dope. Reefer. Whatever it takes to pay the bills.

Once we pass the bodega, Grandmaster Flash pours in through the speakers. The lyrics to his song "The Message" are so true. Where I live is a real live jungle. Full of wildness. In the people. In the land. In the air. And I often wonder if I'll ever get outta here. Escape the drugs and the dark cloud that hovers over Grafton. Break free of the skin-seeping smell of people who are more than happy to be trapped here. Maybe go live someplace where there are real sunflowers and the kind of real sunshine that Toni Morrison talks about.

"That's my song, girl!" Tanisha screams, and she breaks out into a pop and lock when the second verse comes on. She tickles me in my ribs, and I can't help but laugh.

The boys on the corner look at her with needy eyes. None of them look at me like that.

"Come on, Nessy, you know you want to dance! I hope you ain't still tripping over what that fool Curtis said. Are you mad at me for saying the stuff about Miss America?"

"Man, forget Curtis." I smile weakly, adding to my lie. "And no, it's cool. I ain't mad."

On the outside, my game face is serious. Like unbroken concrete. But on the inside, I got a case of twinges in my heart and waves in the deepest pit of my stomach. When Tanisha walks through the door of her apartment, her mother will be there waiting for her. Waiting to hear about her day at school.

In a perfect world, I'd have a mom to talk to. I'd run inside my building, past the pissy-smelling elevator, and dart up to the eighth floor. I'd swing open the door, huffing and puffing, and yell, "Mama! You wouldn't believe what Curtis said today in chorus!" And while I'm telling her the story, I'm popping my neck and snapping my fingers. Mama would throw in a few "Oh no, he didn't!" lines. She'd give me a few crack backs for the next time I faced his braided-teeth self, and I'd be ready for him!

We'd laugh and slap high fives like we been homegirls forever. Then she'd make my favorite dinner: fried chicken, cornbread with honey, macaroni and cheese (with five different cheeses because *all* real moms know how to make it like that), and collard greens to top it off. After dinner I'd help her wash the dishes. She'd listen to my poetry, and we'd paint each other's nails and watch *Jeopardy!* before going to bed. She would tuck me in and kiss my forehead. She'd crack my window so I could feel the crisp Newark air. I'd drift off into a deep sleep under the hypnotizing spell of rap beats and tropical salsa rhythms.

But that world's not real. This one is. The world where I part ways with Tanisha before the sun goes down in Newark. Because we both know the freaks come out at night. Tanisha makes her way to the D building, at the bottom of the hill of the projects, where she has a mom and a dad waiting for her. And I turn a sharp left down the dank alley toward the A building, alone.

And instead of giving myself a heart attack by running up all those stairs, I force myself into the pissy-stanking elevator, where Da'Quan the Dope Fiend is in the corner, having a conversation with his imaginary friend. The elevator moves like molasses, chug-a-lugging its way to the eighth floor. I walk in the house to see Pop Pop passed out on the couch, his empty whiskey cup tipped over on the floor, a newspaper at his feet, and the Bible propped up on his chest. It's funny how drunks and druggies can be the smartest, most religious people you'll ever know. Pop Pop's good leg is propped up on the couch, while his World War II one dangles off the edge. His prosthetic is on the floor, a reminder of all he lost while he fought in what he calls "the white man's war to conquer the world."

The news is playing. Even with fall technically here, we're in for a hot one tomorrow. Temperatures will be in the mid-seventies. In the background I hear TJ in his room, humming some Patti LaBelle. That boy knows he can hit those high notes. Sometimes I wonder what he's dreaming about when he's singing behind those closed doors. Is he dreaming about his daddy? The one who never stayed around long enough to even give him his last name? Is he missing his mama too? The one who moved down South last year with no explanation? Just left a prayerful note to my father, begging him to take care of TJ. Help him grow into the type of man the family can be proud of.

I walk past Daddy's always-locked bedroom door, where it seems he seals away love and good memories, and into my own room filled with posters and newspaper clippings of Vanessa Williams, taped from wall to wall. Behind my closed door, I stare at an image of the type of beauty I long to be. Vanessa and Mama look one and the same. Honey-dipped. Vanilla-coated. Perfect in every way.

I sink into my bed and pull out *I Know Why the Caged Bird Sings*. Sometimes I wish I could read with my eyes closed. Maya Angelou's words almost fly off the page and into my mind. Her own caged bird sings a song, written in the key of fear. But still, in the midst of the unknown, she has hopes and dreams. Like me.

I long for things. Lots of things. Like for Daddy to walk into my room right now with a smile and an embrace. I long for him to do the things that normal dads do. Take me shopping. Go for walks in Branch Brook Park. Stop and play a game of Uno underneath the cherry blossom trees.

Outside my window, the moon shines in the distance. It's starting to rise as the sun makes its way to some other part of the world to bring smiles onto other people's faces. And even though I know it will return again, I can't help but wonder if the sun will ever truly shine on this part of town.

September 22, 1983

This Dang Flyer

Audition for the First Annual
Miss King Middle School Pageant!

WHEN: Friday, September 30, 1983

TIME: 3 P.M.

LOCATION: King Middle School auditorium

WHAT TO BRING: A pair of heels to model in;
a two-minute talent to perform

OVERVIEW: Twelve finalists will be selected.

*Finalists will participate in after-school rehearsals leading up
to our final pageant on Saturday, December 10, 1983.
Segments of competition include talent, formal wear,
onstage interview, and academic achievement.
Each segment is worth 25%.*

PRIZES: Crown, banner, trophy, and $250 ca$h award

And That's That

Mrs. Walton's been posting these doggone flyers every-where in the school. Bright yellow, hawking me in the cafe-teria, the hallways, even the locker rooms. I can't even get dressed for gym without these dang flyers breathing down my neck. Part of me wants to dare myself to take a chance. The other part runs screaming worse than a four-year-old begging her mama to chase the boogeyman out of the closet and off to a place where bad dreams don't exist.

The King Middle girls are excited about Mrs. Walton's pageant. Personally, I been dodging that woman like a con-tagious disease ever since that circus show in class. I can't sit through a replay of my showdown with Curtis. But a small piece of me hopes that she'll shake some good sense into me and make me try out. Tell me I'm just as good as any other girl at King Middle. On the flip side, I'm praying that she'll do what all the other teachers do: ignore me and give me an A, because I'm one of the very few who even bother to do homework.

When I get to sixth period, I see Mrs. Walton has made some big changes in the room. The cavelike walls have been painted a bright blue color. The tissue bombs are still stuck to the ceiling, but I guess she couldn't reach up that far. Posters of musicians are hung all around the room: Ella Fitzgerald, Beethoven, Bob Marley, the Beatles, Marian Anderson. The chairs are gone. All that remain are the piano, the piano bench, and a brand-new Mrs. Walton.

"In this room, we will sing," Mrs. Walton announces sternly. "There will be no rap battles, no copying off your friend's homework for your next class, and no reading"—she turns an icy glare toward me—"unless we are reading music. In this class, we will learn. Am I understood?"

Everybody's whispering. I hear "Mrs. Walton grew some balls," and "She ain't playing around with us no more," among other things.

"Am I understood, class?" She raises her voice, her frame growing ten feet tall.

"Yes, Mrs. Walton," we say in perfect unison.

She starts playing scales like she's possessed. The booming sound causes us all to stand at attention. And we begin to sing up and down the scales. I sing along softly. The voices around me are a mess: some nasal, some off-key, and both are drowning out those of us who could possibly be on key, like me.

"Curtis Dumont." She calls on Mr. Broken Train-Track Teeth, who is still playing around in the back of the class. "Sing the scale. *Alone.*"

The class starts to giggle. I can't help but laugh too. Mrs. Walton taps an F and nods for him to start there.

"Do re *meeee* . . ." His voice cracks into a high, operatic pitch before he can even get to the next note.

Once again everybody's laughing. But I'm intrigued. The boy with the deep speaking voice actually sings like a girl. And even though I'd never tell him this, Curtis sounded . . . *all right.*

Mrs. Walton's lips tighten as she shouts, "In this class, there will be no more insults! You are all capable of singing well. Curtis, you have a lovely, effeminate tone to your voice. You are an alto and will stand in the middle row."

I so want to add, "with the *girls!*"

Curtis sinks his chest in a bit and makes his way to the middle row, away from his brassy-voiced friends in the tenor section.

"Vanessa, your turn," Mrs. Walton calls.

I sigh, but not loud enough for Mrs. Walton to hear. My waistband tightens to the point where I feel like I'm gonna bust a button on my pants. That's if I actually had buttons. Most have been replaced with safety pins. Maybe if I breathe deep, one of the pins will bust open and prick me in the stomach so I can go to the nurse.

I step forward, slow as can be. Everyone's looking at me, and I swear I wanna throw up. It's not like this at church. There I'm free. Whole. Here? I'm only half a person, judged by the way I look, the way I talk, the clothes I wear.

Mrs. Walton begins to play the scales again—this time, she says, in the key of G. I suck in a large breath and pray to baby Jesus.

Please sound good. Please sound good.

My eyes close tight as my voice climbs the scale, reaching the high G like it's nothing. I hold the last note way past the point of Mrs. Walton's piano pedal.

When I have released all the oxygen I can, I fade the note out and open my eyes. Everyone's staring at me.

"Excellent job, Vanessa. Tanisha was right the other day. You can sing. What a lovely soprano voice you have! Make your way to the front row."

Tanisha starts clapping hard, adding in a little squeal and a jump. But nobody else joins her. Just a few teeth-sucking sounds and a couple of whispers: "She think she all that." My insides cave in, shoulders collapsing into my chest.

Beatriz Mendez, decked out in red Reeboks, red earrings, and red lip gloss, rolls her eyes at me. I lower my head, my spirit deflating by the second. My fingers start to shake as I take my place in the front row, next to her. I put my imaginary blinders on and don't even look her way.

Mrs. Walton makes everyone sing like this until the bell rings.

"Vanessa, please remain in class for just a minute. I will write you a late pass for next period," Mrs. Walton says. When the room clears, Mrs. Walton's eyes get all wide, and I know what's coming.

"Remember the other day when I told you I have a friend sponsoring the school pageant?"

I nod my head slowly but don't say anything.

"You *are* trying out for Miss King Middle, right? I think

you'd be great." She pulls out the yellow flyer from her folder, laying it on top of the piano.

I look at it for a second, and when I lift my eyes, Mrs. Walton is straight cheesin'. My stomach is making gurgling noises, and I'm standing there praying that she doesn't hear them.

"Isn't this just wonderful? Especially with all the buzz about Vanessa Williams? This'll be perfect practice for when you eventually try out for Miss America. That's what being in a pageant is all about, you know. Not just being pretty. It's about talent and being a good student. And you are all that! You said you wanted to be Miss America, Vanessa," she says, "so here you go."

"This ain't—" I say, but then I see Mrs. Walton raise an eyebrow. "I mean, this *isn't* the Miss America pageant."

Note to self. No street talk around the white lady.

"No, it's not, but it's a step. How do you think those women in the real Miss America pageant got their start? By doing something small and working their way up. You can do this. You *should* do this," she says, shoving the flyer into my hand.

I bite the inside of my lip to the point where it could bleed any second. Then I flash back to when I watched the pageant. Sure, I pictured myself on that television screen, wearing a bomb-fancy dress, tearing up the stage with some grand, powerhouse song, and in the end having the crown placed on my head. But that wasn't the girl I pictured on the outside. That girl was a lighter, skinnier, prettier version of me. And that was fantasy. If I did this, I'd have to be onstage—the real me—in front of the entire school. Oh heck naw!

"I know what you're thinking." Mrs. Walton breaks my train of thought.

"I'm thinking, why in the world do you care so much?" I admit.

Mrs. Walton swallows hard and clutches her pearls like *How dare you ask me that?*

"Let's just say that at one point in my life, I too wanted to be in the Miss America pageant. Only I didn't have an opportunity like this."

I take one look at that blonde hair, those blue eyes, and throw my head back, laughing toward the tissue-bomb sky. This lady is on something.

"You're laughing, but it's true. Times were tough for me and my family back then. I didn't have anyone in my corner to help me toward that dream. I wasn't as smart as you, or as well read and well spoken. Vanessa, it's 1983 and this country has finally crowned a black Miss America. Sky's the limit for you."

My laughter cuts short.

"You're wondering how you're going to prepare for all of this, right?"

"Well, yeah . . . sorta," I respond.

"I can help you with everything, especially your talent. We can practice in my classroom after school twice a week. And you don't need any help in the academic-achievement portion. I looked at your files. High honor roll every marking period since kindergarten?" Mrs. Walton is talking in one long-winded breath and doesn't even come up for air. "We can also practice for the onstage interview, which shouldn't be so bad, given how much you read. And while I'd love to help you pick out a dress for formal wear, I'm sure your mom and dad will want to—"

"Listen, Mrs. Walton." I cut her off. "Thank you for thinking of me, but I can't do this pageant."

What I really want to say is Mama ain't around and Daddy don't have time for me anyway. So what's the point?

But my words turn into movement. Next thing I know, my feet are pushing me down the hall, my eyes are stinging, every single organ in my body is losing electricity, my hands are crumpling up the flyer and throwing it in the trash. Ain't gonna be no pageant. Not for me, at least. I got better things to do with my time anyway. And that's that.

September 23, 1983

The Beginning of the End

Once upon a time, there lived a little girl
with a mom and a dad and sunshine and love.
Then one day,
the mom ran far, far away,
the dad turned into the big bad wolf,
and the little girl never saw the sun again.
The End.

Dear Darlene,

You know we ain't never been into fairy tales anyway.

—Nessy

Letting Go

"**Nessy, get up.** You gonna be late for choir practice!" The stank of Pop Pop's whiskey-tainted breath burns my nose. The rest of him seems fine. His eyes are clear, not glassy like when he drinks at night. Beneath the faint layer of tart whiskey, I can smell Shield soap, so he must have showered already. He's always good on the weekends, because according to him, the good Lord's looking at him when he walks through the church doors come Sunday.

It's the weekend, thank God. No school. And no dodging Mrs. Walton! All I got is church choir rehearsal today and Sunday service tomorrow.

In the background the news is playing, and the sizzle of something cooking in the kitchen perfumes the entire house. The gritty, bacony, syrupy scent drifts into my room, and I soon forget about the drunken cloud that surrounds Pop Pop.

"What time is it?" I ask, wiping the sleep out of my eyes.

"Almost eleven," he says.

I can't believe I slept this late. I blame that on Mama for seeping into my head and ruining what could have been a perfect night's sleep. Tired of dreams keepin' me awake at night.

"Yo' teacher called here this morning, asking to speak to your mama."

My throat gets real tight. No teachers have ever called the house.

"What teacher?" I ask slowly.

"Lady named Mrs. Walton. Nessy, you didn't tell me you was singing in the school chorus. Well, I'll be!" Pop Pop slaps his good leg. It wiggles, while the World War II one stands motionless.

"She asked for Mama? What did you say?" My voice has elevated two octaves.

"I told her the truth—"

I stop breathing for a second. Oh Lord, here it comes.

"—that she wasn't here," he finishes, and his forehead double-creases.

It is the truth. She isn't here. I don't know where she is. Or if she's even alive, for that matter.

"Listen here, Nessy. I know you got a lot of questions and things on your mind. But it's best that you forget about your mama for now. All you need to know is that she loves you. One day when the time is right, I'm sure your daddy will explain everything. Plus, you got all the love you need right here." Pop Pop spreads out his arms real wide.

But where is she? The question whirls all through my head. It's the same one I've asked him for years, but all I'm ever met with are deaf ears and sealed lips.

He hugs me tight, and I breathe in his whiskey-fading, soapy-scented aroma. I do have love here with him and TJ, and I guess with Daddy.

I breathe a sigh of relief and rise up to get ready for choir practice.

We're singing "Goin' Up Yonder." TJ's singing lead. He's gonna tear the house down come Sunday morning! If only I had his courage to get out in front of an audience like that.

"She done told me about that pageant, Nessy," Pop Pop says, limping to the door.

"Pop Pop, I—"

He cuts me off. "Now looka here. I know you don't wanna do it 'cause you figure your mama ain't around to help you. Your mama would be proud. Heck, I am. I tell you one thing: doing that pageant would be like second nature to you."

"I don't want to, Pop Pop. And how you figure?"

"Just trust me. I think you should try out. Now I know your daddy won't approve, but let me deal with him. You got all the help you need right here. And that teacher who called here this morning seemed to want to help you. Now you march yo' pretty self into that audition next week!"

Pop Pop brushes his hand across my face. I know that in his eyes, I am pretty. And not just the pretty-for-a-dark-skinned-girl comments I sometimes get from the folks at church.

TJ comes walking down the hall, cheesin' so hard his mouth takes up his entire face. All I see are lips, teeth, and that big ole afro.

"I heard all about the pageant, Nessy, and you might as well do it!"

"Yeah, yeah, whatever. I'll think about it."

"I could make all your clothes. I gotta design something for my final grade anyway. Come on. Do it for me," TJ begs.

Pop Pop rolls his eyes. He doesn't dig TJ's fashion-designer dreams too tough, but he knows he has no say. TJ is a Martin. Daddy's nephew. Daddy's problem.

"Do it for us," Pop Pop says, and wobbles down the hall.

I got lead in my feet as I creep toward the bathroom. My back presses against the door, and it slams shut with a booming thud. And then I proceed to do what I do best. Pretend. Shower on full blast. Eyes straight forward. Don't even look at that tub. Fill up the sink with water. Washcloth in my hand. Bath mat beneath my feet. Handle my lady business. Make sure I don't miss an inch. Look in the mirror and tell myself that this is all totally normal. Everybody's afraid of something, right?

I get dressed and make my way toward the kitchen, sunlight pouring in through the window on that sorry-behind sunflower, feeding it with lies. That thing ain't ever gonna live, no matter how hard it wants to.

Pop Pop's made a spread: biscuits and gravy, bacon, eggs, and sweet tea. His southern grandma taught him to cook like this. My stomach is dancing at the sight of all the food, but my mind can't stop thinking about Mrs. Walton's nosy behind calling my house.

I sit at the table and start piling up my plate. It's a long haul to church on Saturdays. Between taking two buses and then walking seven blocks uphill, a girl needs her strength.

When I place a third biscuit on my plate, TJ shoots me a look with his lip upturned and snatches it back. "You are officially in pageant mode!"

"Hey, no fair!" I grab for the biscuit, but it's already in his mouth. TJ's so thin, he could eat a hundred biscuits and not gain a single pound.

In the Miss America pageant, the contestants have to prance around the stage in swimsuits. The flyer for the school pageant said nothing like that. Don't get me wrong, it's cool to watch it on television, but they'll never catch my behind walking around in no swimsuit. No sir! These rolls ain't made for sharing with the world.

We sit around the table, and Pop Pop and TJ are blabbing away about the pageant. Like they're the ones in control and I'm gonna do whatever they say. Both of them are glowing just talking about it, and I start to wonder if the pageant has more to do with them than it does with me.

I can't remember the last time I saw them so excited about something. TJ says he'll make my dress red with silver sequins because red would look good next to my skin. It'll have a train, like those real princess dresses have. He's in design heaven right now.

Pop Pop couldn't care less what I wear. His only request is that I sing his favorite gospel song, "Amazing Grace." Every now and then he makes me sing that song to him while I braid his hair. He says I sound just like Mama when I sing it, except my voice is more buttery than hers. I smile, listening to them go back and forth. I haven't even agreed to do the pageant yet.

A loud thud rattles the front door. We stop chatting and sit up like soldiers.

"Don't say a word. Let me do all the talking," Pop Pop whispers.

Daddy lumbers in, dropping his tool bag in the hallway. The silence in the room is thicker than them biscuits on our plates. He walks over to the counter with his footsteps earth-quaking everything around us. Even the glass jars in the pantry are shaking.

TJ sits up even straighter, puffing his chest out. God, I feel so bad for that boy. Every time Daddy walks through the door, I can hear the iron chains clank around TJ's heart, stripping him of what little dignity he has left.

I stare at Daddy square in the face, hoping he'll look my way. Maybe sit down and have a conversation with me. Ask me how school is going. But his eyes remain straight and unflinching.

"Good morning, Daniel. That job of yours sure got you working all kinds of times these days," Pop Pop says cheerfully.

"Yeah, Pop," he grunts back, gravelly voiced.

My father. Man of many words. There is a pleading in my head, echoing so loud I think all of Grafton can hear. *Daddy, I want to be in the school pageant. Daddy, I want to sing and dress up like Miss America.* The words swirl inside of me, swishing and swooping every which-a-way but out of my mouth.

"Nessy would like to try out for the school pageant, and I say she oughta," Pop Pop proudly announces, squaring his shoulders.

At first Daddy doesn't do or say anything. Just pours himself a cup of coffee, throws a couple of pieces of bacon on a paper towel, and starts to walk out of the kitchen. He stops short in the hallway.

"Pageant? Like that Miss America garbage?" he asks. "The one where them white girls prance around on stage in swimsuits, letting it all hang out for dirty men to feast their eyes on? The one where they finally let a black girl win after all these years? She ain't even all that black, if you ask me! And Nessy wants to do something like that? Now, Pop, of all people you should know better!"

Daddy turns around, and our eyes meet. Mine wounded. His weary.

How would you or Pop Pop know? It's not like that, Daddy. This one's different.

I suck in a long breath, praying that he'll say yes.

"Like hell she'll try out. I can't travel that road again."

Daddy stomps his way to his bedroom, a few drops of coffee spilling onto the floor, and slams the door. The twisting of the locks and the clanking of the chains vibrate through every wall of the apartment. On the other side of that door, Daddy barricades himself in a room that is no doubt filled with nothingness.

And there I sit, swimming in his words. Drowning in his rejection.

"He'll change his mind," TJ whispers. He gestures for me to smile. But I can't. I feel too hollow.

Pop Pop looks at me with pained eyes. "Don't you worry about your daddy. You go on and audition, and I'll deal with him later."

What does Daddy mean, "travel that road again"? There's gotta be a reason why he doesn't agree with me doing the pageant. Maybe he doesn't think I'm pretty enough. Maybe he's right. If you're gonna be black and be in a pageant, you gotta be light skinned with pretty hair. And I ain't got none of that. Mama had it all, though. Me? I came into this world looking every bit like my father, with his blue-black skin, black hair, and even blacker eyes.

It's probably for the best that I don't audition anyhow. What was I thinking to even entertain the idea of being in a school pageant? Who would want to represent that beat-up, run-down King Middle anyway? Some bathroom stalls don't even have doors!

"Y'all hurry up and get on to choir practice 'fore y'all be late!" Pop Pop picks up our dishes and hobbles to the sink. TJ and I grab our things and dash out of the house before we miss the bus.

There's a slight chill in the air today. People are rocking hoodies and combat boots, and you just know the days of summer bliss are long gone. After way too long of a ride, the bus screeches to a stop right in front of Shabazz Park. We hop off and speed-walk up seven blocks to make it to choir practice on time.

The sun beams on the stained-glass windows of Cotton Temple. It's the prettiest building in a neighborhood surrounded by run-down apartment buildings and scattered litter in the streets. I always find my church's name to be a hootin' riot. All those years, black people were slaves, growing cotton and getting whipped over it—why in the world would anyone want to name a church after it?

The organ is thunderous when we step inside. The music crawls through my bones, seeps real deep into my skin. Sister Marie, our choir director, starts to run us through the list of songs we'll sing for tomorrow's service. Tomorrow is Founder's Sunday, which means we'll be celebrating Pastor Evans's father, who started the church back in 1945. It also means service will be extra long 'cause black folk just love celebrating that man. Every year, they go so long I swear I can see his ghost rise up from the dead and take his seat right there in the preacher's pulpit.

When it's TJ's turn to sing "Goin' Up Yonder," somebody screams out, "You better *saaaaaaaang*, Brother TJ!"

My cousin's voice bounces from wall to wall, filling up the entire room. Everyone is feeling it, and I can too. The sound coming out of his mouth is moving, cleansing, freeing. Like Maya Angelou's caged bird being released, flying past the jungle, past the ghetto, and up, up to the heavens. A feeling washes over me, and I forget about everything that's on my mind. My mom. My dad. School. Here I can just let go.

Ain't Miss America No Way

At **seven o'clock** on the dot, Tanisha calls.

"What's up, girl? I saw *Beatrrrrriz* at the bodega tonight." She rolls the *r* extra thick. Just hearing that name makes my fingers twitch.

"And?" I laugh out my response.

"She was talking hard about you and the pageant. How she saw Mrs. Walton asking you to do it, even though you don't stand a chance 'cause you too dark skinned. How she's gonna win, no matter what it takes. How nobody can step to her, blah blah blah. All her friends were laughing and egging her on, and when I got in her face for talking about you, she said she was kidding. But I don't know. There was something about it that sounded like she meant it."

I try my best to pretend like I don't care. "Yeah, well, she can think what she wants. But thanks for sticking up for me."

"Are you gonna try out? Make this chick eat her words?" Tanisha asks.

I suck in a quick breath.

"Hello? You there?"

"Yeah, I'm here. I don't know. Maybe. . . . I will if you do it with me."

Tanisha says nothing back.

"Are you there?" I ask.

"Try out for a pageant? Yeah, okay." The words come out in a giggly, you-must-be-joking kinda way.

There is a silence between us, and I'm struggling to spit out how I'm really feeling. I want to mention that time she made me try out for the basketball team, knowing dang well I couldn't even dribble a ball. That after I made a fool of myself and didn't make it past the first cut, I still went to every single game, every single practice. That I have them all recorded in Darlene. Twelve games and sixteen practices, if we're getting real specific. But I ain't got the guts to say any of that, 'cause having one friend is better than having none.

I finally say, "I probably won't try out for the pageant anyway. I'm 'a be busy with school, so . . ."

For a moment I consider telling her about Daddy and his reaction to me doing the pageant. But what would she know about that? Her father is at every basketball game because he's her coach. Check that. Her number-one fan.

"That's cool, I guess. Plus, who cares about that pageant? It's not like it's actually Miss America or anything."

More silence. That last line lingers in the air, stinging me right down to my toes. *Who cares?*

Well, it's obvious that she doesn't. Tanisha's probably gonna get into Saint Anthony's High School on a basketball scholarship. Me? I got nothing like that waiting for me.

The faint sound of *Diff'rent Strokes* plays in the background on her end. Then Tanisha's mom calls her to come have dinner. I close my eyes real tight-like and picture the spread her mom's made: chicken-fried steak, mashed potatoes with gravy, and buttered corn, all with a side of love.

"Well, I gotta go. Don't forget the season's about to start. I need my favorite cheerleader in the bleachers."

"Yeah. Sure," I say real slow.

When we hang up, I'm feeling more confused than ever. Tanisha's not interested in trying out for the pageant with me, but she made sure to bring up me being there for her basketball. Her hopes. Her dreams. Her way out of Grafton.

Will I ever make it out of here? 'Cause one thing I know for sure, Saint Anthony's not interested in recruiting Tanisha *and* her groupie.

Part of me wants to do the pageant. But even with the strongest game face I can put on, I know that I'm no match for Beatriz Mendez. She can have that crown. Like Tanisha said, it's not like it's actually Miss America anyway.

Goin' Up Yonder

What I love best about Sundays is that not only is Pop Pop sober, but we get to pretend like we're something special, dressed in our Sunday best. Pop Pop wears his mauve bell-bottom suit and veteran's pin. His face is cleanly shaven, and he smells of Old Spice. All his weekday liquor sins are washed away, and I have my grandfather back, even if it's only for one day a week.

TJ looks handsome in his navy blazer with brown suede elbow patches. Since it's Founder's Sunday, all the women wear white. It's a symbol of purity and cleansing. That's tradition at Cotton Temple. My skirt is long and trimmed in white lace, with a white blouse to match.

My usual church shoes no longer fit, so TJ gives me a pair of low heels he got from school, and I can barely walk in them. The white patent leather is scratched a bit, and the bottoms are slightly worn out, but they're better than nothing. Can't go to church in my combat boots. I slip the hand-me-down heels on, and my knees turn inward. I'm so dang tall in these things. I buckle my shoulders to take away from looking like Vanessa the Giant.

"I want you to sing lead with me on 'Goin' Up Yonder,'" TJ says.

"You gotta be kidding. I can't sing that song with you, boy! Everybody in church will be staring at me!"

"We sing together at home all the time. It's time for you to have an audience. You know all the parts, Nessy. Come on, you can do it. This could be good practice for you if you decide to audition for that pageant."

Then I remember one of the poems I wrote in Darlene:

Who travels a road full of twists, turns, cracked earth, and flooded paths?

Only to end up in a place where no one is waiting for you?

And like a lullaby, a tiny voice inside of me sings back: *You do.*

"Umm, yeah, I don't know," I say hesitantly, aware of the uselessness of my dream. Daddy. Mama. Beatriz. Me? Too many bumps in the road. All for a shiny crown.

Because of his prosthetic leg, Pop Pop can't take two buses and walk another seven blocks to church. So we take a car service—a black town car from JP Transportation. Pop Pop fought in World War II with the owner's father, so they give him that good ole battle-buddy hookup. Every Sunday it's like we're Hollywood stars when that car pulls up in Grafton Hill.

Church is on fire, as usual for Founder's Day. Pastor's preaching up a storm, but all I got on my mind is this pageant. Why I should definitely try out for it. And why it's the stupidest idea I ever thought of.

But maybe being in the pageant would open a new world

for me. A chance to step away from the hut-two-three-four military routine that is my life.

Monday through Friday, school.

Saturday, choir rehearsal.

Sunday, church.

Repeat.

Repeat.

Somewhere, pushed deep beyond my fears, there's this thing I got inside me. It's called hope. Hope for Mama to come back. Hope for Daddy to come back to me too. And not as a shell of a man that I call my father. If Daddy gave it a chance, he'd see. The pageant could be a good thing, if only he'd open his mind a little.

The music for "Goin' Up Yonder" starts, and I see TJ stand up from the tenor row and stop at the soprano row. He extends his hand for me to join him.

"I'm gonna ask my cousin Vanessa to join me in singing this song to y'all today."

The church thunders in applause, and I see Pop Pop in the back of the pews jump up and shout, "*Saaaaaaang*, Nessy!"

The spotlight is on me, and the church grows quiet. One by one, beads of sweat form in an arc across my forehead. Fear begins to chew away at my insides. But then that tiny voice returns—bigger, louder than ever, daring me to give it a try.

Next to Pop Pop, a small woman—half his size, covered in an oversized white hat, white blazer, skirt, and gloves— begins to clap. I've never seen her at church, and I'm sure Pop

Pop is back there flirting with her for the whole service. But before I can get a better look, everybody is standing up, clapping to the beat of the song. All of a sudden something pulls me out of my seat, and my feet are moving forward. My mind is screaming at me, telling me to sit my behind down.

Maybe if I close my eyes, then I won't have to feel everyone else's piercing through me. When I do close them, I see her. Mama. With eyes you could swim in. Bluish brown or sometimes greenish gray, depending on the day. Smile so wide, warm, and perfect in every way. With her voice—a perfect blend of silk and honey and hummingbirds—she says, "Go on, princess, sing. Show them what you can do."

Mama caresses my cheek. The heat of her fingertips injects me with confidence. Fills me with her love. Feeds me with what I've been craving all along. I will sing to bring Mama back, even if it's only for this moment right now, right here.

The organ thrums low as the percussion kicks in. TJ begins the first lyrics of the song. Then he passes the microphone to me. Every single hair on my neck stands in military style. I swallow a large dose of oxygen and let go. My voice pours out of me in perfect tune with the music. It is lightning breaking through the clouds. Earthshaking. I am free. And everyone is going wild, stomping and crying and lifting their hands up to the sky.

Mama stands in the front pew, taller than anyone, her shoulders square and proud. Daddy appears, standing beside her, beaming with his big ole hands wrapped around her waist. And it's just like back in the day when we were the happily-ever-after Martins.

The choir joins in, blending in so sweet. Next thing I know, TJ and I are ad-libbing back and forth in harmony over the chorus. We're killing it.

When the song is over, Mama and Daddy melt away like snowflakes falling on wet ground. And everything is back to normal. Daddy's at work like always. And Mama? Well, she's exactly what I've always known her to be. A ghost.

But all around me people are still shouting and dancing. I see Pop Pop catching the Holy Ghost. He's wiggling and stomping that wooden leg of his up and down the aisles. The lady with the big ole face-covering hat is still up clapping, hands raised and spinning round and round. Pop Pop and his new friend are cutting up in the back of the church, having a good ole time.

After the service, I do my regular job collecting the hymnals from the choir rows. Pastor knows how much I love books. The hymnals are like my babies. I dust them off, placing each one delicately in its silk sleeve, and lay them out on the table next to the organ.

Just as I'm placing the last book down, a small hand touches my shoulder.

"I knew you were something special, Vanessa Martin."

I turn around and see Mrs. Walton. She's the little lady in the back of the church next to Pop Pop.

I stand there dumbfounded as Pop Pop wobbles up behind her. "Told you my Nessy here could sing her tail off."

"Indeed you did, sir, and that was quite impressive, Vanessa," she continues. "I can't wait to see you in the Miss King Middle pageant. You're going to be awesome!"

Mrs. Walton sounds worse than a dang cheerleader. I wanna tell her that you can't say the word *awesome* in Newark without somebody looking at you sideways, but what would it matter? Her time here is done, and in the next few minutes she'll be hopping in her fancy car to head up 78, probably to a town where saying a word like *awesome* is perfectly fine.

I try and say something to her, but I'm stuck. I ain't never seen a teacher outside of school. Do they even have a life beyond the classroom walls? Crazy as it sounds, growing up I always thought the teachers lived in school. Seeing my teacher here at church is just weird.

I stand there, torn between wanting to whack TJ and Pop Pop upside the head for scheming behind my back, and trying to figure out why, out of all the kids at King Middle, Mrs. Walton's interested in me.

"You *are* going to audition, right?" She draws in closer to me and stares me down with those hypnotizing, ocean-blue eyes of hers. I breathe her in, and she smells like a mixture of everything nice in this world.

"Umm . . ." I search for an answer.

Pop Pop cuts in and introduces TJ—the third partner in this scheme of theirs. They exchange handshakes. The three of them are small-talking about me, pouring out compliments as I fight the urge to blush.

"That voice is something else," Mrs. Walton says.

"Too bad she won't even consider using it," TJ shoots back.

I try to soak in this idea. Me up on that stage. Voice rising way above the ceiling. People jolting out of their seats. Hands clapping, happy tears flowing, prayers, both small and impossible, heard and answered. I did that here. Today. Maybe I can do it again, at the pageant this time. Bring back that feeling, the memory of Mama and Daddy together again.

"Okay, okay. Yes," I say loudly. "I'll give it a shot."

They throw their hands up and squeal, and there I am, smiling on the inside. My own little cheerleading squad. Mrs. Walton hands Pop Pop two sheets of paper: the flyer for the pageant and a permission slip for the audition.

"Just be sure to have Vanessa's mom or dad sign the permission slip for Friday because we will stay until five o'clock," she says.

Pop Pop and TJ look at me with hesitation in their eyes. "Working all kind of crazy hours, Mrs. Walton," Pop Pop says, "and he ain't never really home. I take care of her, so—"

"Pop, I got this. I can sign it." TJ grabs the paper.

Pop Pop snatches it out of his hands and smirks at Mrs. Walton. "Boy think 'cause he eighteen now, he a grown man." Pop Pop pulls a pen out from his coat pocket, signs his name, and hands it back to her. "There you go."

I keep my eyes fixed on the floor, hoping Mrs. Walton don't ask no more questions. She doesn't need to know nothing about my life. How I'm surviving on empty, waiting and hoping to be filled again.

"Good enough!" she says, and then she wraps her arms around me and holds me tight.

I stand there all stupid-like. Not knowing if I should hug her back. I push slightly away, but Mrs. Walton pulls me in farther, deeper. And then I let her take me in. In that moment an imaginary ax grinds down on my emotions, slicing them in equal parts: happy for the attention, even if it's from a stranger, and angry that it ain't coming from who I need it from most.

"Nice meeting everyone." Mrs. Walton winks at me and then prances to the back of the church and out the door.

Like zombies under a spell, we trail behind her. Our eyes follow her to her car, a pastel-blue Chevrolet Celebrity with shiny silver rims.

We make our way to the town car waiting for us.

"Ooh-wee! That woman know she sho' is fine!" Pop Pop says.

"Yes, Lawd!" TJ chimes in, slapping fives with Pop Pop.

Mrs. Walton's blue car speeds away, past the church, past the garbage, and off to her own little land of sunshine.

September 27, 1983

Me and Darlene Against the Asphalt

Now I lay me down to sleep,
another tear I shall not weep.
Please work your magic through the night,
that I will wake with skin so light.
For this will bring a brighter day,
to light my path and guide the way.
And all the pieces will come together:
love, beauty, family, forever.

Dear Darlene,

Closed mouths don't get fed. Pop Pop would always tell me that when I was a little girl. If you don't say what's in your heart, it ain't never gonna come to you. Never really had no meaning for me until now. So tonight as the moon hovers outside my window, and the music drifts in with the midnight air, I make this my promise to myself. Every night, I'm gonna whisper this poem to the wind. And just maybe those words will turn into reality. Make me beautiful. Free me from the darkness that makes the outside world see me as less than pretty. Take me back to the place where I was once happy. Because here in this jungle, there ain't nothing but weeds and tears and dreams trapped beneath the asphalt.

—Nessy

Pray Myself Invisible

Friday comes fast, and I'm having doubts about this audition stuff. Everybody's been talking about it at school all week. It's almost like Pop Pop is psychic or something 'cause he can sense my nervousness. Right before I leave for school, he gives me a star-shaped brooch to pin on my shirt.

"Your mama used to wear this every time . . ." His voice drifts off.

"Every time what, Pop Pop?"

The light in Pop Pop's eyes dims. "Every time she needed a little luck. She'd be proud of you doing this pageant. Just try your best today, Nessy. And don't worry about yo' daddy. We'll keep it between us."

Another secret to add to the collection in our household. Seems these days you could paint the walls with the secrets we have.

After school Tanisha and I make our way to the auditorium. By the way she's dragging her feet, I can't tell if she's mad because I forced her to come or plain tired from playing basketball during gym. When we get there, it's packed. Every inch of the room is filled with King Middle girls. Some are taking it seriously and practicing their routines. Some are there only to make fun of the ones who look like they don't know what they're doing. I see everything from step routines to praise dancing to rapping and singing.

A small crowd gathers around Beatriz as she stands in front of the first-row seats. She's got on a costume, dressed to the nines. No one told me that we could audition in costumes! Not that I have one anyway, but still. Beatriz has on a bright-red leotard with a long, white, ruffly skirt and a blue silk flower in her hair.

"Dang, *chica*, your outfit is too fly," I hear Beatriz's friend, Maricela Vazquez, say. That girl is Beatriz's number-one butt kisser.

"We know that you'll win the pageant. You got this hands down," Julicza Feliciano chimes in. Butt kisser number two.

Tanisha and I walk down the aisle to find seats. It just so happens that the only ones available are in the second row. Dead behind where Beatriz and her crew are standing.

"My *abuela* sent me this outfit from Puerto Rico. You know when you have an audition you gotta go the extra mile. Take it seriously, especially when you're trying to win. Too bad not everyone got that memo," she says, staring my way, cutting her eyes straight through my skull. Her little audience looks at me and starts laughing.

Tanisha sucks her teeth real loud. "Got a problem?"

A sick feeling buries itself real deep inside me, like a thousand roaches crawling all over me, worse than what we got in our kitchen. And all I wanna do is fill up the tub with Raid and drown myself in it. Not that I even ever set foot in the tub. That thing's got demons in it. Standing at the sink to handle my business is fine by me. That's how they did it in the old days anyway.

Besides, Beatriz Mendez never paid me no mind before, and we've been going to school together since she moved here from Puerto Rico in second grade. But I can't help but wonder if she's right. What am I thinking? I'm not dressed up for this thing. Why'd I even come in the first place?

The teachers walk in, followed by our principal, Mrs. Carlisle. She's all tall and stone-faced, wearing a black-and-white pinstripe suit. As usual she is carrying her bullhorn. That woman carries that thing everywhere. She yells through it to get everyone to stop talking.

Beatriz and her butt kissers take seats in that front row, like it was reserved for them all along.

"Ladies, I would appreciate your attention. Your teachers Mrs. Walton, Mrs. Ruiz, Mrs. Moore, and Mrs. Caldwell have been working very hard to produce a quality event for you. You will behave as young ladies. Four girls from each grade will be selected to participate, and the final results will be posted outside of the cafeteria tomorrow. Good luck."

And just like that, Mrs. Carlisle storms out of the auditorium, with her back so straight and her face so tight that we are hypnotized into silence long after she is gone.

I scan the panel of teachers responsible for choosing the contestants. Mrs. Walton, without a doubt, will pick me. She literally begged me to try out. Seeing her there is enough to keep my behind in my seat. Mrs. Ruiz is the eighth-grade Spanish teacher. She's built like a brick house with mounds of blonde hair, though I'm sure she dyes it that color, because the roots are black. Hands down, she is the best-dressed teacher in the school, always decked out in the flyest gear: designer handbags, blazers with jeweled buttons, and a pair of high heels to match each color of the rainbow. Mrs. Ruiz is extra popular with the Latino kids. Even though I make straight As in her class, I doubt she even knows my name. Beatriz'll probably be her number-one pick. Mrs. Moore is the only gym teacher I've ever known who's actually physically fit. Everybody calls her the drill sergeant. Body made of pure steel. Hair always braided in tight cornrows. Honestly, I think she only passes me out of pity. Every now and then she throws me a little jab to remind me to "make exercise a part of my daily routine." I probably don't stand a chance with her either. Then there's Mrs. Caldwell. Poor, poor Mrs. Caldwell is way past her prime. She should've stopped teaching history a long time ago. She's so old and forgetful that most of the time the students are the ones teaching the class. I'm hoping that in the middle of her dozing off, she'll do me a solid and give me a good score.

For the first part of the audition, everyone has to perform their talent. A lot of the girls take it as a joke. They're up there dancing to rap music and throwing their booty back and forth. I cringe and sink low in my chair. Half of this stuff would never fly on the Miss America stage. Good Lord, what have I gotten myself into?

The teachers announce Tanisha's name, and I get all tingly inside. I'm nervous for her, nervous for me too. She rises up slowly out of her chair and says, "I still can't believe you talked me into this nonsense."

Goose bumps spill out all over my arms. I need Tanisha to get up there and kill it. I need us both to kill it and pass the audition, 'cause I can't do this pageant alone.

The beat kicks in to "The Breaks" by Kurtis Blow. Nobody can resist this style of music, with its hypnotizing beats and poetic rhymes. Next thing I know, Lanetta Gainer and Kayla Knight bust out of their chairs and start popping and locking and singing the song so loud, Tanisha can barely be heard on the microphone. She just kind of stands there, mouthing the words, looking at the floor, not really doing much else.

I'm in the audience, flailing my arms like an idiot, signaling for Tanisha to let loose. It's like Lanetta and Kayla are the ones auditioning instead. Work the stage, Tanisha! Move to the left. Now move to the right. Look at the judges. That's how they do it at Miss America. But Tanisha never looks up, not even for a second.

On the basketball court Tanisha's always showing off, always on fire, smiling and dancing when she makes a three-pointer. On the court she's a true entertainer, and the crowd always goes wild for her silly antics. Who is this person on the stage?

When the song ends, Tanisha breathes a sigh of relief and runs off the stage.

"How'd I do?" Tanisha asks as she sits next to me.

"You did good," I lie. "I'm just happy you came with me." That last part was the truth, though.

Tanisha laughs. "Please, girl. I know I sucked! It's not that easy up there."

Even though Tanisha didn't give it her all, I'm convinced she'll pass the audition. 'Cause when you look like Tanisha, everything comes easy. She's got the triple-L pageant package: light skin, long hair, long legs.

Stephanie Bowles from the sixth grade is called next. She sings "Home" from *The Wiz*. She's dressed up just like Dorothy too. Red bows holding up each curly ponytail, silver shoes, and a white ruffly dress. Not only does she look dope, she's got the whole Broadway singing voice down pat. In front of me, Beatriz and her friends are giggling and whispering, probably making fun of Stephanie.

By this point I'm ready to leave. I'm not about to go up there so they can laugh at me too. Singing in church the other day was different. I had a choir behind me and TJ at my side. There was a church organ playing music and filling up my soul. There was Mama and Daddy in the front row, even though I imagined them there. Here they ain't nowhere to be found. Here I got nothing but a row full of mean girls ready to chew me down in one bite. Here I'm gonna have to go up on that stage *alone*. The aisle leading from my seat to the entrance of the auditorium grows to three miles long. If I leave now, everyone will see me and think that I'm nothing but a punk.

Why didn't I have the good sense to at least dress up for this thing? Why can't I have nice clothes like everyone else?

These other girls have all kinds of extra things to make their talents stand out. They got costumes and music and props. All I have is my oversized sweatshirt, bell-bottom jeans, beat-up sneakers, and this voice. No music. No costume. No frills.

The audience claps for Stephanie. Even some of the eighth graders are giving her props (except for Beatriz and her followers, of course), and that's hard to get when you're an underclassman. Next thing I know, Mrs. Caldwell stands up to read the next name on the list. Her eyes get real wide when she sees my name. "Surprised to see you on this list. Vanessa Martin, you're up."

My entire body is glued to my seat, frozen, motionless. *Surprised? Like a good surprise or a bad one?* Tanisha elbows me in the ribs so hard, I let out a hefty cough. My hand rises to Mama's brooch, and I rub my fingers over each point of the star. On the inside I'm pleading with her to magically appear like she did at church, walk on up there with me. I scan the audience, and all I see are eyes and eyes and eyes. None of them Mama's. I suck in my breath and fear, releasing them as I prepare to walk toward the stage. Then I hear Beatriz whisper to her friends.

"*Mira esa gorda negra,*" she says, and her crew starts giggling.

Nine years of living in the projects, three years of taking Spanish in school, and toss in the countless times I've caught Beatriz cheating off my test during Spanish class? How dumb does this girl think I am?

My feet stop just before the top step. There's a rumble in the pit of my belly, and I let the next scene play out in my head.

"I heard what you said. I got every bit a right to try out, just like you do. Comprendes, chica?" *I look her dead in the face. Chest puffed out. Flames burning in my eyes, shooting out straight at her.*

Beatriz and her stupid friends drop their jaws. Like how dare I talk to the "queen" like that?

The audience breaks out with a few rounds of "Oh no, she didn't" and "Ooh, she told you!" And I'm feeling good.

Next thing I know, all the girls jump out of their auditorium seats and bum-rush me, lifting me up with their hands, marching me around the school, singing my praises for chopping the school witch down to size.

"Um . . . sometime today, Vanessa," Mrs. Caldwell yells out.

I shake my head, snapping back to reality, feet moving me toward the stage. Beatriz Mendez will always be Beatriz Mendez. Her words turn to knives. Those knives cut skin—open, wounded, guts spilling out for everybody to see. 'Cept there ain't no blood. Just a sinking feeling that this ain't where I belong.

Beatriz doesn't have to whisper to her friends that I'm big ("beautifully plump" is what Pop Pop calls it). And she don't have to remind them that I'm dark skinned. They can see it. Heck, everyone can. I'm the one who has to look at myself in the mirror every day and ask God every night to take it away. So far I'm thinking either God's too busy or just plain deaf.

"Vanessa, what will your talent be today?" Mrs. Ruiz asks.

Right about now, running out of here and straight home seems like a pretty solid option. I could forget that all this even happened. Maybe I could change schools so I don't have to look at these people anymore.

"Vanessa?" Mrs. Walton interrupts my rambling thoughts.

"I . . . I'm gonna sing 'Goin' Up Yonder.'" The words stutter out of my mouth.

Confidence, where are you?

"Do you have a cassette tape or any kind of music?" Mrs. Moore asks.

I look down at my sneakers, searching for a way to make myself disappear. Never ever—ever—have I felt so unprepared.

"Well, did you even try to get yourself together for this audition?" Mrs. Caldwell throws her pen in the air, her mouth all twisted up at me like I'm wasting her time.

Mrs. Walton pops up out of her seat and says, "Yes! Yes, she has music!"

"I do?"

And next thing I know, Mrs. Walton's heels are click-clacking their way over to the grand piano below the stage. "Now you do."

She throws me a nod and begins to play the song. And the way she's playing it takes me right back to Cotton Temple. She attacks each chord with vigor, like the spirit done took over her whole body. Each note courses through me, rushing like warm rivers in my veins. Next thing I know, I close my eyes, and I am flying high to that special place. The place where I forget about every mean thing people have to say to me or about me. My first note comes out, clean and pure, and I soar.

I don't get halfway into the song before Tanisha jumps up and starts clapping. Then Mrs. Ruiz and Mrs. Moore get up too. But nobody else does. Not Mrs. Caldwell, but that old fart can barely stand as it is. It's like Beatriz got everyone else in the audience under her spell. Like if they even tried to get up, they'd shatter to pieces the moment Beatriz glared at them. Funny how power works like that.

When I finish, Tanisha and the teachers are hooting and hollering. Screaming like a bunch of fools.

"Wow, Vanessa. That was quite impressive," Mrs. Moore says. "And Mrs. Walton, who knew you play gospel music?"

"There's a lot you'd be surprised to know about me," Mrs. Walton replies, and she winks at me on her way back to the judging table.

As I leave the stage, Tanisha screams, "Girl, you were too fly!"

Señorita Evil Eyes is already throwing daggers my way.

When I take my seat, Tanisha whispers in my ear, "Straight up, I think Beatriz is jealous of you, Nessy."

I suck my teeth. *Yeah, right.*

"Next up is Beatriz Mendez," Mrs. Ruiz calls out.

All of Beatriz's friends and several underclassmen jump to their feet, like they're cheering at a basketball game. Beatriz sashays toward the stage with her ruffly skirt swaying from side to side.

She announces that the song she'll dance to is "Quimbara" by Celia Cruz. The music blasts through the speakers, and Beatriz fires her hips across the stage floor. She twirls her hands and spins round and round to the music. Her skirt flashes red, white, and blue, the colors of the Puerto Rican flag.

When the chorus comes in, Beatriz does this move where her back arches in and her booty pushes out. She gyrates that thing over and over like a snake. A smirk spreads across her face as she sees me hawking her backside. I quickly lower my eyes and pretend I dropped something on the floor and bend over to look for it. What a freaking show-off!

Of course, when she's done, her friends are giving her a standing ovation and so are all the other girls. Probably more out of kissing her butt than thinking she was actually any good. Come on—shaking your booty isn't really a talent. That wouldn't cut it on the Miss America stage.

The next round of the audition is the formal walk. Mrs. Walton explains to us how we should do it. There are four X marks on the stage. We must enter from behind the stage curtains three at a time, stopping at each X before it's time to hit the X in the middle of the stage. Mrs. Walton tells us to put on our heels, and I just about crumble to a pile of dust because I forgot mine.

"Don't worry. You can borrow these as soon my turn is over. That's what friends are for, right?" Tanisha says as she makes her way to the front.

I hate that we're lined up in alphabetical order. Tanisha's up there with all the B's, and here I am standing in my holey tube socks, sandwiched between all the M's and N's, with Beatriz tailing right behind me. She giggles and whispers real low so this time I can't hear her. I sink into my oversized sweatshirt and pray myself invisible.

Soon as Tanisha's done modeling, she runs backstage and tosses me her heels. Her shoes are pretty: black patent leather with a strap connected to a flower. It's almost my turn, so I pull off my socks and slam my feet into the shoes. As soon as I do, my feet puff out worse than a busted-up can of biscuits. Foot fat all fighting to break free. Knees all wobbly and awkward. Everyone else is having a fine time in their heels. No trouble at all.

When my name is called, I wobble to the X in the middle of the stage, imagining that this must be how Pop Pop feels walking on his prosthetic leg. My knees are clapping as I do the pivot turn. The girls on television at the Miss America pageant make this look so easy. I quickly pivot around. My neck whips forward before the rest of my body can catch up. Next thing I know, my arms jut out sideways like an airplane to keep myself from falling, but that doesn't work. My butt slaps against the wood so hard that I swear it might split in half. The low sound of laughter boils the skin on my cheeks, and I jump up and dart offstage, grab my backpack, and fly out the door before it gets any louder. I don't even stay to see how Beatriz does, which I am sure is pretty darn near perfect. Why can't God just snap his fingers and make me the same way? Why didn't I listen to Daddy? He was right. This ain't a road for me to travel.

I don't know what I was thinking, letting Mrs. Walton, Pop Pop, and TJ drag me into this circus show. Tanisha's probably gonna be mad at me for bouncing on her like that, especially since I forced her to try out. But I can't take one more second in that auditorium.

When I get home, I walk past Pop Pop, who is in a whiskey coma on the couch, slam my door, trap myself in my room, pray to God for an escape from my life, and stare at the Miss America posters on my wall, knowing full well I never stood a chance.

"**I didn't get a chance** to talk to you, since I missed church this weekend. I can't believe you played me on Friday. You didn't need to rush outta there like that." Tanisha with her loud voice sneaks up behind me at my locker. It's lunch period, and I need to switch books for afternoon classes.

"Made no sense to stay, especially after my Humpty-Dumpty moment." I shrug my shoulders. "Plus, those auditions were just plain wack. I don't wanna be in the pageant anymore." I strap my backpack on and head toward the cafeteria. The truth is that when I got home from the auditions, I didn't feel like talking to Tanisha, Pop Pop, or TJ.

"So you make me try out for some pageant when you know it's not my thing? You killed it up on that stage! Did you not hear yourself up there singing? Nobody's got pipes like you! I mean that little mousy-sounding Stephanie chick was all right, but if anybody in this school is going to win, it's you."

Tanisha Bennet. My best friend. My counselor. My personal cheerleader.

"Stop lying!" I slap Tanisha on the shoulder. "Did you not see my feet in your shoes? And the way I walked in them? I looked like I was on stilts!"

"Speaking of shoes, I need them back for church this week," Tanisha says.

"Girl, you can have those stilts back with a quickness!" I laugh.

When we get to the cafeteria, a huge group of girls is crowded around the entry door. All I can think is these chicks are gonna have to bounce because a sista is hungry! Then I realize why they're all standing there. The audition results have been posted. I stall for a second and then shake my head. Nah, there's no need to even look.

"Brianna, Lanetta, we got in!" Seventh grader Kayla Knight slaps high fives with her friends.

Tanisha pulls my elbow. "You don't wanna know?"

On the outside I scrunch my face and give her the *girl, please!* look. On the inside every piece of me is drowned in hope. But disappointment is a friend that I know all too well. So I keep it moving and make my way through the cafeteria doors. Tanisha doesn't follow me, though. Instead, she files in with the crowd to take a look at the list.

"Vanessa!" Tanisha screams. "You got in!"

I stop in my tracks. The skin on my arms instantly breaks out in goose bumps. "Wait. What? Really?" *How? Didn't the judges see that I fell?*

Tanisha bum-rushes me, then starts jumping up and down, grabbing me by the backpack straps, making me jump with her. And there we are, jumping like two little schoolgirls who just got a sticker on a spelling test. Out of breath, I bend over, hands planted on my knees. The smell of today's lunch special—tacos—seeps in through my nostrils.

Beatriz, dressed to the nines in a red checkered skirt and white sweater, diva-strolls into the cafeteria, taking a seat at the center table, which everybody knows is reserved for her. Everybody's waving at her, congratulating her, wishing her good luck in the pageant. Maricela and Julicza made it into the pageant too, but you can't tell by the way everybody's kissing Beatriz's behind.

"This is gonna be so much fun!" I say through panted breaths, eyes still glued on Beatriz. "We get to do this together. And girl, am I glad, because I'm going to need somebody to keep me from body-slamming you-know-who!"

I lift my hand up to slap high five, but Tanisha doesn't lift hers to meet mine.

"I didn't get in." The words escape from Tanisha's mouth in one quick, low breath.

The air is still and thick. The everyday noises of the lunchroom are somehow muted, and everything around me becomes motionless.

"What do you mean?" There's a boil starting inside me. I can't do this pageant without Tanisha. "That's it! I'm going to speak to Mrs. Walton right now. She'll fix this."

By now Beatriz is glancing my way. She's got this smile, sly as the devil himself, stretched across her face. It cuts so deep, I swear I can feel the blood rise and fight to bust out.

Stephanie Bowles starts skip-walking toward me and Tanisha. Glasses all crooked. Ponytails all lopsided. I never really got a good look at her until now. Cute as she is, it looks like someone took a bucket of freckles and tossed it beneath each eye.

"So dope we're doing the pageant together, Vanessa," she says.

But I don't feel like being bothered, and I'm sure she can tell by the scowl I got on my face. So I make my way toward the exit. My appetite is gone. Hunger has been replaced by fear, the knee-deep, crawl-under-the-bed-and-hide kind. Tanisha grabs me by the arm before I can even leave.

"Vanessa." Tanisha's face grows serious. "I gotta be honest with you. I blew the audition on purpose."

My jaw drops, lands on the cafeteria floor. Suddenly there's a rumbling boiling up inside me.

"You understand why, right? Basketball and drawing. That's what I'm into. Not pageants. I only tried out because you pretty much threatened my life if I didn't. And I wanted you to go and thought you might not without me. This is your dream, not mine."

Then she adds in this last part to soften the blow: "But look, my plan worked. You got in, right? I'll make it up to you and try to come to one of your rehearsals."

Try? One? As in when you can fit me into your busy schedule?

A quiver darts across my mouth at lightning speed. Deep down, I thought that maybe Tanisha had bombed the audition on purpose. But this tiny voice inside said, *No, Vanessa. She wouldn't do that.*

As much as I hate sports, never once did I fail on purpose when she asked me to try out for basketball. (I actually tried, as pathetic as it was.) And never once did I miss a practice or a home game afterward. I've sat through the torture of the annoying sounds of buzzers, cheerleaders, and rowdy people in the bleachers. All of that to show her my support.

Beatriz and her friends walk past us to head to the lockers, and Tanisha gives them the good ole stare down. I chew on the corner of my bottom lip and try my best not to have a nervous breakdown in front of the whole stinkin' cafeteria. I was counting on Tanisha doing the pageant with me, but it's pretty obvious that ain't gonna happen.

"We still cool, though. Right?" Tanisha slaps my shoulder.

No. We're not cool. In fact, I've reached a whole new level of pissed-offness that I never knew existed. Because I don't recognize you right now. Or us.

But I don't have the guts to say any of that, so I nod my head. "Yeah, it's cool. Hold my spot in the lunch line. I forgot my notebook."

My legs push me forward through the lunchroom door, past the lockers, and straight to the empty bathroom behind the gym. You know the one with no doors on the stalls? The one where if you have to pee, you better have a sweatshirt to tie on the doorjambs and squat at just the right spot so that you have some curtain of privacy? Luckily no one is in there. It's just me, the graffiti, the smell of crushed cigarettes, and three tears. Because three tears is about all I got. One for being happy that I made it into the pageant. One for the fact that I'm going to have to do it all alone. And one for the reality that something about me and Tanisha's friendship doesn't seem right.

Darlene and a Dial Tone

When I get home Pop Pop and TJ don't let me sulk for one second about Tanisha.

"This is about you, Nessy. You need to celebrate the fact that you made it in!" Pop Pop reminds me.

"And you can start by whipping us up one of your slap-yo'-mama dinners." TJ laughs, pushing me into the kitchen.

An hour later, dinner is served. The way they eat up my smothered chicken, corn, and mashed potatoes, you would've thought they'd never eaten before. TJ and Pop Pop are so excited, but I'm still trying to let it all sink in. How much fun is this really going to be if I have to go to practices all alone? Who will I talk to? Who will I sit with? Am I gonna fall on my behind again?

But none of that matters to TJ and Pop Pop. All they care about is what I'm going to wear and how I'm going to sing. TJ says he gonna get all of the fabric for my dresses from school this week. Pop Pop warns him that we can only work on the pageant when Daddy's not home, which is easy enough since he's been doing a lot of overtime lately.

"And we gotta get you a makeover," TJ says. "You need your hair done. I say it's about time you get a perm and some acrylic nails. Girl, we gonna have you looking *good*!"

Just about all the black girls at school have some type of hair style. Jheri curls, crimped hair, side ponytails, weaves, braids, something. Me? My hair is just kind of, um, there. No perm. No relaxer. Most days it's a struggle to get a comb through this carpet. I usually just wear it out and natural. And when I really want to be adventurous, I'll stick a headband over it, hoping to make myself look somewhat girly. My clothes? Well, they're a disaster too. I can't even remember the last time I went shopping for myself. Most of my clothes are hand-me-downs from the ladies at church. Now that I'm in this pageant, maybe I have a real shot at wearing something in style.

I'm happy that TJ can make my outfits because Lord knows I will sure need his help. And it's a good thing he can get everything from his school. We can't afford nothing new. I've never had a makeover before, and I pray that TJ can do something—anything—to make me look anywhere near as pretty as Vanessa Williams. And even though all of this sounds great, I can't help but feel empty real deep inside. I'm supposed to be doing this kind of stuff with my mother.

After dinner TJ and I take a power walk around the neighborhood because according to him, "pageant boot camp has begun." When we return, we watch television in the living room with Pop Pop. The six o'clock news is on. Pop Pop always keeps the TV loud so he can hear with the one good ear he has left since the war. TJ sketches dress ideas as I sit on the floor, finishing up *I Know Why the Caged Bird Sings*. Usually I'm able to block out the noise, but the latest news story breaks my concentration.

There's an outrage over making Dr. Martin Luther King Jr.'s birthday into a federal holiday. Two white senators from North Carolina say that Dr. King isn't important enough to have a day honoring him. They're on that television criticizing the greatest civil-rights leader known to man, and all he ever wanted was to bring peace to this country. I can't help but think that the United States of America isn't so united after all. They say Dr. King is un-American because he was against the Vietnam War.

"Yeah, and if Dr. King was the president, there wouldn'ta been no stupid war!" Pop Pop yells at the television as if the reporters can hear him.

I swear my grandfather cracks me up. A black man as president? Here in America? Even I know I won't see that in my lifetime! They already let us have our first black Miss America. That's probably about as far as it goes. But you gotta love Pop Pop and his big dreams.

The front door swishes open and slams closed. TJ shuffles to hide his dress sketches. Pop Pop stuffs my pageant paperwork underneath the couch cushion. Daddy drops his tool bag on the floor and walks into the kitchen to grab the plate I left for him on the stove. Even though I always leave him dinner, I never know when he'll come home from work to eat it. A sudden rush floods over me as I hear him remove the foil from the plate. Did I put one piece of chicken or two? Is the food still warm? I wish we had one of those microwave ovens. But since they cost almost four hundred dollars, we won't be getting one of those anytime soon.

I tiptoe into the kitchen. Daddy sits with the plate in front of him. He's humming as though he's happy at the sight of the meal I made. My stomach swirls, and I crack a smile, begging for him to ask me to join him.

Daddy stops singing when he notices me standing there.

"You want me to reheat your food on the stove, Daddy?" I ask. "Can I get you something to drink?"

"No." His voice is short. "Food's just fine."

Hardheaded, I rush to the refrigerator and grab the pitcher of cherry Kool-Aid I made earlier. My hands tremble as I place a cup on the table next to his plate. When I go to pour the juice, my hand shakes, and next thing I know, the juice pours out so fast, it knocks over the cup and spills everywhere.

"Vanessa!" Daddy screams as he jolts up from the table. His keys and stack of mail go crashing to the floor. But not the plate. The chicken is saved. Thank God.

"Sorry, Daddy! I was just trying to pour you some juice."

I grab a stack of napkins and start to sop up the liquid on the floor. Daddy grabs a towel from the sink and wipes his pants and shirt.

As I shuffle through the mail, a bright-yellow envelope catches my attention. It's addressed to me. I've never gotten anything in the mail. Ever. I can barely make out the wording from the sender. *Edna Ma . . . ?* The rest of the letters are blurred in juice and ink mixed from the spill. Who is Edna? But the address is clear. The letter is from Clinton, New Jersey. Where is that? Far, far away from Grafton Hill, I bet.

"Daddy, this letter is for me?" I pick it up and rise slowly from the floor.

I never seen Daddy whip around so fast. He snatches that thing right from my hand. He hesitates before speaking. His eyes grow cold and dark. The veins in his neck bulge out as he prepares to answer me.

"Just some papers to renew your health insurance. None 'ya business," Daddy says.

None of my business? But I thought our insurance was called Blue something. Either way, the envelope has my name on it. The words grow paralyzed on my tongue. It is fear that leaves me this way. A deeply rooted fear of my father and those stone-black eyes. It wasn't always like this. Once upon a time his eyes were the color of love.

From the living room Pop Pop yells, "The Italians got Columbus Day. The Irish got Saint Patrick's Day. The Chinese even got their very own New Year. But you mean to tell me black folk can't have Dr. King Day? Come on! Give me a break!"

Daddy grabs the soiled mail and shoos me away. My back is turned, and I can still feel the scowl on his face.

Inside the darkness of my room, I pull out Darlene and sit by the window to catch a piece of moonlight to guide my words.

My heart bleeds, blood blackened to a crisp.
For I am a ghost, a mere reminder of memory's bliss.

The eye is blind, unkind to the here and now,
forgetful of the then, forgetful of the how.
Secrets float between us, begging to be revealed.
Not caring how it's done, not caring how we feel.
She existed once in our tight-lipped lives, so I existed too.
Yet she's gone, a whisper in the wind, and now your love is
    through.

Loneliness settles in, rattling through my bones. Daddy imprisons himself in his room, but what else is new? Sometimes I've wondered if Daddy is keeping Mama in that room with him 'cause he wants her all to himself. Mama was a magnet like that, you know. Once she stepped into a room, everybody floated straight toward her. Silly, I know, to think she'd be locked up in there with him.

TJ's stepped out, under the cover of darkness. He's been doing that a lot these days. Once the moon comes out, it's like he ain't got time for me. Pop Pop lies on the couch, wheezing whiskey-scented breaths in and out. I pick up the phone to call Tanisha. She takes five years to answer.

"Hey, girl. You busy?" My tone reeks of *I need someone to talk to.*

Tanisha's voice comes out real quick, like she ain't got time. "Yeah. 'Bout to shoot some hoops at the community center."

I pause for a second, waiting for her to invite me to go with her. Or at least ask me what's wrong. Can't she hear the desperation in my voice? But she doesn't, and I decide not to invite myself either. She's probably going to play ball with her dad.

"Basketball season, ya know? We'll chill . . . later? Miss you."

"Yeah, sure. Later. Miss you back."

Tanisha hangs up first, and all I'm left with is the dial tone humming a wordless tune in my ear.

October 24, 1983

Closed Mouths Don't Get Fed
Now I lay me down to sleep,
another tear I shall not weep.
Please work your magic through the night,
that I will wake with skin so light.
For this will bring a brighter day,
to light my path and guide the way.
And all the pieces will come together:
love, beauty, family, forever.

Dear Darlene,

So far I've said this poem every night. Seems Pop Pop's little saying ain't got no merit to it. I open my mouth, whisper my heart's wish into the wind, but the pieces still remain broken. There is no love. No family either. Maybe there is beauty, trapped somewhere deep beneath this black skin. After all, I did get picked to be in a beauty pageant. So tonight I say my poem twice, just in case the winds didn't hear them the first go-round.

— Nessy

Tell Me What?

Tanisha's version of later is starting to feel like a heaping load of never. The more time that passes, the more alone I feel. During pageant rehearsals I stay to myself, trying hard to ignore the staring, the whispers, the *she don't stand a chance* giggles.

The weeks go by, blending one into the other, and I haven't been seeing much of Tanisha except for sixth-period chorus and church. And even then we don't sit in the same vocal sections. We don't walk home together anymore either, 'cause she's always off to practice.

Today is Halloween, and normally we'd be together, even if it meant me following her around like a puppy to her activities. But things are different this year. She's got practice after school, and I've got rehearsal. Still, I at least managed to sit through one basketball practice last week. Tanisha has yet to come to any rehearsal. Today would've been nice. Pageant practices are getting lonelier by the day, and I'm really missing my friend.

My schoolwork is piling up too. Three tests: one for advanced

English, one for algebra, and one in US history. Plus a paper about women's suffrage. And that's all due today. So much for the teachers easing up on us in time for Halloween. Most of my free periods are spent in the library. At home I'm just as busy. Pop Pop and TJ make me practice every single night when Daddy's not around.

At this point I'm starting to realize that I have to do most of my homework at school because both TJ and Pop Pop pounce on me as soon as I walk through the door. TJ makes me walk with him around the neighborhood at least three days a week. He says that exercise is important when you're doing a pageant. The more I exercise, drink water, and eat right, the more I'll "glow" onstage. We circle the perimeter of the projects five times. It takes about thirty-five minutes, and by the time it's over, I'm soaked in my own sweat.

After that we go home, and I work on dinner while he works on the dresses at the kitchen table. Both dresses are looking real fly. For talent, he's making me a white dress with a silver halo and silver wings. Pop Pop says I'll look like an angel as I sing "Amazing Grace." For evening wear, TJ's designing a red, flowy gown with silver sequins around the neckline.

After dinner TJ works with me on modeling in heels. Crazy thing is I'm not the only one wearing them.

"This is how you stand, Nessy." TJ screws up his face when he sees my horrid pose. "It's called a model's T."

"You doing that thang a little too good now, boy!" Pop Pop lifts one eyebrow at TJ.

"Just playing the role, Pop. For Nessy." TJ stands even taller.

I look down at how his feet are positioned, and they don't look like a T. It looks more like the letter Y. My knees are twisted outward, and I got a bad case of airplane arms.

"Step with your right foot. Then step with your left foot. Now, pivot around and tuck your foot back to the model's T. Don't forget to inhale!"

Do this. Do that. Stick out your butt, suck in your gut. This is too much to think about. I sigh loudly to show just how much I'm enjoying all this.

"If you want a fighting chance, you gotta listen, Nessy." TJ deepens the tenor of his voice. "This is how the models at my school do it when they're showing off our designs."

"Oh, okay! I see your style, ole boy! Going to that there fashion school to get closer to the ladies!" Pop Pop says.

"You know it!" TJ replies, smiling weakly.

TJ bends down to fix my crooked feet. I follow him as he's modeling, but all I do is stumble. TJ holds me up to break my fall. "Ooh, Nessy baby. We gotta lotta work to do, but you gonna get there!"

When modeling practice is done, they make me sing my talent song. My microphone is an empty Coke bottle. Pop Pop suggests I start the song in a lower key and then make the key higher by the end of the song. TJ adds that I need to cover the whole stage and not just stand there and sing. He's got me doing hand motions and bending my knees to show emotion when I hit the high notes.

The last thing we practice each night is the onstage interview. This part of the competition really makes me want to vomit. I'm so nervous about speaking in front of an audience, especially when I have no idea what the judges will ask me. What if they ask me about nuclear weapons in the Soviet Union or something like that? What the heck would I say?

Pop Pop says that even if the questions are tough, with all the books I read and the news I watch, I'd be able to answer them easily. I'm not so sure. Reading is one thing. But talking? In front of an audience? Oh dear.

TJ says when in doubt, pause, smile, and repeat the question before answering it. That will buy me some time to gather my thoughts. I sure hope he's right.

When practice is over for the night, I close the door to my room, sinking low into my bed. Thoughts of Mama boil up inside and push me harder, deeper under my blankets. I crack open my window and whisper my poem into the wind, praying it will carry the message to her, bring her back to me. I need her here with me on this journey of fear and excitement and possibility.

The clanking of glass in the living room lets me know that Pop Pop is having his nightcap. A little later than his usual start, but I guess this pageant stuff has kept him so busy lately, there isn't enough time to drink all day. Which is a good thing. He's trying to stay sober for our practices. I can dig it, because a sober Pop Pop is much better than a drunk one.

A ripple of cool air flows into my room. Eight floors below, I hear the mix of salsa and rap over the scatter of nighttime voices and the movement of people out causing mischief on Halloween night. I wonder if any of those people clothed in their masks and costumes, hustling about the city, are the Edna who wrote to me. Who is she, and what could have been in that letter? A message about my mama? A clue to whatever truth Daddy continues to hide from me?

To take my mind off of things, I decide to call Tanisha. She always knows what to say. Always ready to make me laugh with a funny story about school or church or her own mama. Anything to make me forget. Though I'd never admit it to her, it is nice to hear that sometimes she's got "mama drama" too.

Tanisha answers the phone, and I'm greeted with the sound of laughter. More than one voice for sure.

"Hey, girl, what you doing?"

"Nothing much . . ." Tanisha's voice is shaky, nervous. More laughter echoes in the background.

"Sounds like a party over there."

Tanisha pauses before responding. "Yeah, after practice I went trick-or-treating with Amaryllis."

Insert awkward silence. This is starting to become our new normal. "Rodriguez?" I ask.

If Tanisha is the number-one girl on the basketball team, Amaryllis would be a close second. But they ain't never hung out before, not that I've heard of.

"Well, I guess I'll let you get back to your *friend*." I make sure I say the last word extra stank.

"Yo, T, got any more Laffy Taffys?" Amaryllis calls out.

82

T? She even got a nickname for Tanisha now?

"Um . . . you wanna come over for a little bit? We got a lot of candy left," Tanisha says.

It's almost eight o'clock. Not to mention it's a school night. Tanisha knows better. Plus it doesn't seem like I was a part of the original invitation anyway. Not that I had a Halloween costume this year, or any other year for that matter. But at least in the past I'd go trick-or-treating with her—even if my costume was random: some ripped-up jeans, one of Daddy's work shirts, and some powder thrown on my face.

"Nah, I'm good. I'll check you later." I slam the phone on the base before I even allow Tanisha to say good-bye.

At two in the morning, the front door blasts me out of my sleep. Daddy's home from work. His footsteps are heavy and angry-sounding, as usual. The plastic on the couch screeches. Pop Pop clears his throat and mumbles a hello to Daddy.

I tiptoe to my cracked-open door.

"It's that time of year again," Pop Pop says. "You know where I'm going soon, right, son?"

Daddy lets out a heavy sigh. He takes a seat on the couch, the sound of the plastic covering echoing through the hall-way.

"Not now," he mumbles.

I take a small sip of oxygen, clutching onto their every word.

"I'm tired of telling you this, Daniel, but that child needs to know," Pop Pop says to Daddy. "She ain't no little girl no more. She's got eyes, and she smart too."

"When the time is right, Pop, I'll tell her," Daddy replies.

"She's thirteen, 'bout to turn fourteen! She gonna be a woman soon. Don't you think she got a right to know? It's time to forgive and forget. Move on, before you lose her too."

And with that, Daddy huffs and walks to his bedroom, slams the door, and chains up the locks on the other side. In that room he locks up everything. Himself. My letter. His secrets. His love.

Part of me wants to bust down that door and demand that he let me in. But instead I go back to my bed and ready myself for a sleepless night. Daddy's words echo in my head for the next four hours.

When the time is right, he will tell me. Tell me what?

November 10, 1983

Holding On

November rolls in like a lion,
stomping its way into Newark with a thunderous roar,
devouring days of long suns and bearable, brisk winds.
Replacing those with a cold so bitter, so biting,
its teeth sharper than the lion's fiercest enemy.
And in the midst of it all, of the cold,
of the short days that turn into long, dark nights,
I'm still trying to hold on.

Dear Darlene,

I sure hope you're hanging on too. Just a few more pages to go before you're all filled up. But don't worry. Pop Pop will come to the rescue real soon. He always does.

—Nessy

Dumb and Dumber

My clothes don't fit right anymore. I've already poked two new holes in my belt to hold up my jeans. That's never happened before. Pop Pop says I'm getting taller, which is the last thing I need. Five foot nine is tall enough. Most of my pants are high-waters now. It's bad enough my clothes don't match with the latest fads, but wearing high-waters is considered social suicide in middle school. I need TJ to bring me home some clothes, stat. He's not around as much these days. It's like he ain't got time for me anymore either. He's been skipping out on our walks or slipping off in the middle of the night when no one is around to question his every move.

At rehearsal this week, Mrs. Walton announces a big surprise. The Miss New Jersey pageant is sponsoring a trip for the contestants in our pageant to visit Convention Hall, complete with a pool party at a hotel and dinner at a fancy restaurant. Atlantic City, here I come! I'm going to get to stand on the same stage that Vanessa Williams was crowned on. Sweet! The messed-up part is that Vanessa Williams herself can't be there. She's a superstar now and travels all over the country.

The teachers give us permission slips for our parents to sign.

As the days turn into weeks and weeks turn into months, the secret of me being in the pageant slowly grinds its teeth at me. Daddy should know about it and support me, but instead he's too busy keeping his own secrets, leaving me in the dark.

We need an escort for the evening-wear segment of the competition. The person has to be a male and could be a father or relative, teacher, or friend. They have to look all handsome and gentleman-like in tuxedo suits. All the girls are raving about having either their dad or their crush walk with them onstage. I don't like anyone at this school, because all the boys here are plain dumb-acting and behave like they have no home training. Exhibit A: Curtis and his braided teeth.

As much as I love my Pop Pop, I can't imagine both of us walking all wobbly legged on that stage. And Daddy is out of the question. It's bad enough he doesn't know I'm in the pageant. Even if he did, he wouldn't do it for me, and I don't need his reminders that I don't belong. That I'm not worthy of his attention, his time, his love. I guess that means TJ will have to do it, but that boy might upstage me and win the whole darn pageant even though he's not a contestant! But I know that he'll be proud to be up there, standing next to the dress he made special for me.

The stage in King Middle auditorium is massive, which is nothing compared to the Miss America stage, I'm sure. But never in my life have I felt so small standing on that thing. The janitors polish it every Monday. So much so that the stage glows like the sun, bright and slippery, and all I can think of is me falling again—in front of Beatriz and her crew sitting in the audience, in front of the whole school laughing, pointing at me as I go tumbling down, shaking the whole auditorium.

I'm standing behind the stage curtain, waiting for my turn to practice my evening-wear modeling. Stephanie Bowles is center stage, walking in them heels like it's nothing. Back all straight, big old cheese painted on her face. Like she was made for this stuff.

"Vanessa, why don't you go next?" Mrs. Caldwell nudges me in the back. "Try to stand a little taller and not slouch, so you don't look so . . ."

FAT. Just say it, lady. So I don't look so doggone fat.

But Mrs. Caldwell just puts a fake smile on her wrinkly-behind face and shoos me center stage.

Beatriz sits in the audience, hand covering her mouth, whispering to her friends. And man, are they hawking me up and down. My pants are slowly falling down. Any second now the crack of my behind will be playing peekaboo with the whole stinkin' audience.

The sound of giggling, soft and piercing, simmers low from the seats.

"Straighter, Vanessa," Mrs. Caldwell whispers from behind the curtain. "Suck it in!"

The heel of my shoe catches in a tiny crack in the stage. More giggling. I search for the exit doorway in the back of the auditorium, but the stage lights blind me. I wanna leave so bad—get out while I still have a small piece of me left.

Mrs. Walton bolts out of her front-row seat, probably to try and catch me before I fall flat on my behind. "Let's run that again. And girls in the audience, show some respect or consider yourself disqualified!"

Boy, they all shut their traps after that.

Mrs. Walton grabs my shoulders, shaking me a bit. She stares me down with those eyes of hers. *Focus*, her eyes plead.

Mrs. Ruiz and Mrs. Moore, sitting in the sound box on the second level, run the music once again. The music pours out of the speakers like waves crashing against cliffs. The saxophone is the star of this nameless song, with the drums and piano blending with it in perfect harmony. It's called jazz, and Mrs. Walton's been teaching it in chorus for two weeks now. I let the melody bleed into my skin. I close my eyes, take a deep breath, and Miss Americafy myself. Next thing I know, I'm like Vanessa Williams, tall and demanding, gliding across that stage.

My left-foot turn is smooth. I don't break for one second. My right foot wobbles a bit, but my hands fan out like a swan ready to soar, preventing my would-be fall. Not a sound in the audience. No giggling. No whispering. Moments later I hear a clap. First one, then two, then a few. And then a loud cheer from Stephanie Bowles.

"Go 'head with your bad self!" she screams.

"Nice job, *chica*," Beatriz calls out, and her groupies all start nodding.

Maybe Beatriz is just saying that to be funny. I lock eyes with her as I do one last pivot on the runway, and she throws me a thumbs-up. My stomach dances a bit, and I force a smile back.

Practice lets out early, which is good because I need to study before TJ gets home.

The beats of Grafton move at a lightning-fast pace. Little kids play double Dutch in the empty lot, their braided ropes thwacking against the cold asphalt. Thumping, pumping, vibrating concrete pushes my feet home. Past the empty lot, past the liquor store, past the alley, and down the hill, deep into the projects. But first I make my way to the bodega to pick up Pop Pop's newspaper. He wasn't home this morning when I left for school. Sometimes he walks to the bodega to get a *cafecito*—I think buying coffee is a way to be eyein' Mrs. Mendez.

"Yo, Vanessa," a loud voice screams out from way down the block. "Wait up." Beatriz runs toward me and stops short, huffing and puffing.

"Dang, you walk fast." Her cheeks turn redder than her bomber jacket.

"Yeah, well, I've had a lot of practice these days," I say, but I don't stop walking.

"I just thought we should talk is all." Beatriz's voice lowers to a whisper so soft, I can barely hear her over the music. "You know, make a fresh start. I really didn't mean anything when I made fun of you during auditions. I was just clowning around, you know."

She pulls a piece of crinkled paper out of her pocket and hands it to me. It's her phone number.

I stop in my tracks and look at Beatriz with my mouth twisted to the side. We stand in front of the entrance to the bodega, no words between us. Just the blast of *bachata* coming from inside her mother's store.

"Going to Atlantic City will be fun, huh?" She changes the topic fast like the wind.

This is the girl who giggled. This is the girl who whispered. This is the girl who pointed. This is the one who tried to chop me down. And now here we are, standing with the winter chill nipping at our noses, forcing ourselves into a conversation. Minus the fat-black-girl jokes.

"Um, yeah. S-sure," I stutter, doubtful.

"Maybe you can sit with us on the way down." Beatriz gestures to her friends standing halfway down the block. They wave at us and keep it moving. "Do you like to play Uno? I'll pack my cards."

"You know, I don't understand you. You're mean to me basically all our lives, and now you wanna play nice? I don't bother you. Heck, I don't bother anyone at that school. So why—"

The door to the bodega flies open, and out comes Beatriz's mom. Mrs. Mendez is a little lady with hair like midnight and a mouth that starts at one ear and wraps around her entire skull. The way she carries herself, you'd think she was six feet tall, but she can't be an inch over five feet. She's the type of woman that when she steps in the room, your knees turn to Silly Putty.

Mrs. Mendez sashays her way over to us. "Ay, Beatriz, who

ju friend?" Her English is thick and broken, syrupy and hypnotizing.

Beatriz and I look at each other, not saying anything at
first. *We're not friends, lady. In fact, up until this very moment,
your daughter has been a* bruja *to me.* I want to say all of that.
But of course I don't. Nobody wants to be told that their
daughter is a witch. I'm pretty sure Mrs. Mendez thinks hers
is a perfect angel.

"Mami, this is Vanessa Martin. She's in the pageant too."

"Ay, the *chica* you tell me she sing so good." Mrs. Mendez
smiles at me. "Vanessa, you giving my Beatriz a run for the
money, eh? I making her practice all the time because of you."

"Mami!" Beatriz raises her shoulders, fists clenched.

"No, no. I think is good. Is like you two can push each
other to be better." Mrs. Mendez points her finger in our
faces.

Then things get real quiet even though the beat coming
from the music in the store switches from mellow *bachata* to
earsplitting salsa.

"I have an idea. Why don't you come inside, Vanessa? I
show you how I start my business in Puerto Rico making the
best empanadas ever. You know what those are?"

"She speaks Spanish, Mami."

"*Si, empanadas son mis favoritas,*" I say.

Mrs. Mendez's eyes widen. She claps her hands and
throws her arm around my shoulder. "*Ay, que bueno!* Come
and let me show you just why the Mendez Bodega is the best
mercado in all of Newark!"

How can I say no to empanadas? Those delicious, fried, cheesy, meaty pockets of joy. Plus it's kind of hard to turn down a woman like Mrs. Mendez. It's like she's got a spell on everybody in the neighborhood.

Next thing I know, Mrs. Mendez is pulling me into their apartment above the bodega, with Beatriz trailing the steps behind us. I don't need to look back to know that the look on her face is just as dumbfounded as mine.

Baby Steps, Girlfriend!

🌹**When I get home,** Pop Pop's still not there. Then I remember that sneaky little conversation him and Daddy had a few weeks ago. *You know where I'm going soon, right, son?* And now that I think about it, it does seem like every year around this time he disappears for the day. Stays out for hours but always returns by the time the streetlights come on. That man can't be out in the cold for too long with that leg of his.

TJ and I take our power walk around Grafton, all the while hoping to run into Pop Pop and tell him to hobble his half-legged self back home. It ain't autumn no more.

We walk uphill and downhill, followed by a light jog twice by the river. All the while, the icy air is biting at every exposed part of me. Something about it, though, cleanses everything that's crowding my mind. Tanisha. Daddy. Beatriz. The pageant. The secrets.

My hands are stuffed deep inside my hoodie, hopeful for the slightest bit of warmth. I touch the paper Beatriz gave me and sing the numbers in my head.

555-9345. 555-9345. The notes come out clean, thunderous,

pitch-defying, until that number is permanently etched in my memory.

Beatriz Mendez gave me her phone number. Beatriz Mendez wants to be my friend. Beatriz Mendez wants to sit with me on the bus for our trip to Atlantic City. These days it feels like I have no friends. Tanisha's too busy being basketball buddies with Amaryllis *Rodrrrriguez*, making new Halloween traditions that don't involve me. Come Thanksgiving and Christmas, I'll probably be left out too. She's too busy trying to make it out of Grafton and leave me behind. Maybe it's time I start to think about making some new friends of my own and planning my own exit out of here.

"What song are you humming?" TJ asks, breaking me out of my thoughts.

"Huh? What?" I stumble on my words. "Oh, it's nothing." I decide to forget about what's on my mind and focus on TJ.

"What's up with you stepping out in the middle of the night all the time? Bad enough Tanisha ain't got time for me these days—now you?"

This ridiculously wide, cheesy smile breaks across TJ's face. "I've been seeing somebody." The words float out of TJ's mouth like clouds, all fluffy and thick.

"Ooh! Who? One of those models at your school in New York?" I squeal.

"Maybe. Maybe not. You know I don't kiss and tell! Let's just say this person is *muy caliente!*" TJ says, pushing my back with his hand. That's my signal to stop asking questions. Walk harder, jog faster, push longer.

When we return I slip on a pair of heels and cook dinner, even though I'm still full from Mrs. Mendez's empanadas. I try to ignore the veins in my feet pulsing in and out. I look pretty silly in my blue hoodie, gray stonewashed jeans, and white patent-leather heels. But I need all the practice I can get at this point.

Tonight's meal of fried bologna, french fries, and eggs means only one thing. The first of the month can't come soon enough. That's when Pop Pop gets his veteran's check and TJ does the food shopping. Pop Pop takes care of the groceries. Daddy pays rent and utilities. We eat real good for the first two weeks: turkey wings, steaks, and whole chickens from the bodega. Sometimes we go all out and send TJ to get whiting from the Portuguese fish market in the Ironbound. But once the money runs low, we resort to the cans we have left on our pantry shelves. And sometimes that doesn't include meat. Tonight, though, I discover a hidden treasure when I find four pieces of bologna wrapped in wax paper behind an empty carton of milk.

After dinner TJ and I start to practice, even though Pop Pop still hasn't come home yet. TJ has me try on the dresses again, since it's been a while. My angel costume is fitted like a large choir robe, so I slip that on in the living room over my clothes. TJ attaches the angel wings by wrapping elastic over my shoulders.

"All you gotta do backstage is get Mrs. Walton to help you with the wings," he reminds me.

The last piece is the halo, which is covered in all things

sparkly: glitter, sequins, and rhinestones. When the stage lights hit, my halo's gonna shine all through that auditorium.

For the red dress, I go to the bathroom to try it on. TJ says I can't have no clothes on underneath or it'll ruin the fit. My skin is covered in goose bumps as I remove the dress from the hanger. I've been waiting for this moment for weeks.

The satin tickles my skin as I pull up the zipper. In the mirror the dress hangs lifelessly around my stomach and hips. It doesn't cling in all the right places like Miss America's dress did on the night she won.

Just as I'm stepping out of the bathroom, the front door of our apartment kabooms as it opens. Pop Pop wobbles in, both hands planted on his cane, wheezing like he done sucked on a pile of ashes.

TJ and I run to the door, help him take his coat off, and get him to the couch.

"Now, now. I don't need no help. What y'all think, I'm old or something?"

"You really want us to answer that?" TJ can barely get the last word out before Pop Pop is whacking him upside the head.

TJ falls over backward, laughing something awful, but I don't find a darn thing funny.

"Why do you pull this trick every year? Disappearing like you don't have a family. I was worried about you." My hands are on my waist, and I got my head cocked to the side like I'm his mama.

"Just took me a little day trip is all. It was nothing."

"Where do you go, Pop Pop, when you leave like that? Who do you go with? Seems like you and Daddy got a lot of secrets around here!" I ain't letting up on this old man. *And I still wanna know who Edna is.*

"Well . . . you know. I don't wanna talk 'bout that right now." Pop Pop's cheeks go red.

"Awwwww shoot, Pop's got him a little lady friend!" TJ rolls up off the floor, holding up his hand to slap fives with Pop Pop. Only Pop Pop don't raise his hand to meet TJ's.

"Brought you back something." Pop Pop reaches into his sweater pocket and hands me a brand-new Darlene made of pressed sunflowers, full of pages and pages ready to be filled with my words.

I grab my grandfather real tight, no longer mad at him for staying out past dark. Darlene the Ninth is a nice consolation gift.

Pop Pop pushes me away from him, squeezing hard on my arms. "Nessy chile, you done changed. You losing the meat on your bones."

My face turns hot, not knowing how to respond to that. Is that a bad thing? Where Pop Pop comes from, being on the fat side is a badge of honor. Means you eat well.

"This is your dress for the pageant? You swimming in that thing," Pop Pop says, looking me up and down.

"It's too big, right?" I respond.

"Well, when she tried on the mock-up a few weeks ago, this was her size. Now there's at least three inches of material that's loose. See. Look."

TJ places a mirror in front of me. When he pulls the dress tighter with some clamps, I can see a waistline. It curves in, and the dress hugs firmly at my hips. It's not the boxy, shapeless, boyish body I'm used to. I look . . . like a woman.

"Nessy, you just growing up is all. Don't worry, TJ will fix the dress," Pop Pop says. "Everything'll be just fine."

Tanisha calls me later on that night. There is a new air in our conversations, short and choppy, so hot that the effort suffocates us both. Our friendship seems like rotting fruit trying to hold on for one more day, begging for anyone—anything—to save it from complete spoil.

"Yo, Nessy, where you been? I called you hours ago."

"Thought maybe you'd be hanging out with Amaryllis. Either way, rehearsal ran late, and then I had a lot of homework."

The lie pours out smooth, effortless. Tanisha's had secrets recently. Seems our friendship is soaked in them. Little secrets are like seeds in a garden. But not every garden is full of pretty flowers. Sometimes there're weeds in there. The unpretty ones. Way I see it, I got a right to have my own secrets too.

So I tell myself it's none of Tanisha's business that I did my homework at Beatriz Mendez's house today, practiced for the pageant, and played Uno. I won't tell her that Beatriz showed me how she picks the lock to her brother's room. (Crazy what a butter knife and a hanger can do!) I don't tell her how his collection of Adidas, herringbone necklaces, and stacks of one-hundred-dollar bills is insane.

I won't tell her that Mrs. Mendez fed us empanadas and

mango milkshakes and listened to my stories about my family, though I never revealed too much. Only said that Mama ain't around no more.

Everything about my time at the Mendez house felt . . . real. Once upon a time I had that with Tanisha. She used to invite me over, and we'd spend time in the kitchen, kickin' it with her mom. Now it's like she couldn't care less.

"It's been a while since we chilled. Wanna shoot some hoops or something after school?"

I fight the urge to let out a long, breathy sigh. "Tomorrow I can't. I got so much going on with—"

"Let me guess. The pageant." Tanisha sighs instead.

"Well, yeah, but it's not just—"

"Whatever, yo, just hit me up when you have time." Time no longer exists, at least not for us.

"What about Thanksgiving break?" In the background *What's Happening!!* is blasting from her television.

"What about it?"

"Maybe we can hang out then?" *Thanksgiving is two weeks away. Can we survive another two weeks?*

"Yeah, I guess. My mom said she wanted to take us skating as an early birthday present for you. We can go after choir practice."

Tanisha and I used to spend lots of Saturdays at the roller-skating rink in downtown Newark. Laughing. Dancing. Scoping out the cute high-school boys. That was over a year ago. Before things got weird and hectic. I do miss those times. I miss us. Maybe we still have a chance. Maybe there is hope after all.

"Sounds like a plan. Check you later."

After that the line goes dead. For a second I consider calling her back. Tell her about Beatriz. Tell her about Daddy and the letter I found. Tell her about the pageant and the trip to Atlantic City. But a tiny voice inside stops me. *Baby steps, Vanessa. Baby steps.*

November 15, 1983

Chains
I got a piece of me
chained behind that steel door,
suffocating in the sun-sucking room,
dancing with the gray-skinned ghost.
Can you hear it
calling me to break it free?
Click,
click,
click.
Time stands still beyond those walls,
though behind the chains I can hear
a voice. . . .
Shameless,
nameless,
blameless.
Problem is,
I ain't got no key.

Dear Darlene,
How far would you go to learn the truth?
    —Nessy

Rise of the Undead

The muscles in my legs squeeze to the point where I feel like they could burst at any moment. This exercise stuff is really putting a hurtin' on my body! Pop Pop says the best way to soothe the soreness is to sit in a bath of Epsom salt. But that ain't happening. Not today. No thank you.

I walk past the tub, purposely not looking at it. I fill up a large bowl with hot water from the sink, sit on the toilet top, and place my throbbing, biscuit-can-busting feet in there. Man, it feels like heaven. I swear, the more I wear pageant heels, the more I can see corns and bunions in my future.

The rest of my body is screaming for a dip in that hot water, but I can't do it. There's demons in that tub, just waiting to pull me under, and I kinda like being able to breathe. So I do what I've done for years. Turn on the shower. Let the steam fill the room. Stand at the sink and try to cleanse more than just my body. Wash away the mental clouds of everything that's been going on.

As I stand hunched over the sink, rinsing the shampoo out of my hair, thoughts of Mrs. Mendez surface. Being with her the other day was beautiful and sad, all at the same dang time. What in God's eyes did I do wrong to not have a mom like that? To make me feel . . . I don't know. Whole?

Don't get me wrong. I got somebody. But loving Daddy comes at a high price. With secrets. Like that letter he took from me months ago. Who wrote to me? Mama? But her name ain't Edna . . . is it? When I was four, Mama was the moon and the stars. Only name I knew for her was Mama. Leave it up to Daddy and Pop Pop with their tight lips and hushed words, and it's stayed that way for years. But these days, I ought to call her by another name: Monster.

Speaking of creatures, I don't recognize the one staring at me in the mirror. Different. Naked. Growing. Man, my body has changed a lot. I mean I've always been big, but now I can see the arch of my waist extending to my hips in the shape of the letter S. I turn sideways and suck in my stomach to flatten it out, like Mrs. Caldwell reminds me to do at every single pageant practice. My back pulls up straight, and my chest protrudes forward, showing curves I ain't never seen before. Not quite as curvy as Beatriz, but I like what I see, sort of. Now if only I could get this dark skin of mine to lighten up a bit.

I wish I had a mother around to talk to me about puberty. I remember "the talk" in fourth grade. The school nurse kept all the girls in from recess. We had to sit through this God-awful video that went something like this: one day you will grow boobs, pimples, and pubic hair, then bleed every month for the next forty years of your life, and somewhere in between you'll squeeze a couple of kids outta your lady business, your period will stop, your hair will turn gray, and then you'll die. The end.

I still haven't gotten my period yet. Part of me wonders if something is wrong with me. Seems like everybody else in eighth grade got it except me. 'Cause technically, I should have it by now, right? But the other part of me is kinda glad. I will never understand how a woman can bleed for a whole week and live to tell about it.

When I go to bed that night, I make a promise to myself. No matter how bad it hurts, one day I'm going to find Mama. I don't care if it's tomorrow or ten years from now. I don't expect us to all of a sudden forget the past and become home-girls. But I do want answers—a key to help me understand why she left. No mother would leave her daughter without a good reason. There has to be an explanation. And that explanation starts with my father. Was it somehow his fault? Whether he likes it or not, he will tell me what happened. I'm a young woman now, like Pop Pop said. I can handle the truth.

That night I am carried off into a deep sleep, lost in dreams about Mama. I can hear the quiet whooshing inside my head, like the tide swelling, bubbling over, and crashing its way up the shore. I see myself fighting the waves, pushing and pushing to move forward. But the ocean is violent, angry, and pulls me back. In the distance I see her. Mama. The sun creates a glow around her. Her white dress dances with the ocean breeze, her silver wings shimmer in the sunlight. She's wearing the same dress that TJ is making for me for the pageant. She smiles and extends a hand for me to join her on the cold, wet sand.

Under the sound of the tumbling waves, she whispers, "I'm so sorry, Vanessa. I never meant for this to happen."

My body is fighting against the current, trying to get to her. I have so many questions. Why did you leave? Is your name Edna? Are you still alive? Where are you?

One wave after another comes pounding down on me, pulling me under, deeper. Gallons of ocean water fill my lungs, the saltiness tearing up my insides something good. I frantically gyrate my body upward to come up for air. But I'm no match for the ocean. The waves pull me under deeper, faster. I open my eyes, and she is right there with me, falling as I fall. Dying as I die. And suddenly it makes sense. The halo. The angel wings. Mama's dead.

The waves stop pulling me under and return to a calm swooshing. My body no longer has to struggle, and I butterfly my way through the water. Slowly I swim to the shore, looking back with each stroke. But she ain't behind me. Mama is gone, gone, gone.

My body bolts upright, covered in sweat. The dream has weakened me, leaving my stomach bubbling, twisting, moaning. Mama must be dead. All these years gone by and Daddy never said one word. What did he think? That I wouldn't handle it too well?

Suddenly I'm praying harder than ever, hoping my dream isn't true. I throw on my slippers and tiptoe to the kitchen for a cup of hot tea, hoping we at least have lemons in the refrigerator and tea bags in the cupboard. This is a bad time to be reminded of how stinkin' poor we are. With pains like this, I need more relief than a cup of hot sugar water can provide.

In the darkness of the hall, Mama's ghost is hawking me,

following me on my way to the kitchen. I cannot see her, but I know she's there. The weight of her memory is like lead on my shoulders.

Seeing Daddy in the kitchen nearly scares the daylights out of me. I thought he'd either be at work or locked away in his room, sleeping. But there he is, seated at the table with his head in his hands, taking in small sips of air. I guess seeing me shocks him too, because he shakes his head and wipes his eyes. Red swollen balls of fire stare back at me, matching my own crimson eyes. Has he dreamed about her, like I did? Can he feel her in the room like I can right now? I wanna touch him. Want him to hold me. Tell me it gets better than this.

"Nessy, you should be in bed."

"I couldn't sleep. I had a bad dream . . . about Mama."

Daddy holds his breath, pulling in every ounce of oxygen in the room with him.

"You dreamed about her too. Didn't you? What happened to her, Daddy?" I fall slowly in the seat next to him.

"Best you forget about your mama now. She's gone."

"Is she dead?" I ask him, long and slow.

His face distorts in pain. He moves his hand toward my forearm, circling his finger around my elbow. He used to do that when I was a little girl. I ain't felt his touch in a long time.

"Might as well be." He stops touching me, abruptly getting up.

Don't leave, Daddy. Stay.

I pause for a moment and soak in this opportunity. He's

still got a little love for me left inside. Maybe he'll see things differently about the pageant, if he just lets me explain.

"Daddy, I wish you'd let me do the school pageant. It's not what you—"

He sharply turns to face me, anguish surfacing in his eyes. "Nessy, not right now. This ain't up for discussion."

Not now? Then when? The pageant is in a few weeks. I want him there. I *need* him there. He just walks away to his chamber of emptiness.

I never do get that cup of tea. All I want to do is wish myself back to sleep and hope that I can get through the day.

The Left Behinds

My private practices with Mrs. Walton are my escape. In that music room there are no reminders of home. It's just me, her, and the music. Soul-shaking rhythms that take me away from it all, and I play the role of the girl Mrs. Walton believes me to be.

We've been meeting up twice a week since September. She helps me go over every segment of the competition. For evening-wear modeling, she makes me walk with an encyclopedia on my head.

"Why do we have to do this again?" I ask her every time.

"This will give you poise and balance when you're walking in your gown," she reminds me.

If you ask me, I look crazy wack with that thing on my head. It's hard enough trying to walk in heels, but I have to balance a five-pound book too?

Mrs. Walton uses a tape recorder to record my responses when we practice the interview segment. When she plays it back, my answers are filled with "um" and "you know what I mean." I sound like a nervous little lamb.

"You must be mindful of that, Vanessa. Be . . . *smooth.*" She holds the "oo" extra long.

"Word, yo. I dig it," I respond.

She squints her eyes at me and cocks her head to the side.

"Yes. Yes, I completely understand," I say, laughing.

Mrs. Walton likes that my speech is like a light switch: I can go from news reporter to 'hood girl in a split second. But for the pageant, she doesn't want to hear me speak any street talk, or, as she calls it, colloquialisms. Sometimes I wonder if she's trying to make me talk like a white girl. Like her.

My favorite part of our practices is talent. The way Mrs. Walton plays "Amazing Grace," you'd think she's been playing in the black church all her life.

We review breathing techniques. When I inhale, my stomach must inflate like a balloon. Mrs. Walton says that taking deep breaths will help me reach the high note at the end of the song. When I exhale, my stomach starts to deflate like air being let out of a balloon. That trick really gives "meat" to my lower notes, she says.

"You're doing an awesome job, Vanessa. The committee received everyone's report cards for the academic competition portion of the pageant, and yours is by far the best one," Mrs. Walton says as we pack up for the day.

It's nearing four o'clock, and she knows I can't stay much longer. The skies darken earlier since the clocks turned back.

"Thank you, Mrs. Walton," I say. "I've been working real hard with TJ and Pop Pop at home."

She scans me and says, "I can tell, and you're getting taller too. Might be time for you to get some new clothes?"

I can feel her glancing at my high-water pants. My white ribbed socks do a poor job of hiding the skin peeking out.

"Tell you what." She points that scrawny little finger of hers. "Since we have Thanksgiving break this week, how about we go shopping on the weekend? Do you have any holiday plans?"

Thoughts turn into words. Words turn into lies. "My family has a big turkey dinner. At my grandma's house. Out in the country."

The lie greets me like an old family member who comes to visit but won't go back home. There is no grandma to celebrate the holidays with. Both of them passed away before I was born. And there ain't no house in the country. Though in my dreams, that's where I sometimes picture Mama waiting for me.

The only family I'll have with me on Thanksgiving is Pop Pop and TJ. Most of Pop Pop's people are either down South or out West. And Daddy's family stopped having us over during the holidays years ago. They didn't feel like locking up their liquor cabinets from Pop Pop. They turned their noses up at TJ 'cause "caring about fashion and hair just ain't normal for a young man." And I'm sure it took every bite of the tongue to stop them from telling me I needed to fix myself up. It never mattered that Pop Pop lost his leg in battle or knows the Bible inside and out. It doesn't matter that TJ's talented and can bring the whole congregation to their knees with that voice of his. And they couldn't care less about my good grades, not when I walk around looking the way I do. To them we are the broken pieces of the family. We are the left behinds.

Daddy doesn't stick around for the holidays. Says he's gotta work extra hours 'cause he planning something big. But I think he just doesn't want to be around us, especially at the dinner table, where there's always one empty seat.

"Okay, maybe we can go shopping on Saturday then. Do you like Bamberger's?"

Who doesn't like Bamberger's? What she should be asking is if I can afford to shop there. The people in my neighborhood hang out in downtown Newark, but I ain't never heard of nobody actually shopping in Bamberger's. That's for people with money, like the folks who work at the Prudential building. Those people make the big bucks. People like me, from Grafton Hill, simply walk past the window displays to check out what's inside, but we never buy anything. Bamberger's is one of the flyest department stores in downtown Newark. I pass by it every now and then, especially during the holidays because that store has the nicest Christmas displays. There's even a merry-go-round in the store where you can take pictures with Santa Claus. But I've never actually been inside. I can only imagine how much those clothes are gonna cost.

"I'd love to, Mrs. Walton, but my folks don't get paid until after the holiday."

"No, no, this'll be my treat. In fact, I have a little surprise for you." She smiles. "And how about we keep this between us and your family? We wouldn't want to make the other contestants jealous. What do you say?"

I never had a teacher take me shopping before, let alone buy me anything. Why is this woman being so nice to me? Because she missed out on her Miss America dreams?

"Um . . ." My voice comes out all shy-like. "I mean I guess I can go, only if I can pay you back. I still don't get why you're doing all of this."

"Oh, hush!" Mrs. Walton throws her hand in the air. "I already told you. You're on the brink of something big, Vanessa. I didn't get that chance when I was younger. I'm happy that I'll be around to see you make your mark. That, my dear, is payment enough."

She pulls out a sheet of fancy blue stationery. "Here. Take this note to your grandfather. Ask him to sign it so you have permission to go, and I will pick you up Saturday. Let's say nine in the morning?"

"Um, sure," I say.

Mrs. Walton puts on her ice-blue wool coat. "I can park and come get you at your apartment if you like."

I can imagine the scene now: Mrs. Walton cruises into the projects in her fancy pastel-blue Chevrolet Celebrity with chrome rims. She walks up the eight flights of stairs and picks me up at my door. When we return to her car, it's sitting on cinder blocks, and all that's left is a shell. The wheels, doors, seats, steering wheel, speakers, and radio are all missing and probably on their way to some drug dealer's house so he can sell them.

"That's okay. I'll just meet you downstairs," I say quickly.

"Great. Have a happy Thanksgiving, Vanessa."

"Thanks, you have a nice one too."

I grab my things and head home, painfully reminded that tomorrow is Thanksgiving. That tomorrow there will be two empty seats at the table, yet again. That really there ain't much to give thanks for at all.

A Thankless Thanksgiving

The only thing that takes my mind away from what little food we have to eat is the fact that the Macy's Thanksgiving Day Parade is on. It's my favorite part of the holiday. From the time it starts to the time it goes off, I am sucked into the pageantry of it all. Trumpets blare and bands march in uniform steps, and Miss America herself, Vanessa Williams, stands on top of a beautifully decorated float and for me, is the highlight of the whole parade.

Her fur coat is bad to the bone. Underneath she wears a sequined top and twist-tie skirt. Times like this, I sure wish we had a color television so I could get the full effect of her outfit. But nonetheless, my girl is looking fly!

"Go on, Miss America! With yo' fine self!" Pop Pop screams at the television, like Vanessa Williams can actually hear him.

All around, people are yelling her name as she waves to the crowd. What I would give to live a moment like that. To have someone make me feel beautiful, like Miss America.

When the parade is done, it's time to get creative in the kitchen. There are a few cans of Spam in the pantry, along with some mixed vegetables, and a couple of rotting onions in the refrigerator. Things we never run out of are sugar, flour, and cornmeal.

I scoop the Spam into a serving bowl and add two eggs and seasoning salt, and I chop up the last few pieces of old bread we have. I blend all the ingredients together real good and then form the Spam into the shape of turkey drumsticks. They almost look like the real thing. There's enough to make six drumsticks. Hey, that's better than last year! We only had enough cans to make three. I place them in the oven and heat them at 350 degrees for thirty-five minutes until they're crispy on the outside and soft in the middle.

While that's cooking, I pick at the rotting parts of the onions. The outside of the onions is varying shades of greens and browns with white patches of fuzz, but on the inside the flesh is bright and good enough to eat. I wonder what Miss America will eat for Thanksgiving. One thing's for sure, she doesn't have to pick through no spoiled onions. Miss America probably gets a full spread with candlelight and flowers on the table and real fancy china to eat her food on.

I cut the onions into perfect circles, toss them in some flour, and throw them in a pan with a little bit of oil that I saved from the last time I fried chicken. The scent of the onion rings travels throughout the whole apartment.

The can of mixed vegetables is our last one before Pop Pop gets his check. God, the first of the month can't come soon enough for me. I throw a little salt in the saucepan with the vegetables.

"*Ooh-weee*, it sho' smells good in here, girl!" Pop Pop hobbles in just as I'm finishing up.

The table is set as festive as I can get it. In the center there's a turkey I made out of paper towels, and beside each plate, I fold pieces of toilet paper into the shape of a feather. This is about as much Thanksgiving as I can create from what little we got.

If I had a mother, our Thanksgiving dinner table would look a lot different. There'd be no way that she'd allow me to serve turkey-leg-shaped Spam balls. Mama would've roasted us a big turkey, even if she had to go out to some remote woods and kill the dang thing herself. There would have been macaroni and cheese, collard greens with smoked ham hocks, and sweet-potato pie with a side of vanilla ice cream for dessert.

TJ comes into the kitchen, and we gather at the table to say our family prayer in unison.

Father in heaven,
sustain our bodies with this food,
our hearts with true family ties,
our souls with thy truth,
for Christ's sake,
Amen.

We all stare at our meal and then at each other in silence. Pop Pop breaks it by saying, "Let's dig in. Nessy sho' outdid herself."

"Yeah. Looks real good, Nessy." TJ says.

The lie pierces deep inside my heart. There ain't nothing good about this. The two empty chairs stare at me, taunting me. Daddy doesn't care to be here with us. He'd rather be working, rather be away from us. From me. And this food isn't good. It's barely enough.

The need for escape tugs at me harder than ever before. When I saw Vanessa Williams on that television screen today, I was reminded that there's hope. That leaving is possible. That maybe one day I too can make it to the Miss America stage. Win twenty-five thousand dollars like she did and bounce up outta this jungle. Go somewhere with a house big enough for all of us: TJ, Pop Pop, Daddy, and even Mama. She'd come back if she knew that we could be together again somewhere real nice where the sun always shines and the grass is green and the air smells of honey.

Vanessa Williams ain't never done a pageant before Miss America. Like me. And she had everything standing in her way. They ain't never let no black girl win before. That crown wasn't meant for her. That Miss America dream was for white girls only. But Vanessa didn't cave. Could I one day do the same thing? 'Cause like Daddy and Curtis said, Vanessa ain't even all that black. My black is blacker than hers will ever be. Darker than the deepest crater on earth. Could the world see past that? See me as beautiful too?

November 26, 1983

Water
The tide rolls in angry like a bull,
pulls me out to sea.
Body fighting,
waves growing,
arms flailing,
earth all-knowing.
Time is no longer mine.
I sink deeper,
slower,
until the water calls me home.

Dear Darlene,

Last night I dreamed of water. Tell me this. How is it that
something that feeds the earth with life can kill you just the same?

—Nessy

The Case of the Rusty Tiara

When Saturday morning comes, I wake up extra early to figure out what the heck I'm going to wear for my shopping trip with Mrs. Walton. I can't go to Bamberger's in overalls and a sweatshirt!

The whole house is quiet except for the trickle of the water coming from the shower in the bathroom. Daddy must be getting ready for work. Lord knows when he'll be back. I swear that man is a horse. Work, eat, sleep. Repeat.

I gotta find a way to make me look halfway decent today. Once I read in a magazine that you can make lipstick by mixing Kool-Aid with petroleum jelly. I decide to go with that, but first I need some gear.

I tiptoe into TJ's room to check out his closet. He's knocked out on the bed, snoring, mouth wide open, drool spilling out of the corner. Any other day I'd play a prank on him, like the time I poured a packet of hot mustard in his mouth and then ran back to my bed. (Best prank ever!) But today is too important to focus on silly stuff.

TJ's closet has a split personality. The front is full of men's church suits and street clothes. Tucked behind that, it's filled with all his original designs. I find a black faux-leather jacket with lots of silver zippers, almost like the jacket that Michael Jackson wears in the "Beat It" video. Next I grab a silver, shimmery shirt and a black wraparound skirt. I already have black pantyhose and my black combat boots. TJ even has a jewelry chest. I grab a pair of silver cross earrings, and my look is complete.

"Where you going this early in the morning, big head? And stealing my stuff too!"

Jewelry and clothes are spilling out of my arms. "I'm headed to Bamberger's with Mrs. Walton." I can barely hold in how excited I am.

"Ooh, big stuff. I sure hope you picked the right outfit. You can't be looking crazy around them white folks!"

I hold up what I picked out, and he gives me a nod of approval.

I throw the things on my bed and get ready to wash up, but Daddy is still in the shower, taking his sweet time. So I decide to go to the kitchen to grab the Kool-Aid, but as I pass Daddy's room I swear I hear something. Soft and whispery like the wind. And my feet kinda stop short, like my slippers done filled up with concrete. What's Daddy keeping from me behind those doors? And why for so long? Curiosity takes over, and from that moment, time moves like light. Pushing my feet past the locked room, past Pop Pop snoring on the couch, and into the kitchen hallway, I soon forget what I needed in the first place. Next thing I know, I got a hanger from the closet in my left hand and a butter knife from the sink in my right. Like wings, my feet fly me to Daddy's door.

You remember what I showed you? Beatriz's voice creeps deep inside my brain. And I am transported to the memory of her breaking into Junito's room. In this moment Vanessa the good girl does not exist. She is sneaky and conniving, and I do not like the way it feels. But at the same time, the rush takes over as I rig the hanger in the doorjamb and softly unclick the bottom lock. I feel one step closer. But closer to what?

The first and last time I saw Daddy's room was when we moved here when I was five. It's tiny inside. A twin-size bed with ratty gray sheets is pressed against the wall. A small dresser with a lonely lamp on top is placed beneath the window. Colorless, lifeless walls. No pictures. No family. No love. My room is so much bigger and better looking than this dungeon.

In the bathroom the shower is still running. Just enough time to do a little digging. The top dresser drawer whispers to me. *Open me, Vanessa.* A large cookie tin that says "Royal Dansk" stares back at me. My favorite cookies! I open the tin, ready to steal a few of the butter-flavored ones, praying Daddy won't notice any are gone, praying he won't realize I broke in here in the first place. Except there aren't any cookies. Just a rusty tiara and the yellow envelope that came in the mail that day. Whatever was inside that envelope is long gone. What did Daddy do with the letter? And why would he hide this from me?

The tiara, dainty and petite with several stones missing, is delicate in the palm of my hand. Why would Daddy have this? Maybe I used to play dress-up with it as a little girl? Still, why would he care to keep it when he barely has two words to say to me now?

The sound of Daddy pulling back the shower curtain echoes throughout the apartment. I stuff the envelope in my housecoat pocket and put the tiara back in the cookie tin. Next thing I know, I dart outta his room, push the bottom lock in, and slip into the kitchen before he catches me.

"Dang, girl, you ain't dressed yet?" TJ's voice scares the living daylights out of me. "And what boogeyman are you trying to kill with those things?"

He's sitting at the table, eyes half open, clutching a cup of tealess tea. I realize that I still have the hanger and butter knife in my hands.

"Umm . . . I'm going now." My voice is shaky. "I was just clearing some stuff out of my room before I go."

"Well, don't take your sweet time in the bathroom, sucking up all the water from the shower and the sink like you always do. Sometimes I don't understand you, girl."

And then I do what comes naturally. Smile. Hold it in. He got his secrets. I got mine too.

TJ places his cup on the counter and walks back to his room.

By the time I'm done washing up and getting dressed, Daddy is gone for the day. The dungeon is sealed yet again. I take a look at myself in the bathroom mirror. What I see on the outside can't make up for how I feel on the inside. Blind. Somewhere in that cookie tin was the truth, but I couldn't see it. What did I miss?

The image staring back at me shows that the Kool-Aid trick worked. My lips are cherry red and glossy. The clip-on cross earrings squeeze the life out of my earlobes, but beauty is pain, right? My hair is a different story. I dip my head in the sink, rinse out the conditioner I left in overnight, and ring my hair dry with a towel. My damp hair curls up a little, and I throw on a thick headband. I got no time to fuss with this bush. It's almost nine o'clock, and I gotta run down eight flights of stairs. I've been trucking up and down those stairs at least four times a day. Not to mention TJ and his drill-sergeant walks around Grafton. No wonder my clothes don't fit!

I grab the note from Mrs. Walton and go to Pop Pop, passed out on the couch. When I pat his face to wake him up, he just snores even louder.

"Pop Pop," I whisper softly in his ear.

"Don't go near that rock! It could be a grenade!" Pop Pop bolts upright and covers his ears with his hands.

His forehead is covered in sweat, and he breathes out hard before staring me square in the eyes. There're ghosts in Pop Pop's eyes. Trapped behind the speckles of gray and green.

"Another war dream?" I ask, knowing he never likes to talk about it.

"Oh, it's nothing," Pop Pop lies. "What you got there, Nessy?"

"Mrs. Walton's taking me shopping downtown to get

some things for the pageant, remember? You gotta sign the permission slip for me to go."

Pop Pop smacks his lips together and wipes the sweat from his brow. "Downtown, huh?" he mutters. "Hold on, and let me put my leg on. I'm 'a go with y'all." Pop Pop shuffles to get up.

"Um, that's okay. You can hang out with us on a different day. This is a girls' day. I just need you to sign this, and I'll be back later this afternoon."

"But what about choir practice, Nessy?"

"It's just one practice. Please, Pop Pop."

"Okay, fine, but you ain't missing church tomorrow."

"Promise."

Pop Pop lets out a slow yawn, and his eyes roll back in his head. He leans over and reaches inside his prosthetic leg and hands me three dollars.

"Ain't much, Nessy, but get yourself something nice." Pop Pop leans back on the sofa, and within seconds he's snoring again.

I place the pen in his hand, but he immediately drops it. His fingers are too weak to even grip the pen and write his name. I squeeze his hand around the pen and help him write his signature. When I kiss his forehead, his eyes open, revealing his pupils. They're dilated, frightened, drowning in wartime memories, maybe drowning in his own dreams of his daughter, my mama. Then he smiles and goes right back to sleep.

Mrs. Walton, Please Stop Dancing!

The cool air is dancing with the rush of the Passaic River behind my building. Once upon a time I swam in that river. Back then it was so dang clear, you could see your feet at the bottom. Now it's black, dirty, ugly, and a sad sight, at least in our part of town. Somewhere in some town on the other side of the river, the sun is shining and the water is sparkling like it did when I was a little girl.

Mrs. Walton pulls up in her fancy blue car with the radio blasting. The bass is booming, and the whole car is vibrating. The Eurythmics' "Sweet Dreams (Are Made of This)" is playing. Mrs. Walton greets me with a smile and an awkward, in-the-seat, body-jerking movement. Is she dancing? I wanna tell her so bad that you can't play that white-girl music in the 'hood. If you pull up in the projects with a fancy car, you better be playing some New Edition, Whodini, or DJ Kool Herc.

"Ready for a fun day?" she yells over the noise as I hand her the permission slip.

I nod my head, and she pulls out, up the hill, past the projects, past the bodegas and the liquor stores with men sleeping on the cold asphalt, out of the ghetto and to the hustling, bustling scene of downtown. To Broad and Market Streets.

I'm used to seeing Mrs. Walton at school in her suits and heels. Her hair is always pinned up in a conservative bun. Every lash is always perfectly mascaraed. Both cheeks lightly rouged. Today is a different story. I ain't never seen Mrs. Walton like this. She's wearing jeans. Gray stonewashed Levi's with a sharp crease down the middle, an olive-green Members Only jacket, and an argyle sweater. Her hair falls past her shoulders in loose waves, not a bobby pin in sight.

She's not wearing any jewelry. She barely has on any makeup, yet her skin still looks like porcelain. Pecola from *The Bluest Eye* would worship the ground Mrs. Walton walks on. She's everything that Pecola hoped to be. Blonde. Blue eyed. Beautiful.

I don't say much during the car ride. What do you say to a teacher outside of school? What student hangs out with a teacher on a Saturday? Oh Lord, this is awkward.

We pull up to a parking lot where you have to pay to leave your car and guards watch it to make sure no riffraffs come in and try to jack it from you.

"I'm so excited. We're gonna hook you up, girl!" Mrs. Walton pays for parking, and we head toward Bamberger's.

From wall to wall, Bamberger's is decked out for the holiday season. Extra-long silver ribbon hangs between all the columns. The stair railing is decorated in red, green, and silver tinsel. A huge Christmas tree stands right in the middle of the children's department. Even though Thanksgiving was just two days ago, it seems like they got to Christmas fast.

The women's department is huge. All the clothes are color coded. To the left are the winter whites: wool coats, mink hats, wool sweaters. I look at the price tag on a simple shirt, and it's nineteen dollars! For a little shirt with barely any material? These people are buggin'.

"So, I know TJ is making your talent dress and evening gown for the pageant. How are they coming along?" Mrs. Walton says, combing through the racks.

"Everything looks really good so far. Both the dresses are a little big on me now. TJ has to take them in and add a few more sequins."

"Great! I can't wait to see them. Now you only need the essentials. Do you have a business-style outfit for the onstage interview? What about matching jewelry?"

"Um, no," I mutter.

Mrs. Walton wrinkles up her nose. "What about shoes and pantyhose?"

"I guess I could wear the white patent-leather shoes from TJ's school or borrow Tanisha's, and I have two pair of pantyhose at home. One pair is running a little, but I can put some clear nail polish on the rip to keep it from tearing."

"Hmm," Mrs. Walton huffs. "Let's get you some new shoes, and a girl can never have enough pantyhose."

Mrs. Walton grabs me by the hand and leads me to the dressing room. I feel a pair of eyes hawking me. It's an old lady with so many creases on her face, I lose count. She's probably trying to figure out what the heck I'm doing here. I feel like telling her that I'm wondering the same darn thing.

Next thing I know, Mrs. Walton's chatting it up with this woman, and they start bringing me all kinds of things to try on: a white wool sweater with black polka dots and a blush-pink, knee-length skirt; a cranberry-colored sweater dress with a black shoulder wrap; a green, pink, and blue striped silk blouse with pearl buttons and a matching blue silk skirt.

When I try on the first outfit, Mrs. Walton tells me to come out and stand on the pedestal in front of the mirrors. The sweater is itchy and tight. I reluctantly walk out to the mirrors and realize I have an audience.

Three salesladies. Two customers. And Mrs. Walton.

Great.

"Vanessa is my most talented student. She's going to be in her school's first-ever beauty pageant." Mrs. Walton beams with pride. The rest of the ladies size me up. I bet my bottom dollar that when they hear the word *pageant*, they don't quite picture a girl who looks like me.

One of the salesladies clears her throat and says, "Pageant, huh? Well, what's your talent?"

At this point I want to run away because I know what's coming next.

"Vanessa is a singer. She's got a gift from the good Lord himself," Mrs. Walton chimes in. "Go on, Vanessa, sing a little something."

I give Mrs. Walton the stare of death. Shouldn't she know by now that I hate being put on the spot?

"The pageant is coming up real soon. And you're going to have to sing in front of a bunch of people you don't know, plus a panel of judges."

Sing? Here? Now? In the four corners of the music room, there's only me and Mrs. Walton and gospel music rattling through my bones. I sing my heart out because no one is there to hear me. I sing because there is no one around to judge. But this is different. Foreign. Terrifying.

Mrs. Walton's voice rings loud and clear inside my head. If I can't sing here in front of this small number of people, what in the world will I do when there's three hundred people in the audience? A volcano erupts in my stomach, and I look at the floor, willing it to open up and swallow me whole. Water rises slowly into my eyes. I can't do it. I look at Mrs. Walton and shake my head.

But the next thing I know, Mrs. Walton places her hand in mine and begins the first line of "Amazing Grace," so sweet, so pure. Her stare is magnetic. It's her way of reminding me to look past the nerves and let go. I gulp in a large dose of oxygen and join her in harmony. There's something about this song that pulls me away from it all. The fear. The doubt. It all melts away, and it feels, well, *amazing*.

Together we sing the first verse in a low key, just as we've practiced. She says that B-flat major is my sweet spot and gives me the most room to transition from my chest to my head voice when I climb up to the high F at the end.

When we finish the verse, she lets me continue the song alone and steps away from my shadow. When I sing the last line, I open my eyes and realize the original crowd of six has turned into a mini-audience of about forty gathered around me.

They clap and whistle loudly. I smile nervously, half happy that I did it, half embarrassed that I almost didn't. Mrs. Walton hugs me so tight, she lifts me off the pedestal, and for a second I think we'll go tumbling to the floor.

A short, bald white man steps forth from the audience. He is dressed up in a crisp navy suit with brown suede elbow pads and dark-brown penny loafers. He extends his hand forward to shake my hand. His handshake is firm and darn near crippling.

"Wow, Fernanda, *sobrinha*. You no kidding when you say this girl has talent!" the man says to Mrs. Walton in a thick Portuguese accent.

I stand there smiling weakly, looking dumbfounded.

"When have I ever lied to you, Tio Ronaldo?" Mrs. Walton kisses the old man on each cheek.

"Vanessa, I'd like for you to meet my uncle, Ronaldo da Silva. He's the general manager here and is in charge of the Bamberger's Community Outreach Program," Mrs. Walton says, holding my shoulders with a death grip.

"My niece calling me for weeks bragging about you, how lovely you sing. When she asking me to have store sponsor part of your pageant wardrobe, I telling her to bring you here. And now I see for myself that she no lying. I think we have winner here, eh? What do you say, everybody?" Mr. da Silva turns around and rallies everyone to start clapping all over again.

Both Mrs. Walton and I are cheesin' like two schoolgirls, though I'm sure the red in her cheeks is much more visible than mine.

In the crowd I hear a lady say, "You know they recently crowned a black girl for the first time at the Miss America pageant."

As people leave, they wish me luck in the pageant. Mr. da Silva leaves and returns with a store-credit check in the amount of two hundred dollars. I blink my eyes to make sure I read it correctly.

"I'll be waiting for autographed picture of you in your pageant tiara. I make lot of copies and hang around the store, yes?" He smiles. "And Fernanda, dinner next Sunday, eh? Good luck to you, Vanessa."

Mrs. Walton blows him a kiss. Then this man—or should I say angel—simply walks away. Who has that kind of money to dish out based on me singing one little song?

That Mrs. Walton is full of surprises. We take the check and get everything I need for the pageant, plus a little more. The salesladies and Mrs. Walton decide I should wear the green, pink, and blue striped silk blouse with pearl buttons and matching blue silk skirt for the interview portion of the pageant. It has the best fit and makes me look real fly. Mrs. Walton picks out a bad-to-the-bone pair of blue patent-leather heels to match and some tan-colored sheer pantyhose. A pair of pearl clip-ons tops it off. Next the ladies pick out a rhinestone earring, necklace, and bracelet set to wear with the evening gown that TJ is making. Last they have me try on a pair of formal shoes that I can wear with my talent dress and evening gown. They look like glass, like the ones Cinderella wears, straight out of a fairy tale.

Mrs. Walton says I should also get some clothes for school, especially a new pair of jeans. The way I been dressing these days, I don't argue with her. We pick out two fly pairs of Guess jeans—one blue stonewash and one gray acid wash. Finally I'll have something that's name brand. Then Mrs. Walton picks out some shirts: a red silk blouse with black buttons, an off-the-shoulder sweatshirt, and an argyle polo shirt.

Next up is makeup. We head to the Fashion Fair counter. Mrs. Walton tells me that it was the first makeup product made for black women. "Will your family be okay if we get you some makeup for the pageant? It's just to help you glow more onstage."

I want to blurt out that not only would TJ be okay with the makeup part, he'll probably be stealing it as soon as I get home. I'm sure Pop Pop won't mind. He knows that the Miss America girls have to wear makeup for the pageant. Daddy, on the other hand, is a different story. But since he's not coming to the pageant, he'll never have to know.

"Vanessa, I have to run to the ladies' room. Do you need to go too?"

"No, I'm good. I'll just wait for you here."

"Okay, be right back. In the meantime, pick out some things you like. Maybe this young lady can help you." Mrs. Walton points to a pretty black girl behind the counter and scurries off.

The girl scans me over suspiciously as I look at all the makeup options. Even though I'm not looking directly at her, I can tell what she's thinking. I need one of everything.

"So you're the big commotion in the store today," she says when she finally speaks.

I lift my eyes to meet hers. Her eyes are almost as black as my skin. "I don't know. I guess." My voice is shy, awkward.

She's dressed to the nines. Makeup flawless. She can't be much older than nineteen. She starts going on and on about the type of makeup colors I'll need for my complexion. Nutmeg-colored blush. Amber-toned lipstick because red tones are too drastic for a pageant. Black mascara to thicken my lashes.

Everything goes in one ear and out the other because something else steals my attention: an advertisement featuring a black woman in "before" and "after" pictures. In the "before" picture, her skin is chestnut brown. She's wearing a frown on her face something fierce. In the "after" picture, she's at least two shades lighter, and she looks happy. A crowd of men is gathered around her, offering her roses. The slogan reads: *Wonderful things happen when your complexion is clear, bright, Sol-Glo light.*

Maybe this is what I need. The ad says results guaranteed in two weeks. Just in time for the pageant. I look at the price tag. Five bucks. Pop Pop only gave me three dollars. I wouldn't even fix my mouth to ask Mrs. Walton to get it for me. I don't feel like hearing one of her "you're beautiful the way you are" speeches.

"Like what you see?"

"Um, yeah. But does it really work as good as it says?"

"Of course it does. It worked for me." She runs her fingers across her honey-coated face, then leans in and whispers, "I used to be a lot darker. Started using this stuff, fixed up my wardrobe, my complexion cleared up, and I got me a fancy gig right here in the finest department store downtown. You wanna have a shot at the pageant, right? You and I both know what type of girls they look for. This might be your ticket."

She sounds like a dang commercial. But she got me thinking. Suddenly I'm picturing myself with lighter, clearer skin, onstage in my pageant gown, ready to win it all.

"I'd love to get it, but . . ."

"It's expensive, I know. No worries," she says, touching me on the shoulder. "I'll give you a few free samples with your makeup. You do want these, right?" She points to what she's picked out.

In the distance I hear Mrs. Walton's signature click-clack strut as she makes her way toward the counter.

"Do me a favor and put the samples in a separate bag," I whisper softly so Mrs. Walton won't hear.

She winks at me and does as she's told, slipping the bag in my hand so I can stuff it in my coat pocket real quick.

"All set with makeup, Vanessa?" Mrs. Walton walks up to me, out of breath.

"Sure thing."

The makeup girl throws me a wink and a smile and mouths, "Good luck."

When Mrs. Walton and I get to the register, our items ring up but don't even hit the full two hundred. Everything adds up to 135 dollars.

"*Obrigado!* Thank goodness, we're under budget! Now that's what I call clearance-rack magic," Mrs. Walton squeals. "Let's pick out one more thing. Ooh, how about that dress?"

Mrs. Walton darts from the register and stops in front of a mannequin dressed in an ivory princess-style gown. The bodice is covered in lace with pearls woven in between the seams, and the bottom flares out and brushes the floor.

"It's beautiful, isn't it?" she says.

"Yeah, all ninety-nine dollars of it," I reply. "Plus I already have a gown for the pageant. I told you that." This feeling starts building up inside. Does she think TJ won't make a dress that's good enough?

"Yes, yes! TJ is making your dream dress, but who says you can't have a backup one? I say we get the dress anyway. If nothing else, you'll have it for something in the future. Maybe the eighth-grade social?"

I've been so busy practicing for the pageant that I forgot that there's a social at the end of the school year. All the eighth graders get decked out for this event. It's the party to attend before graduation.

Before I even have a chance to respond, Mrs. Walton waltzes to the register, dress in hand, and adds it to the rest of my order. With the addition of the dress, the new total is 234 dollars.

She pulls the remaining balance out of her wallet like it's

no big deal. Thirty-four dollars. That's enough to cover the light bill. Or groceries for the week. A decent Thanksgiving meal, even. But I don't say nothing. I just shut my mouth and take my blessing.

Feeding Our Souls

By the time we're done with all that shopping, all I can think about is that bleaching cream in my pocket and how I can't wait to get home and try it. But my stomach is screaming, and my feet are throbbing inside my combat boots.

"Let's get something to eat," Mrs. Walton says. "What would you like?"

"Oh, I don't care. The lunch counter at Woolworth's is good enough. I think they have specials on Saturdays."

"Woolworth's? They don't serve meals fit for a pageant queen. Let me take you to my favorite spot."

We round the corner of Broad and Market and head down toward Halsey Street. The sun is out something fierce, but that doesn't stop the cold air from constantly smacking us backward. We fight our way through the bustling streets and land in front of Je's Restaurant.

"Um, Mrs. Walton, this is a soul-food joint. I'm not sure if this is what you were looking for."

"Oh, yes. This place is my favorite. The collard greens are to die for!"

Mrs. Walton throws her hands in the air like she's praising the Lord, and I swear my jaw drops past my shoulders.

Soon as we walk in, two waitresses double-team hug Mrs. Walton. And they strike up a conversation like they been waiting for her. It's like Mrs. Walton is family up in here.

"Fernanda's here, y'all! Get those pots ready!" one waitress says.

"That's right, Janet!" Mrs. Walton high fives her.

"And how's your daddy doing, Fernanda?" the other waitress asks.

Mrs. Walton's face turns serious.

"Oh, you know, Kim. Same old, same old. He sends his love."

"Well, make sure you stop by and grab him a plate before you go visit him upstate. I'm sure by now he's got a hurtin' for our greens!" Kim says.

The owner, Mr. Sutton, strolls over and introduces himself to me and grabs our coats.

We sit at a table by the large window at the front of the restaurant. The movement of feet hustling through the streets of Newark matches the tip-tap of the Motown music playing inside. "Get Ready" by the Temptations comes on the radio, and Mrs. Walton breaks out into her awkward chair dance.

I try my best to hold it in, but I can't help it any longer. So I bust out laughing.

"What? You think I don't know soul music? I grew up on this stuff, honey!"

Mrs. Walton starts singing the lyrics, and her voice blends

in perfectly with the male lead singer, only hers is an octave above. Her singing is great. Her dancing? Not so much.

Janet sashays over to our table, and she and Mrs. Walton start singing together. When the song fades out, they slap five like they just gave a sold-out concert at Symphony Hall.

"Will it be the usual?" she says to Mrs. Walton.

"You know it."

"And what will the young lady have?"

I haven't even looked at the menu. I've always wanted to eat at Je's but never got the chance. More like never could afford it.

"Just tell her what you like, and they can create something special for you," Mrs. Walton urges.

I hear Pop Pop's voice inside my head, reminding me to order the cheapest thing on the menu "'cause we ain't Rockefeller." But hunger wins. This girl's gotta eat.

"I'd love to have some macaroni and cheese, collard greens, and baked turkey wings, please." This will more than make up for the turkey-shaped Spam balls we ate for Thanksgiving. I really want to order something fried, but the last thing I need is my face looking like a pepperoni pizza come the day of the pageant.

"Comin' right up!" Janet smiles and heads toward the kitchen.

There is an awkward moment of silence between Mrs. Walton and me. I can't even find the words to thank her for one of the most fun days I've had in a real long time.

"Mrs. Walton, why are you doing all this?"

"All what?" She smiles.

"You know. The shopping, this fancy lunch, accepting me into the pageant even though I fell flat on my behind. I don't get it. Why me?"

Mrs. Walton reaches forward and places her hand briefly on top of mine.

"First of all, you could have fallen through the stage and landed in the school basement, and you still would've passed the audition because of your singing and your academic records. Second, I have a daughter. And when she gets older, I want her to be as smart and talented as you. And believe it or not, Vanessa, I see a lot of myself in you."

This lady has got to be out of her mind. We couldn't be any more different. My face must've given away my thought because Mrs. Walton keeps talking.

"No, I'm serious. Did you know that I'm from Newark? Well, Portugal by way of Newark."

I almost spit out my Coke. "Say what?"

"I was born in Portugal. My family immigrated to the Ironbound when I was very young. We lived together in a three-room house over by Ferry Street—my father, grandfather, Tio Ronaldo, and a whole load of cousins and great-uncles from Portugal. My family came here with nothing, and they worked for pennies in the factories." Mrs. Walton laughs. "And then they rushed home before nightfall to hide from the immigration-raid vans. Scared me half to death as a kid."

Mrs. Walton places her hands on top of mine again.

"Now do you see why becoming Miss America was never in my future? Being a poor immigrant was rough. And not having a mother to help me was even rougher. How was I supposed to be Miss America? I didn't lose my accent until I was out of college, and I didn't become a citizen until I got married. There was no place for someone like me in Miss America. But you, Vanessa? Ah, you can make history!"

This is a lot to sink in. Living in a house smaller than what we got in the projects? Hiding and being hunted like animals? Working for barely any pay?

"Well, what about your mother? Where was she?" I ask before I realize that I shouldn't have.

Mrs. Walton pauses. "She up and left before I could even walk."

She gets real quiet for a second and then starts scratching the corner of her left eye. Maybe we got a lot more in common than I thought. I want to ask where her mother went, but that'll probably make her ask questions about my own mama.

Mrs. Walton starts talking again. "After years of working in a factory, my family finally saved enough to start their own business: Da Silva Dry Cleaners, right in the heart of the Ironbound. Life was good here until the riots in '67. Then it got so bad, a lot of Portuguese immigrants packed up and left. We stayed even though times were hard. But when rioters burned down the business, my father moved us up to upstate New York. I always knew I'd come back eventually. After I got married, my husband and I moved back to Newark. Then I was offered a job to teach at King Middle, and I couldn't turn that down."

"Wait! You *live* here?"

"Well, of course. Where'd you think I live? In the suburbs somewhere? Don't be fooled. I'm a city girl through and through!"

I can't picture Mrs. Walton living here during the race riots or even now. Though the riots happened two and a half years before I was born, some parts of the city are still damaged. There are still some buildings boarded up, with the windows busted out and replaced by paintings of would-be windows with curved drapes. Those busted-up buildings are now a hangout spot for the dope fiends and homeless people. I've seen pictures of what old Newark looked like before the riots. Back then, Newark was like a city of gold.

"If you didn't have a mother around, then who taught you how to dress like you do? And where on earth did you learn about gospel and soul music? Aren't Portuguese people Catholic or something?"

Mrs. Walton chuckles. "Yes, I grew up Catholic, though my family worked so much, we didn't go to church often. But trust me, there were no songs like 'Goin' Up Yonder' at Sunday mass! Mrs. Boxley taught me all kinds of music, from Bach to the Supremes. She was my music teacher at Ann Street School and the only black teacher there at the time."

Talking about these memories brings a smile to Mrs. Walton's face. "She was very popular with all the students. Mrs. Boxley took me under her wing and taught me how to play the piano and the church organ, and how to sing all styles of music, like classical and Broadway, but mainly gospel and soul music.

She didn't teach me only how to sing the music, she taught me how to feel it in my gut. Every Sunday she'd drive from her house in the Central Ward all the way to the Ironbound to bring me back to Central to go to church with her."

Mrs. Walton's eyes pace the ceiling as though she's looking for something.

"Where is she now? Do you still see her?"

She clears her throat and lifts the napkin to the corner of her eye. "Once my father moved us to New York"—Mrs. Walton's voice cracks—"I never saw Mrs. Boxley again."

I feel the beat of my heart slow down in my chest. Mrs. Walton lost not one mother but two. Dang.

The waitress comes out with our food, piping hot, but suddenly I don't feel like eating. Mrs. Walton's order looks like a buffet table. This woman's got a plate of grits with fried whiting, biscuits in white gravy, three thick slices of beef bacon, and a side of candied yams with marshmallows and raisins. To top it off, she has a pitcher-sized cup of sweet tea. Compared to my meal, hers looks like a heart attack on a plate. Make that several plates.

Smokey Robinson's "The Tears of a Clown" blares through the radio.

"Enough of the sad talk now. Today is about fun!" Mrs. Walton breaks out into her white-girl dance while she takes large bites of her food. Next thing I know, I'm dancing and tearing up my food too.

When Mrs. Walton drops me at home, everybody is gawking at her ride. You'd think black folks ain't never seen a white woman driving in the projects before. Who am I kidding? I ain't never seen one either!

I thank Mrs. Walton for everything and make my way toward my building with my hands full of shopping bags.

"Hey, Vanessa. Do you want me to help you bring your things up?" Mrs. Walton yells from her car window.

I look behind me and see Junito and his crew walking down the hill. "Um, no thanks, Mrs. Walton. You better head home. Before the sun goes down."

With that, she throws me a wink, spins her car around, and speeds up the hill, past the Diablos, past the garbage, past the pipes, and to the thumping, jumping rhythms of her own piece of Newark.

Up in the apartment, as I pick up the phone, I'm already asking myself why I'm dialing the number. Maybe it's because TJ's not home (again!), and I have no one to talk to about my amazing day with Mrs. Walton. Maybe it's because I know that if I even tried to call Tanisha, she'd "conveniently" be unavailable. Or maybe it's because Beatriz gets it. Gets me. Gets the pageant. Gets my dream.

"May I speak to Beatriz, please?"

"Vanessa? Hey, *chica*. I heard you were hanging out in some fancy blue car today."

"Um, yeah, I was—"

"*Chica*, everybody knows that's Mrs. Walton's ride. Teacher's pet!"

"We were just—"

"You don't have to explain anything to me. It's all good.

Wanna come over and practice for the pageant? We can play Uno. Mami's making *arroz con gandules* for dinner."

Maybe Beatriz and I are becoming real friends. She knows I can't turn down her mom's rice and beans.

"*Claro que sí!* I'll be over around six."

November 30, 1983

Empty Promises
Wonderful things happen
when your complexion is clear.
Bright.
Sol-Glo light . . .

Dear Darlene,

I've been using this stuff all week. And so far, *nada*. My skin seems blacker than the skin I started with. Each day I ask why the heck I'm doing this. To look like Vanessa Williams? To look like Mama? Or maybe to fix what's on the outside, hoping the Sol-Glo will take care of what's left inside too?

—Nessy

New Friend, Old Problems

My gear's been decked out for school every day since I went shopping with Mrs. Walton. Today I'm wearing my gray Guess jeans with a blue-and-orange argyle polo and a pair of shiny brown penny loafers TJ got me from school. My outfit is tucked in all the right places, showing off curves that I ain't never had before.

From the stares I've been getting all week, I can't tell if people think I'm looking fly or think I'm new to the school, because I definitely don't look like the nerd they're used to seeing in the back of the class.

Right before lunch I change books for the last periods of the day. Curtis and his boys walk toward the cafeteria, right near my locker. Curtis winks at me and blows a kiss, and I just about throw up in my mouth. Then one of his boys slaps him in the ribs and says, "Yoooo, that's Vanessa Martin!"

Curtis does a double take and says, "What the heck? She ain't look like that last week!"

I just roll my eyes and keep packing my books. Idiots.

Tanisha comes out of the bathroom and heads toward my locker.

"Well, hello, stranger. So nice to be in your royal presence. You know you ditched choir rehearsal Saturday." She's got this stank-attitude, eye-roll look smeared all over her face.

"I know. I went shopping for the pageant with Mrs. Walton."

"You hung out . . . with a teacher?" Tanisha's voice is loud, so I hush her so no one else hears.

"Guess you forgot we had plans to go roller skating. My mom was going to take us as an early birthday present for you, remember?"

Shoot! I did forget! I was too busy hanging out with Mrs. Walton. And Beatriz. Suddenly I feel sick. "Tanisha, I'm sorry. There's so much going—"

"Look," she cuts me off. "I get that the pageant is coming up and all. And you know I got your back in all of this, but—"

Just then Beatriz strolls up with her crew, all of them wearing red jeans and white button-down shirts like they're some type of R&B group. Beatriz smiles at me and looks me up and down.

"Nice outfit, *chica*. You wanna sit with us at lunch?"

Well, this is awkward. Does she mean both me and Tanisha or just me? "Nah. I gotta go to the library and finish up my lab report."

Tanisha crosses her arms and sucks her teeth.

"Wanna come over my house again after practice?" Beatriz asks.

"Um, I'll let you know."

Fire shoots out of Tanisha's ears, scorching my face.

Beatriz winks at me, rolls her eyes at Tanisha, and struts with her crew to the cafeteria.

"Hang out at her house? Again? These days you ain't got time to chill with me, but it looks like you got plenty of time for her. Since when did you two become friends?" Tanisha asks. Her eyes look hurt and sad.

"Oh, stop it! It's not like you're not hanging out with a new friend these days." I slap her on the arm. "Come on. You know who my best friend is. *You!*"

I'm half laughing, but Tanisha ain't cracking a smile. "We've just been helping each other practice for the pageant. It's nothing, really."

"I can't chill with you if you're gonna be hanging out with her. I don't trust that girl. Ever stop and wonder why she wears red to school almost every day? That's the color of her brother's gang. That girl ain't nothing but a snake in the grass, and I told you that a long time ago. Hit me up when you got time for your *real* friends."

"Oh, don't be like that! You're wrong about Beatriz. She's not so bad once you get to know her."

I say all of that hoping that Tanisha will turn to face me, tell me she overreacted, tell me she's sorry because she's the one who started dissing me in the first place. That she'll let me know she hasn't given up on us yet. But Tanisha doesn't say a word. She keeps it moving to the cafeteria, not even looking back.

Junito Shatters the Earth

🌹 **On the walk home** from pageant practice, Beatriz grooves to the rhythms of Newark traveling in the air. The cool-cat bass of Kurtis Blow is playing low under the hip-grinding sway of Celia Cruz. Beatriz's steps match the different beats: a slow tread through the grassless patches of black soil, followed by a faster two-step on the cracked concrete. I'm walking a half beat behind her, not really feeling it.

The homeboys hanging on the corners keep trying to step to Beatriz. It's like I'm nothing more than her shadow. "What's up, *boricua linda*? Can we walk you home?"

Their words linger in the winter winds. Beatriz has light skin, so she's pretty in their eyes. I'm reminded yet again that I'm too dark—invisible—and not worth an ounce of their attention.

Beatriz sucks her teeth and throws her hand up in the air. As each group of guys calls out for her, Beatriz carries herself taller and arches her back to show off her curves. I pull my stomach in and do the same, but I don't look as good.

"Ahhh. I'm so nervous for the pageant!" she says.

"Yeah, me too," I say, finally letting out a cold breath.

"I ain't gonna be able to look at my family in the audience. Junito and my cousins will probably be laughing at me. And Mami will be too busy trying to tell me how to walk and how to talk."

I pause, painfully reminded of what little family I have coming to see me in the pageant. "Be happy your mom will be there. Only my grandfather and TJ are coming. Tanisha was supposed to come, but I doubt it now."

"Oh," Beatriz speaks slowly. "Look, I'm sorry if I said something earlier that maybe Tanisha didn't like. It's just that, you know, she's always giving me a hard time. Talking caca about me."

"Don't worry about her. She'll come around. I bet the three of us will chill together one day like nothing ever happened."

"What about your dad? He had a change of heart, right?"

I nibble on the inside of my lip, thinking about how to answer that. I wanna tell her how I broke into his room. How I found an empty envelope and rusty old tiara. But I can't.

"I'm gonna do the pageant. Without his permission. What he doesn't know won't hurt him." The words spill out like water.

"Hmmm. So you mean if I want a shot at winning the pageant, all I gotta do is rat you out to your dad?" Beatriz raises an eyebrow, and my breath cuts short. Then she laughs so hard, all of Grafton can hear.

"I'm kidding, *chica*! Real friends don't do stuff like that to each other. It's your dad's loss if he doesn't come and see you."

There's this uncomfortable silence between us.

"So when are you going to invite me over and show me the gown Mrs. Walton got you?" Beatriz asks.

"Oh, my cousin's making my gown," I blurt out. Dang. The last thing I want is for anyone to know that TJ makes clothes for girls. The family story is that he's in school for the business side of fashion. Which is a bald-faced lie.

Beatriz stops walking and raises an eyebrow. "Wait. You mean TJ? You didn't tell me this. Well, excuse me! What does it look like?" She's all up in my business now.

"It's nothing special," I lie. "Red with silver sequins."

I'm not the bragging type, but my dress is fresh to death. No, it's not a fancy brand-name dress from some expensive boutique, but the fact that my cousin's making it means it's special to me. TJ is putting the finishing touches on it at school and bringing it home on my birthday, the day before the pageant.

"What about your dress?" I ask. "All the times I've been to your house, you haven't showed me yours either."

"That's because my *abuela* hasn't finished making it yet. She's shipping it up from Puerto Rico. It's white and simple." Beatriz throws her hand in the air, a sign that she ain't got nothing else to say. She then takes her other hand and runs her fingers through her hair. They glide through the silkiness in one smooth, napless sweep. Part of me wants to reach out and touch that hair, grab a thick chunk, and brush it against my cheek. Feel what it's like, even for a second, to have nice hair. But she'd probably call me out for being a weirdo if I did that.

Deep down I know Beatriz is lying about her dress. That girl never does anything simple. Beatriz Mendez is a living, breathing, walking edition of *Vogue* magazine. I can only imagine what her dress will look like. Probably like something straight out of a Gucci ad. Maybe she won't tell me because she doesn't want to make me feel bad. Beatriz's mom owns several bodegas, so she has the money to buy the most expensive fabrics in Puerto Rico and dress her up all nice. Me? I ain't got none of that.

"TJ went to Barringer High, right?"

"Yeah, he graduated last year."

"I remember him. He went there with my brother. They used to be cool."

Junito dropped out of high school when he was a sophomore and started selling drugs in the neighborhood. He even has pushers in the elementary school selling that poison for him. There is a pause as though she can read my thoughts.

"Junito says that TJ is . . . different?"

"Different how?"

"As in he likes boys. You know, that kind of different," she replies.

Beatriz is all up in the Kool-Aid and she don't know the flavor.

"You mean, like, gay? Oh, girl, don't listen to that crap. Plus, TJ has a girlfriend. In New York. He's with her all the time."

My voice sounds confident, but on the inside I'm asking myself a million questions.

"Oh, I didn't know that." Her voice is hesitant, almost as unconvinced as mine. Beatriz twists the corners of her lips. "Sorry, *chica*. I just thought I'd ask. I believe you, though."

When we get to the corner, Junito and his crew are hanging out in front of the bodega. They're all dressed in red and smoking something that looks like cigarettes, but I know better. That ain't nothing but reefer wrapped up in a cigarette disguise. Beatriz asks if I'm coming in for some empanadas. I'm starting to think about what Daddy would say if he knew that I was hanging out in a house where a known drug dealer lives.

"Mami made extra for you to bring home this time."

Just then the number 25 bus screeches to a halt in front of the bodega, coughing out a thick puff of black smoke before the doors open. Out comes TJ.

"Yo, Nessy," he says, walking up to me and giving me a hug.

TJ fixes his eyes on Junito, then smiles and waves at him. Through his coat, through the thick smoke of wintry air, I can see TJ's heart pounding out of his chest.

For a split second, the look in Junito's eyes is different. Soft, longing. Not his usual hardened, thugged-out getup.

"Why the hell this fool waving at you?" one of Junito's boys says, stepping forward like he's ready to start something.

Junito turns stiff, cold, and angry, and he draws his eyes away from TJ. In that one second, that one moment between them, I can tell something ain't right. TJ's cheeks turn pink, and I stand in front of him like a mother bear protecting her cub.

"Hell if I know. I don't deal with *maricónes*, so step!" Junito stomps his foot so hard, the earth about shatters beneath us.

TJ jumps back. I don't need to turn around to see the fear and hurt in his eyes. I can smell it on him—wild and fresh and unwavering.

The Diablos start talking about TJ in Spanish. *Mira esa maricón.* The way they're looking at him and gritting their teeth, you don't need to speak the language to know that they're calling him gay in the worst way possible. TJ stands there for a second as though he's waiting for something. But Junito only responds by slapping high fives with his boys as they go on and on about TJ, the neighborhood sissy.

"I'll take a rain check on those empanadas, Beatriz. We gotta go help my grandfather with something."

Beatriz stands there with this look on her face that's hard to read. Half satisfied. Half abandoned puppy. "Okay, Vanessa. See you tomorrow for the trip to Atlantic City. Don't forget to pack your swimsuit *and* that you're sitting next to me on the bus!"

My stomach gurgles as soon as I hear the word *swim*. No sir, there will be none of that for me. I grab TJ by the wrist and start to walk away from the bodega, down the hill toward the projects.

"I don't want to talk about it, Nessy." TJ releases himself from my death grip.

"Why did Junito look at you like that, TJ? What's going on with you two?" I grab him again, but he yanks away and walks faster.

"I said not now." There is an air of sadness in his voice.

The truth. The lies. The secrets. Knew deep down all along.

It's what we all knew. Pop Pop and Daddy. Shoot, even the roaches could tell! But we were too busy trying to lock it up, throw it in with the other secrets piling up within the four walls of the place we call home.

"That's who you've been sneaking out to see at night? Junito? He's your *muy caliente* lover?"

TJ throws his hand over my mouth. "You don't understand, Nessy. That back there was just an act. Something to prove to his boys." His voice is stern, like he's trying to convince himself.

I'm not so sure.

"Look, I know what I'm doing. Junito wouldn't hurt me. We're even talking about leaving this place. Maybe going to San Francisco. My friend from school Donnell always talks about how life is so much better over there. His brother moved there last year. People don't look at him so funny no more. Junito and I need that. Promise you won't tell Pop Pop or Uncle Daniel."

Tell them that you're exactly what the rest of the family thought you were all along? Or tell them that you've been hooking up with the biggest gangbanger in all of Grafton?

"I won't say anything, but I think you should stay away from him, TJ. He's never gonna let you ruin his street cred. That boy is bad news."

"Says the girl who's hanging out with his sister, who's equally bad news." TJ laughs, as though he's trying to make himself feel better.

But TJ is wrong. Beatriz has dreams. Like me. Real dreams

of making it out of Grafton. Doing something with her life. Going where the sunshine is always smiling and never forgets to return. She ain't nothing like Junito. I just have to find a way for both TJ and Tanisha to see that.

TJ reaches in his backpack and puts on a ball cap to mask the real him. He speed-walks past the river, past the alley, past Pop Pop drunk on the couch, past Daddy's dungeon door, and into the safety of his room.

December 2, 1983

Me and Darlene Sing to the Winds
Now I lay me down at night,
I sing to the winds, please make things right.
Make all the pieces come together:
love, friends, family, forever.

Dear Darlene,

I rewrote the poem. What you think? I figured if I shorten it,
God will hear this time, 'cause I'm starting to slowly fall apart. I need to
know that TJ will be all right. That he's making the right choices,
because I don't like this secret one bit. I need Tanisha back too. Need
to hear her voice, her laugh, that way of hers that pulled me away from
it all.

I called her tonight, hoping to smooth things over, but her mother
answered the phone and gave some scripted response.

"Tanisha is sleeping right now, Vanessa."

On a Friday night? Please!

If only I could find a way for both Beatriz and Tanisha to be my
friends. But somewhere in the back of my mind the reality is clear.
I'm pretty sure I've already lost my best friend.

—Nessy

A Long Way from Our World

Before the bus arrives, the teachers and contestants stand motionless in front of King Middle. Our silence screams that we'd all rather be sleeping at the butt-crack of dawn on a Saturday. Except for the sixth graders. They're hyper, huddled together and squirming around like a bunch of preschoolers. Stephanie Bowles is the most excited of them all.

The sky is a cloudless black with no peek of sun in sight, and the neighborhood is deathly still. Then this bus that looks like a house on wheels cruises down the block and comes to a halt in front of us.

"Here we are, ladies," Mrs. Ruiz announces.

We all perk up when we see our ride for the day. The outside of the bus is royal blue with shiny chrome rims, and the windows are covered in white linen curtains. The total superstar treatment. It's enough to take my mind away from the fiasco with TJ the other day. Like he said, he knows what he's doing. As for me, I'm still trying to figure out my own problems.

Beatriz grabs my hand as soon as we walk on the bus. "Sit with me, *amiga!*"

These aren't your average back-breaking, seatbelt-missing

school-bus seats. These seats are cushioned and covered in a soft velvety material with a built-in pillow on the headrest. A girl like me could get used to this!

The aisle is a lighted runway that makes me think of slapping on my heels and practicing my pivot turn and model's T. For a second I think that maybe this was part of the teachers' plan. To make us strut our stuff all the way to Atlantic City.

I've never been to Atlantic City before. Heck, I've barely traveled outside of Newark. The highway is covered with bare trees. The winter chill has swept away the fall leaves, and the grass beneath them is frozen. On the ride down, Beatriz tries to cheer me up about TJ and Junito. "Don't worry about my brother. Him and his boys were just playing around. They do that sometimes."

My smile is weak and hopeful all in one. Maybe it was all talk. Nothing more than a bunch of thugs jivin' around. I fight back the urge to ask Beatriz if she knows the truth. That beneath the drug dealing, beneath the gangbanging, far below the thugged-out shield that Junito hides himself in, he is *different* too. Does she know that he and TJ *loooove* being different together?

But I chew on my words and keep my thoughts on the inside. Tell myself it's best to keep those questions between me and Darlene.

An hour and a half into our trip, the faint smell of salt pours in through the tiny cracks in the bus windows. Mrs. Moore rises out of her seat and tells us it's the smell of the Jersey Shore. A few of the girls peel back the curtains to see the changing landscape. We're a long way from our world, our 'hood. Miles and miles of ocean expand on both sides of the bridge. Docked boats sway in the current. The sun has made its entrance, and the sea-blue sky is dotted in white puffy clouds.

Atlantic City is a land of lights, with its tall buildings and flashing marquees. I've never seen anything like it. There's a huge sign in front of Convention Hall that says, "Welcome Miss King Middle School Pageant Contestants."

Mrs. Caldwell walks up and down the aisle, taking pictures of each of us.

"Beautiful smile, Kayla!"

"Brianna and Lanetta, pull in closer. Ahhh, lovely!"

Mrs. Caldwell is pouring on the compliments. Then, she gets to the back of the bus where, me, Beatriz, Julicza, and Maricela are seated.

"I'll have to turn on the flash for this one." Her words hit me like a ten-pound weight in the chest. I mean, maybe she didn't mean anything by it, but come on. Everyone knows you gotta use the flash when taking a picture of something really dark.

The bus comes to a halt just as Mrs. Caldwell is hobbling her way back up to the front. For a second I hope that the sudden stop will fling her hateful behind straight through the windshield.

A smallish woman with her hair swept up in a loose bun and a smile painted on her face greets us at the door. "Hello, young ladies, and welcome to Atlantic City. My name is Margaret Sconiers, and I will be escorting you inside."

She walks us into the huge waiting area and leaves to get our tour guide for the day. Convention Hall ain't at all what I imagined it to be. It's like a huge barn out on a farm in the middle of nowhere. Like at any moment a bushel of hay could roll right past us. It sure looks a lot fancier on television.

When Ms. Sconiers returns, she has company.

Suzette Charles.

Let me clear my throat and say that again.

Suzette! Charles!

Our very own Miss New Jersey is going to show us around all of the famous Miss America monuments. Seriously, I can't even hold it in. I'm looking around, and none of the other girls seem to even know who Suzette Charles is. Beatriz, Maricela, and Julicza stand there doing their usual: whispering, pointing, and giggling. Today Stephanie Bowles is the target. Poor thing was doomed the second she put on those corduroy high-waters and no-name sneakers.

Part of me wants to scream, *Hello, people! Stop dissing, and let's take in the moment. This is the woman who is first runner-up to Vanessa Williams! Did you not watch the Miss America pageant?* This is a big deal, because even though Vanessa Williams is the first black woman to win Miss America, Suzette Charles is the first black woman to win Miss New Jersey. We got a real live piece of history standing in front of us. But I don't say none of this out loud because I don't want to look like some crazy pageant-queen stalker.

In person Miss Charles is much shorter than she looked on television. I look like bigfoot standing over her. Every strand of her hair is curled to perfection. Her burgundy lip gloss matches her wine-colored cashmere sweater dress. And her crown? It's like that thing is stapled to her head, not flinching one bit. Shoot, if I had a crown like that, I'd never take it off.

"Hello, there. My, you're pretty. What's your name?" she extends her hand to shake mine.

A real live Miss America contestant is talking to me! And she called me pretty. As in beautiful. As in gorgeous. Just throw me in a casket and send me straight to heaven right now!

Miss New Jersey's comment catches Beatriz's attention, and her focus shifts from Stephanie to me. From the corner of my eye, I catch her cheeks turning redder than her Reeboks.

Mrs. Walton is standing a few feet behind Miss New Jersey, and I see her give me a look that says, "Act like you have some home training." But I already know I can't clown around with this lady.

"Good morning, Miss Charles. My name is Vanessa Martin. I saw you on television in the Miss America pageant. Congratulations on placing as first runner-up. You did New Jersey proud!"

Mrs. Walton gives me her nod of approval. Miss New Jersey smiles at me, her cheeks blushing the faintest pink. There's so much more I want to say, like *Where'd you learn to sing like that?* and *Where did you buy your evening gown?* and *How did it feel to be on television?* but Mrs. Caldwell's hot breath in my ear stops me.

"See you tryin'a talk all prim and proper," she whispers, lifting her nose up as she moves down the line. My shoulders cave in, smile fading like the sunset.

One by one, Miss New Jersey greets the rest of the contestants, so gracious, poised, and well spoken. I eye her every move, from the way she stands with her Miss New Jersey crown perfectly balanced on her head to the way her eyes smile as she's answering questions. All these weeks of practicing, and I still don't look half as good as that. Everything about Miss New Jersey is regal, but not in a conceited, uppity, stank way. If she went to my school, she'd be the most popular girl in the whole building. I don't think Beatriz could handle that.

We spend the next few hours being shown all the Miss America memorabilia. Miss New Jersey shows us some of the previous winners' dresses. It's funny to see how the styles have changed from the 1920s to now. The flapper dresses the contestants wore back then were wack like that! I wouldn't even call them dresses. More like knee-length, baggy tank tops with pearls around the edges and funny-looking capes. And the crown that Miss America won back in 1922? A doggone mess! Big and floppy looking, like a jack-in-the-box. The newer dresses are the types I'd want to wear. Silk, chiffon, and all decked out to the nines.

We take turns taking Polaroid pictures with Miss New Jersey as she holds her crown above our head. When it's my turn, I bend my knees and close my eyes, and I can see myself on the Miss America stage. I'm modeling my dress, the same one TJ is making for me. The light hits at all the right angles, and when I look real deep, I am happy with the image of the girl in my head. Even though I'm still trapped in this blue-black skin and this big, tall body of mine.

For the final part of our tour, Miss New Jersey takes us to the Miss America stage to practice our model walk. I swear, if I weren't looking at her, I'd think that was TJ up there teaching us because she shows us everything TJ's been teaching me at home. We practice our model's T and pivot turn. Then, one by one, she lets us take a walk down the same runway that Vanessa Williams graced when she won Miss America. When I watched the pageant on TV, the stage and runway seemed so small. But now I realize this thing is a mile long.

As I walk, I'm cheesing and doing the traditional pageant wave. In the rows of empty seats, I picture my own little cheering squad: Tanisha, TJ, Pop Pop, Daddy, Mama. It's a perfect vision. Pure and sweet, lovely and clean.

We wrap up our stage practice at Convention Hall, and Miss New Jersey announces, "I hope everyone packed their swimsuits! It's pool time!"

On the way to the hotel, all the girls are hyped to get a little slice of summer, even though Old Man Winter has already arrived. In the locker room, everybody's putting on their swimsuits. Part of me is cooking up any excuse to get out of this. First of all, I don't even own a swimsuit. Can't recall the last time I swam. Me and water obviously don't get along like that. I do have an oversized T-shirt and some shorts packed. I figure maybe I can just read on one of them comfy-looking chairs at the pool, instead of actually swimming.

"What kind of swimsuit is that?" Julicza says, laughing as I come out of the stall.

Beatriz squeezes Julicza on the arm, forcing her to let out a pitchy squeak. "I mean, that's cool." Julicza changes her tune.

"Maybe she doesn't want to swim," Lanetta Gainer says innocently, but that doesn't stop Maricela from giving her the evil eye.

"She's right. Swimming ain't my thing anyway," I say back, trying my best to brush off Julicza's dis. I pull out a copy of Alice Walker's *The Color Purple* to show her and everyone else that reading was my plan all along. "Maybe I'll put my toes in the water, but that's about it."

Miss New Jersey leads us through the locker room. The walls are made of glass, the air smells of mint, and harps are playing through the speakers. Everyone's oohing and aahing at how fancy this place is. Meanwhile Beatriz busts out with, "Yo, enough of the classical music. They need to play some rap and salsa!"

Mrs. Walton stops short, turns around, and cuts Beatriz the most hateful look. "Decorum, Miss Mendez."

But Beatriz can't help being loud. "What in the world is a decorum? Some kind of decoration or something?" Her voice echoes against the glass.

All the girls start laughing. I pretend I dropped my hair tie and start looking on the floor so Mrs. Walton won't think I'm part of Beatriz's shenanigans, funny as she is.

"Means manners. Have some manners." Stephanie Bowles's chipmunky voice breaks everyone out of their laughter.

Before Beatriz can even crack back, Miss New Jersey lets out a loud cough and swings open the doors of the pool hall.

The pool at the Seaside Suites is dope! First of all, it's indoor and heated, so no battling the cold weather outside. Second, they got the most comfy chairs to chill in. Palm trees are everywhere, like we're in the Caribbean. Third, not only is there a pool, there's a Jacuzzi too. We are really rolling big-time in Atlantic City. Miss New Jersey rounds up the teachers and leads them to the double doors just outside the pool.

"We'll be right over here, ladies. We have to sign some paperwork," Mrs. Moore calls out to us as we place our swim bags on the chairs.

"May I take your drink order?" a waitress walks over to me, Beatriz, Julicza, and Maricela.

Beatriz orders Shirley Temples for all of us. Doesn't even ask if that's what we really want. But I don't say a word. I ain't never had that drink anyway. There's a first time for everything.

Next thing I know, I hear Stephanie, Lanetta, Brianna, and Kayla ordering the same drink. And then a few more of the girls.

"Such followers," Maricela says, popping a piece of Bubblicious in her mouth.

Melissa Hoffman, one of the seventh graders, starts roaming around and comes across a radio, right by the entrance doors. "Hey, guys! Look what I found," she calls, her voice all sneaky sounding.

Beatriz starts to chant, "Do it! Do it! Do it!" And all the girls chime in.

Melissa changes the classical stuff and moves straight to rap. Run-D.M.C.'s "It's Like That" starts booming through the speakers. Melissa turns the volume up, and the girls begin jumping in the pool, swimming and jamming to the beat. Maricela puts her drink down, squeezes her nose, and cannonballs to the deep end.

I sit near the edge, but not too close, while everyone else swims. Beatriz and Julicza each finish off their Shirley Temple. Stephanie's lagging behind, not because she doesn't want to get in but because she is literally putting on every piece of swim gear imaginable. Hair cap, goggles, nose clip, earplugs, flippers. The girl is turning herself into a doggone scuba diver.

I scope out the scene. The sun's pouring in through the glass windows, and the trees outside are whipping with the ocean winds, like they're fighting to feel the warmth we're soaking in. The music seeps into my soul, lyrics transporting me to a place far beyond the moment. Like the song suggests, you gotta search for meaning in life. One thing's for sure, I been looking for answers, that special something to make everything all right. It's out there, waiting for me. I close my eyes, and the bass courses through my spine.

The beat drops. Earthquaking from wall to wall. Suddenly my back kicks in. Something snaps like branches tumbling to the ground in the middle of a tornado. My body lunges forward. Cold. Wet. Sinking. The floor disappears beneath me. I open my eyes, water stinging like acid. Close them up again, fighting to stop the burn. My throat fills, swells with water. My arms, like wings, spread out, but they fail to send me soaring. It's like the visions in my night terrors, only this time come true. Somewhere beyond the gushing waters, my ears catch the faintest of screams.

Two arms. One heartbeat. Lifting me from the depths.

Air catches hold of my throat. Fills me up. I am panting. Coughing. Crying.

"You okay, *chica*?" Still gripping me tight, Beatriz pulls me so close, I'm sure she can smell the fear on my breath.

By now all of the girls are swimming fast our way, and the teachers are busting through the doors.

"What in God's name happened?" Mrs. Walton is screaming over the music.

"Turn that crap off!" Mrs. Caldwell orders someone to silence the radio. Kayla Knight hops out of the water and quickly does as she's told.

The teachers hoist me out of the pool while Julicza covers me with towels. I'm coughing violently, throwing up the water I still feel burning me up on the inside.

"Some jokes aren't funny, you know," Julicza says.

"Yeah, not cool, *Stephanie*," Beatriz adds.

My breath cuts short. Stephanie Bowles pushed me in the pool? For what?

Stephanie's face turns stone blue. "I didn't! Wait, you can't possibly think I—"

Mrs. Ruiz throws her hands on her hips and puts her face real close to Stephanie's, like she's searching for the truth in her eyes. "Young lady, did you push Vanessa into the pool? Did anyone see what happened?"

Everyone starts shrugging their shoulders, except for Beatriz and Julicza, who point straight at Stephanie.

All of a sudden the tears start flowing, and Mrs. Ruiz and Mrs. Caldwell are escorting Stephanie, the sad scuba diver, out the doors and to the locker room. Some of the girls start whispering.

"Why would she do that?"

"Didn't she know Vanessa didn't want to get in?"

"Dang, she's so immature. Sixth graders!"

"We didn't see anything, 'cause we were doing headstands under the water."

Julicza's got this smirk on her face, like she's happy Stephanie's in the locker room getting reamed out. All the contestants gather around me and Beatriz, seated on the cold, wet floor.

"You gotta learn how to swim, *chica*," Beatriz whispers softly in my ear. Both her arms are folded around my shoulders, fingers locked tighter than Daddy's chamber door. She breathes in. I breathe out. Together, like the perfect lyric over a hip-hop beat. The swelling on my insides has faded away, but that feeling I've been trying to shake long before today lingers. Sinking, sinking, sinking.

Waters Rising Higher

After we leave the hotel, the teachers take us to have dinner at the Boathouse, which is a restaurant shaped like a boat right on the boardwalk. The buffet is laid out with the dopest spread I've ever seen. There's a carving station with turkey, roast beef, pork shoulder, and leg of lamb. Each meat has its own dipping sauce. Honey barbecue. Mint jelly. Wild mushroom. My taste buds are doing backflips, especially because I emptied the contents of my stomach back at the pool.

There's a dessert station with an assortment of pies, cakes, and ice cream. The salad bar has types of lettuce greens I've never seen before and at least twenty toppings. Then there're plenty of sides: mashed potatoes, macaroni and cheese, green-bean casserole, corn on the cob, rice and beans. My mouth is salivating at the sight of all this food. I swear I want some of everything!

"Now, now, Vanessa." Mrs. Caldwell creeps up behind me in the buffet line. "Go light on that plate of yours. You wouldn't want to put on—"

Mrs. Walton's click-clacking heels cut her off. "Vanessa,

get what you'd like and go take a seat with the girls. Mrs. Caldwell, may I have a word with you?" Mrs. Walton's got this stank attitude painted all over her voice.

I add some green beans to the barbecued chicken on my plate and do as I'm told.

"Vanessa, can I talk to you?" Stephanie touches my arm as I'm walking toward the table. The freckles under her eyes are darker and more clustered than usual. Her lips are cherry red, like she been biting on them to stop the words from coming out.

"I don't have much to say to you." I look her straight in the eyes, expecting to see some kind of sign of why she'd play me like that. Immaturity? Jealousy? Anything? But all I see is fear.

"It wasn't me. I didn't do it."

"Well, if you didn't, who did?"

Stephanie's eyes dart toward Beatriz and Julicza seated at the table, and her lips start to quiver. "Please don't say anything."

"Girl, you're bugging! Clearly you didn't see the way Beatriz jumped in the pool to rescue me." I'm all up in her face now. "She wouldn't let me go until she knew I was okay. But your immature little prank coulda got me killed!"

Stephanie's eyes start flooding, and I throw one more jab to harden the blow.

"So spare me your boohooing and your fairytales and just own up to what you did." I roll my eyes at her, do a perfect pivot, and sashay my way back to Beatriz.

Our tables are in front of a large window overlooking the Atlantic Ocean. I take my seat in between Beatriz and Julicza, and Maricela sucks her teeth at me like I done committed a crime. I think about saying something to her, but I'm too busy trying to calm my nerves over Stephanie's stupid behind.

I catch sight of Mrs. Walton and Mrs. Caldwell still standing near the buffet line. Mrs. Walton's ice-blonde hair is whipping side to side, and she's popping her neck and snapping her fingers all up in Mrs. Caldwell's face. I'm not sure what they're talking 'bout, but it ain't pretty.

Everybody starts talking about our day. Meeting Miss New Jersey, practicing on the Miss America stage, and how dope the pool party was until *somebody* ruined it.

"Did you see how sparkly Miss New Jersey's crown was? I wonder if those were real diamonds," Maricela says.

"Girl, I'm gonna be the first Puerto Rican Miss America!" Beatriz chimes in. Julicza tosses her mass of dark hair over her shoulder and slaps Beatriz high five.

"I wanna do the pageant too," Stephanie's mousy voice chimes in on the conversation.

"*En tus sueños,*" Beatriz says. Maricela and Julicza start bust-a-gut laughing. The smile on Stephanie's face is replaced with flushed cheeks and a look of pure confusion. It's like she knows the joke is on her, but her Spanish ain't good enough to respond. Not that she would anyway. A sixth grader wouldn't dare step to an eighth grader. Especially not Beatriz Mendez.

At the beginning of the school year, I was the butt of

Beatriz's crack backs. My, how the tides done changed! At least Beatriz ain't cracking on me, but boy is she trashing Stephanie something good. Stephanie doesn't talk much after that. It's like her whole spirit up and died.

I remain quiet as I listen to the girls go on and on. My eyes stay fixed on the view outside the restaurant window. The sun begins to set, and the sky glows orange, pink, and blue. I smile as the girls continue to rant and rave about our day here at the shore, a long way from Grafton Hill—our 'hood, our world. Someday I'll find my way back here. Maybe even end up on that stage in Convention Hall and have my moment in the spotlight. Then everything would come together.

We end the day at the souvenir shops on the boardwalk. Pop Pop gave me four dollars this morning and told me to buy something nice for myself. I scour the aisles, looking for something reasonable, but everything is so dang expensive. Most things are in the ten-dollar range. Beatriz's mom gave her twenty-five dollars, so she's racking up a T-shirt, saltwater taffy, and a coffee cup. By the cash register, there are baskets with items for a dollar and up. I buy a shot glass that says Atlantic City for Pop Pop (which is probably the last thing he needs), an Atlantic City keychain for TJ, and a small pin shaped like the Miss America crown for myself.

When we get on the bus, everybody's showing each other what they bought. Everybody except Stephanie. She sits in the back row alone—knees raised to her chin, high-waters rising higher—lonely, quiet, staring out the window. It's like Beatriz cast a spell on everybody to not talk to Stephanie for the rest of the day, even the sixth graders. I sink low in my seat next to Beatriz and try to block out the noise of the screaming, giggling Miss King Middle contestants.

I clip the pin I bought onto the collar of my shirt and fall asleep, picturing the Miss America crown being placed on my head.

Ain't a Little Girl

By the time I get home from Atlantic City, my legs are sore something awful. Between exercising so much lately and the long trip, my body is screaming for relief. As I apply some Sol-Glo to my face and neck, I feel a presence in the bathroom. The bathtub. It's staring at me. Begging me. Please come in. *Not today.* One near-death experience for the day is enough for me. Tension fills up in my chest, and I shuffle to my room, share my day with Darlene, and hit my pillow hard, unable to shake the uneasy feeling that's settled in my bones.

Sleep doesn't come quick, and it takes a long time before I slip into that place of broken memories. Light pours in, and Mama appears before me. Only this is a different version of the mother I'm used to seeing in my dreams. Her beauty is gone. Something done ate it up real good. Got her eyes all weary and bloodshot. Her skin, once vanilla-coated and scattered with freckles, is now grayish and sickly looking.

In the background, cartoons are playing, and I'm in my high chair, laughing and singing along with the characters. She puts a plate of food in front of me, and I stuff my face. Guess some things never change. Then I throw up all over myself. The rancid smell fills the room, and Mama's lips get real tight. That dismal face of hers turns cherry red, and spit starts flying outta her mouth as she screams, "Girl, I just gave you a bath!"

And then it's almost like the devil takes over her body. The veins in her neck and forehead protrude so much they're fighting to break through her skin. In one swift grab, she shakes me out of my high chair. My neck jerks like it wants to detach itself from the rest of my body. I'm sobbing salty tears, molasses-thick. Heaving, breathing in and out, each breath twinged with a high-pitched wheeze. Mama grows angrier, shaking me harder, and all the while a voice inside me begs, *Please, Mama, stop.*

But she doesn't. So I close my eyes, and suddenly I'm at the summer carnival in downtown Newark. A happy place. Daddy hoists me up onto the black stallion on the merry-go-round. Mama's standing behind the gate, waving, smiling, snapping Polaroids. The ride cranks up, and we spin round and round, and I'm screaming, "Whee!" There is no pain here. Only smiles and warm breezes and love. It's the type of feeling that I'd give all twenty fingers and toes to have again.

Mama yanks me back into reality, peeling my vomit-soaked clothes off and walking me to the bathroom. She throws me in the tub with a rubber duck toy and storms off to her bedroom. The slamming of her door sends my world into a hurricane-like spin, and I dive face-first into the hot water.

Darkness takes over. I can't see nothing. No black stallion. No smiling Daddy. No happy, picture-snapping Mama. My other senses are working overtime. I can taste metal in my mouth. Smells bad, like flesh rotting in the desert sun. Feels scalding hot, heat seeping through my nose, torching up my insides something bad.

The sound of sirens and high-pitched screams swirl around me. Mama is crying. Daddy is yelling. The fight to hold my breath is intense, but I can't hold it in anymore, so I just . . . let go. Water rushes in, the blackness is fading, the white light swallows me whole.

Suddenly a loud car horn blasts all the way to my eighth-floor window. My body jerks forward, hitting the tiled floor with a thud. In and out, in and out, my lungs gasp in the stifling heat of my room, life flowing through me. The walls feel extra close, slowly inching their way toward me as I lie there in the fetal position. I do not understand this dream I had, the meaning of it all. It doesn't make any sense. I'm not dead. I'm here, living and breathing and longing and feeling. Empty. Like my bed. I look around and realize that everything is on the floor: the top sheet, the covers, the pillow.

I crawl up and look at my bed as I pull back my curtains to let the moonlight in. A small, round pool of blood stares back at me. I crack the window open to let out the heat trapped in my room. A ripple of wind pours in with a whistle that sings a telling message: "You ain't a little girl no more."

Desperate Times Call for Homemade Pads

It's funny how when a girl gets her period for the first time in those cheesy-behind maxi-pad commercials, she's happy, smiling, and dancing with her friends. I'll never understand how cramps and bleeding could make somebody wanna bust out in song and dance.

When Pecola gets her period in *The Bluest Eye*, her foster sisters tell her that she could get pregnant now. Now I'm not that stupid. I know that you gotta do the nasty to get pregnant. There's plenty of girls in Grafton Hill who do it right in the alley among the garbage and the foul smells. Shameless. Some of them as young as me. Skanks is what Pop Pop calls them. And I ain't interested in being a skank.

It's four in the morning, and there aren't many people I could call to help me with my situation. As I sit there staring at the blood on the bed, I can feel it continuing to slowly gush out of me. My skin turns to sparks. The sparks multiply to flames. Somebody should be here right now with me, helping me clean and turn over this bloody mattress, bringing me a cup of hot tea to calm my achy stomach, giving me a maxi pad wrapped in pink-flowered plastic packaging, and talking to me about the birds and the bees. But all I have are broken visions and this new nightmare.

Even though I'm sure my sweet grandfather wouldn't mind helping me, I doubt very seriously that he knows how to use a pad. He probably wouldn't buy me the name-brand ones if I asked him to. I could see him now, hobbling to the bodega to get me some random, no-frills girlie diapers because that's the kind he can afford. But knowing Pop Pop, he'd rather give me a raggedy cloth and a belt and tell me that's what women did in the old days.

TJ wouldn't be much help either. As much as he knows about all things girlified, I know for a fact that he's grossed out by the thought of girls getting their period.

I already know better than to ask Daddy for money for pads. I can just hear his response now. *I pay the rent and the utilities. Pop puts food on the table. Anything else you need, it's on you and TJ.*

So I figure it's best to take care of the problem myself. I tiptoe to the bathroom so I don't wake nobody up. How hard can it be to make something that looks like a pad? It's made of tissue anyway, right? Plus, Beatriz can give me some freebies from the bodega at school this week. She's had her period since she was nine. I wrap several sheets of tissue around my hand until it forms a thick rectangular shape. I use Scotch tape to seal the four corners and place my invention on the lining of a clean pair of underwear. I rinse the bloody pair in the sink, place them in a plastic bag, and put the bag at the very bottom of my hamper. Then I hide the bloody sheets in the back of my closet. I put clean sheets on the bed. The last thing I need is for TJ to wake up, go to my room, and see this crime scene. I can see him now—wailing and flailing his scrawny arms worse than a white girl in a horror movie.

My insides are pulsing like someone took my intestines and wrung them out like a mop. A cup of herbal tea sounds like heaven. When I get to the kitchen pantry, the box of Lipton is empty, much like the rest of the shelves. Tomorrow TJ will go food shopping. I heat up water in the kettle and coat the bottom of a coffee cup in sugar. In the refrigerator, there's a lonely lemon. It's more brown than yellow, but the juice inside is still good enough to flavor my tealess tea.

Outside our small kitchen window that faces the river, the sun begins to make its entrance onto our side of town. In the living room the plastic on the couch screeches. Pop Pop wakes up, hobbles his way to the kitchen, and says, "Mornin', Miss America. How was your trip?"

"Oh, Pop Pop, it was so dope! We met Miss New Jersey and got to practice on the Miss America stage, and we had dinner overlooking the ocean," I say all cheese-like, totally covering up what happened at the pool party. I don't need that old man worrying about me.

Pop Pop flashes a smile and switches on the radio on the windowsill above the sink. The sounds of Nat King Cole pour through the speakers, and Pop Pop breaks into song. He hovers over me and extends his hand for me to sing "The Christmas

Song" along with him. I tickle the tip of his nose, and he scrunches his face. Then I join him in perfect harmony.

Mrs. Walton is a good music teacher and all, but Pop Pop is really the one who gave me my first vocal lessons. He taught me how to sing with my heart. Pop Pop's voice is warm and smooth with a layer of deepness that would make Barry White jealous.

"You better come on and start getting ready for church," he says when the song is over. "TJ's already getting dressed, and the car's gonna be here in a half hour. Now that you're Miss Diva, I'm sure it's gonna take you a while to get dressed, so hurry yo' tail up."

My chest sinks inward a bit, and I look down at the kitchen floor. "Pop Pop, you mind if I miss church today? I'm not feeling all that well." Telling him that my period came ain't even an option.

Every crease in his face sinks to the floor. "You done missed two choir practices and now Sunday service? I don't want this pageant stuff being more important than going to church, Nessy. What's really going on with ya, baby girl? Is it your daddy?"

And Mama. And TJ. And Tanisha. And apparently every single person who steps in and out of my life.

"Nothing too bad," I lie. "I just feel a little sick. With the pageant coming up this Saturday, I don't want to be all messed up for it. Can't I just take some medicine and rest?"

"Well, what ya sick with?"

"Um, my stomach hurts." Technically that is the truth.

"You ate something bad on that trip yesterday? I told you about trying new food. They probably took you to some fancy restaurant, 'round all them white folks, and you ain't know how to act!"

"Pop Pop, it's not that."

"You got gas?"

"No," I respond. My left eye is itching now, and I can barely stand to look at him.

"What you got? A case of the dookies?" He laughs and slaps his half leg.

"Pop Pop!" My grandfather is just plain ridiculous.

"All right, all right! I'll give you two more passes—one for today and one for the pageant on Saturday since you'll miss choir practice again. But after that, no more. It's right back to normal, young lady."

"You got it, Pop Pop."

Like a robot, I finish my tea, return to my bedroom, and shut off that internal switch to make my real feelings go away. Pretend that everything that I'm going through is nothing more than a figment of my imagination. All I want to do now is drift away into a deep, thoughtless sleep where confusing visions of Mama don't exist.

December 4, 1983

W-o-m-a-n
I'm a woman now,
and so I must rise,
phenomenally,
before the sun kisses the sky.
Cleanse my sheets,
my body,
my soul,
the undying need to feel whole.

Dear Darlene,

Right about now would be a good time for you to turn yourself into human form. Some things just ain't meant to be experienced alone.

—Nessy

The Sun, the Moon, and the Truth

Thank God for Kotex, and thank God for Beatriz. She gives me enough maxi pads to last me the next two months. Tanisha, on the other hand, been dodging me left and right. Every time I call her, I'm given the same scripted responses. She's either sleeping or studying, which I know is a dang lie. That girl's allergic to schoolwork.

After school I go to Grafton Hill Laundromat up the hill, next to the liquor store. I've slacked off during the past week because of all the homework, the pageant practices, and the trip to Atlantic City. I've got at least four loads to do. I put in a load with all the towels and sheets, including the bloody ones from the other night. Mrs. Mendez told me if I pour in a cap of vinegar with the detergent, it will get rid of the stain. I sure hope she's right. The next load is for all the dark clothes, mostly Daddy's work uniforms. The third load is for all the whites. And the final one is for all the light colors. As I toss the final items of clothing into the washer, a piece of paper falls out of my housecoat pocket and onto the floor. It's the envelope I stole from Daddy's drawer. I had forgotten about it. I start the wash and take a seat with the envelope in my hand.

The address is clear and easy to read: 30 County Route 513, Clinton, New Jersey. The final letters are blurred out from the juice I spilled on it. Could the rest of the letters spell out Martin? Why can't I remember my own mother's first name? And why would Daddy say that Mama might as well be dead? I try to make sense of it, but frustration starts boiling up in me all over again.

Old Man Lee is the owner of Grafton Hill Laundromat. He's a little man who always greets you with a smile, a piece of candy, and some random quote from one of his books on Buddhism. Today's message: *There are three things you can't hide from: the sun, the moon, and the truth.*

Old Man Lee knows something about everything. He's traveled all over the world. Started out where he was born—China—then went to parts of Europe and up and down the East Coast of the United States before settling in New Jersey.

"Mr. Lee, you ever been to Clinton?" I ask.

"Clinton Avenue?" he says. "Yes, stay away from there. Trouble, trouble."

"No, Mr. Lee. Clinton, New Jersey."

"Oh! Yes, very nice place. Very far. In the country. Lots of cows and grass. Up, up, up 78 West."

Is this where Mama could have been all these years? In the country? While I'm stuck here in the ghetto? I instantly picture meadows filled with wildflowers and animals roaming free.

"How do I get there?" I ask.

"You drive, of course!" Mr. Lee laughs and claps his hands, applauding himself for being funny. But I'm dead serious.

"It's a straight shot, but it'll be a long trip if you're taking the bus," someone cuts in. I turn around to see that the voice is coming from an oversized, heart-shaped butt. A woman is bent over, hurling her whites into the dryer.

She stands up, reaches for her box of fabric-softener sheets, and looks my way. She's crazy short with cheeks like pillows and a mouth as wide as the Nile River.

"What you going to Clinton for? That's an awfully long way to travel."

I bite my bottom lip and think of a very careful way to respond. "To see . . . my grandmother."

"Oh, well, that's nice. I've been there lots of times. Used to work for a chiropractor there before he retired and moved to Germany. It's a lovely little town. Now here's what you gotta do."

I grab a pen from Old Man Lee's countertop and start writing the directions down like mad.

The lady says I have to take a bus into Penn Station in downtown Newark. Then walk down to Commerce Street and get on the New Jersey Transit bus, which'll take me right to Route 513. When I hop off the bus, all I gotta do is walk until I find the house number. She warns me to be careful not to fall asleep on the bus, though, or else I'll miss my stop. There's no way I'd doze off on that trip. I'd be too nervous to miss a moment of it.

I thank her for the directions and Mr. Lee for the pen. I finish up my laundry and think of a plan. When will I go up there? After the pageant. Yeah, definitely after the pageant.

Mrs. Walton says every contestant is getting a trophy, no matter what. So even if I don't win, I'll show up to Mama's big fancy house in the country and show her my trophy. Maybe it'll be enough for her to let me in. Maybe it'll be enough to let me stay.

Take Me Back to the Merry-Go-Round

My period finally went away. Thank you, sweet baby Jesus! It's the day before the pageant. December ninth. My fourteenth birthday. Tanisha usually decorates my locker with balloons and cards. I'm pretty sure that ain't happening this year. Even still, I'm holding out hope that maybe we'll fix things.

My nerves got my stomach in a balled-up, knotted mess. But everything for the pageant is almost set. My interview outfit is freshly pressed, and all the matching accessories are packaged with it. Mrs. Walton bought me some garment bags and had me label each one so there'd be no question of what I need to wear when I'm changing backstage. My angel costume is done and all that needs finishing is my evening gown. TJ has to take it in two more inches at school. He says he'll have the dress for me when he gets home tonight. And, boy, I can't wait!

I decide to dress up real nice for school. A fly outfit will put me in the birthday and pageant spirit. I slip on an off-the-shoulder, hot-pink sweatshirt. To that, I add a black leather-and-lace skirt I stole from TJ's closet the other day. My makeup skills are getting better. TJ's been teaching me all the latest makeup tricks: how to contour my cheekbones before applying blush, how to moisturize my face before adding foundation, and the best way to line my lips before applying lip gloss. Today I keep it simple, with a little blush, some silver eye shadow, and sheer lip gloss. The girl staring back at me in the mirror breaks into a wide smile.

On my way out the door, I head to the kitchen to grab some breakfast: a piece of cornbread and an apple. Since it's the beginning of the month and TJ went grocery shopping, we'll live the good life for the next two weeks. Our fridge is stocked with all sorts of goodies: fresh fruits, meats, and vegetables. I grab a bunch of grapes and wrap a piece of foil around them.

I'm listening to my Walkman and humming my talent song. Mrs. Walton made a tape of herself playing "Amazing Grace" on the piano and gave it to me to practice with at home. Since we don't have a tape player, Mrs. Walton got me the Walkman as an early Christmas present. God, I love that woman! Now I just have to figure out what to get her for Christmas. Hopefully, if I win the pageant, I can use some of that money to buy her something nice. Maybe a herringbone necklace. She'd look real fly in that.

Just as I'm hitting the high note, the door slams. It's eight o'clock in the morning, and Daddy's just getting home from work. The smell of smoke, garbage, and a hint of whiskey drift into the kitchen. I ain't never known Daddy to drink or smoke before. God, I hope he's not taking after Pop Pop. One drinker in the house is about all I can handle. I turn slowly from the kitchen counter, hoping that Daddy will notice the new me.

It's my birthday. Please say I look pretty, Daddy. When I raise my eyes from the floor to meet his, I can see the red veins fighting to break through. His eyes turn to slits, and his lips curl inward.

"What in the hell do you have on your face? And what are you wearing?" His voice is so loud, it ricochets from both walls and explodes in my ears.

"It's just a little blush and lip gloss, Daddy. I wanted to look nice"—my voice quivers—"for my birthday."

"Birthday? Or do you mean pageant?" His voice is elevated, and spit darts from the corners of his mouth. Daddy's all wobbly, barely able to stand. He grabs hold of the kitchen table and continues his verbal lashing.

"I told you a long time ago that you were not allowed to try out for that damn pageant. And after all this time, I find out the truth. That you've been sneaking behind my back for months. Without my permission! You defied me!"

I swallow the lump in my throat. It pushes down deep and slowly crawls to my gut, where it settles for good. "Daddy. Let me ex—"

He cuts me off. "Wanna know how I found out? I stopped at the bodega this morning to pick up a paper for Pop, and I met your little friend, *Beatrrrrriz.*" Daddy rolls the *r* extra long, and I swear I wanna die right here, right now.

"She told me that your sneaky behind is in that pageant.

So since you want to keep secrets, since you think you running thangs 'round here, you ain't doing that pageant tomorrow. And that's that!"

The word *secrets* dangles off his lips, almost to the point where it's a joke. I'm not the only one with secrets in this house. Daddy carries his with him and keeps them in that room, in that cookie tin. Never once did he stop and think about my side of things. That this was about more than just being in a pageant. This was about a connection. Holding on to a memory. Holding out for the hope that something like this might bring us back to that forgotten place of smiles and love and family. But like a vacuum, he sucked it all away.

My whole world is spinning. I close my eyes and wish myself back on the merry-go-round I dreamed about, but nothing helps. At this point I'm praying for somebody—anybody—to come and rescue me from this nightmare that I call my father.

The music in TJ's room lowers. He's listening, frozen still behind the locked door of his bedroom. Pop Pop's not even home. The covers on the couch were neatly folded when I passed by this morning, which is normal for a Friday. That man spends all week drinking, and then come Friday, he's walking around the neighborhood trying to sweat out all his demons to prepare to enter the good Lord's house on Sunday. By Monday he's drunk all over again. Pop Pop is usually there for me, and I need him right now more than ever.

My mouth opens, and out comes this shaky, whispery voice. "I'm so sorry, Daddy. But the pageant is tomorrow. I've worked so hard."

Daddy hobbles two steps forward, towering over me. His shoulders are hunched, and he's close enough to slap me in the face if I turn the wrong way. I can see the sweat forming on his forehead, one bead at a time. He curls his lips so tight that only his two front teeth are showing. And when a parent looks like this, it means only one thing: you're about to die.

"I *said* you ain't doing that pageant! *Do I make myself clear?*"

Daddy's words cut deep to the bone, and right there I realize we'll never be okay. We'll never be us again. Our old selves are buried deep in our pretend selves. We pretend that this life is normal, that it doesn't matter that Mama's not around, that it's okay to live like this—hungry and angry and empty and wanting.

I fight to hold back the tears swelling in my eyes. This man will not see me cry. I sharply turn my back to him, run to my room, slam the door, drop to my bed, bury my face in my pillow to the point of suffocation, and give myself permission to let the tears do what they will. Sobbing. Screaming. Cries trapped in the thickness of my pillow.

I hate my father.

I hate my father.

Hate. Him.

Hate! Him!

The front door of the apartment slams closed with an echoing thunder. The boogeyman has disappeared, but that doesn't stop the pain. I drift away into a deep, salty-teared slumber.

Finding Mama

There is a soft tap on my door. I'm not even sure how long I slept. Feels like hours.

"Nessy, you okay?"

Good question, TJ. I'm doing just dandy other than the fact that my father has ruined my life. I wipe my face and tell TJ to come in.

There is a silence between us, but the meaning is crystal clear. Daddy is a monster. Daddy has no heart. Daddy has no soul. Daddy will never love me 'cause I'll never be *Mama*. Daddy is wrong, wrong, wrong.

"I saw that you had fallen asleep, so I wanted to give you some time. What are you going to do?" TJ asks.

"You mean before or after I kill Beatriz? I can't believe she played me like this. What did I do to her? How can I just drop out the day before the pageant?"

And I start to cry all over again. TJ holds me close and strokes my tear-soaked hair. I should have listened to him. I should have listened to Tanisha. Instead, I chose to get caught up in Beatriz's web of lies and hurt. At that moment I make a promise to myself. I'm never talking to Beatriz Mendez again.

"Why do you think Uncle Daniel doesn't want you in the pageant?"

"Because he's ignorant. Because he wants to keep me trapped here. Because he feels that something like a pageant could open me up to the possibility of a world outside this place. So I won't leave . . . like Mama did."

And then it hits me. I can't stand to be in this house one more second. I gotta make my move. It's now or never. "TJ, you about to head out to Penn Station?"

"Yup, I was gonna go up to school to close out the last seam on your dress, but—"

"Good, I'll go with you."

TJ twists his face and cocks his head to the side. "Nessy, your school is right up the hill. Not to mention you're about two hours late at this point. Where do you think you're going?"

I wipe the last tear from my eye. Blood speed-racing all up inside me, I look him square in the face and say, "To find my mother."

Well, Her Name Ain't Edna!

🌹**Today, is gonna be** a day of firsts. It's my first time cutting school *ever*. It's my first time taking a bus by myself. It's the first time I'll (hopefully) see my mother since she left all those years ago.

"I can't believe you're doing this. Do you even have a plan?" TJ speaks through the biting wind as we approach the entrance to Penn Station.

"Sure I do. You'll go to school and fix the dress. I'm going to go see my mother. She'll give me the answers I need. She'll convince Daddy. She'll even come. And Daddy won't have any say."

"So you just have this all thought out, huh?"

Part of me knows that this is stupid. That maybe I'm getting my hopes up for nothing. That I'll get to the door, and it won't be her at all. But I don't care. I grab Darlene and my coat and hustle out the door.

It's already past eleven, and I know the ride will be long. We decide to meet up at six-thirty at the top of Grafton Hill in front of the bodega. This way we'll walk down the hill and into the house together. All three of us: me, TJ, and Mama. She will be right at my side and put Daddy in his place. And maybe when it's all said and done, she'll let me come live with her. Pull me out of here. And I'm hoping she'll let Pop Pop and TJ come too. Daddy can stay locked away in his chamber of inner demons all by himself. He don't want us no way anyhow.

Outside of Penn Station is bustling with people trying to get to their destinations. A dark-skinned black man dressed in a Santa suit is clanging a bell next to a Salvation Army sign. He asks me for money for needy children. I feel like telling him I'm one of those needy children, so he needs to be giving me some of that money in his kettle.

TJ hands me a few dollars before we part ways. He says it should be enough to get me there and back with a little left over for lunch.

"Not necessary," I say, throwing my hand in the air with my pinky pointed to the sky. "Mama lives in the country, so she'll probably make me a fancy lunch like English tea and watercress sandwiches."

TJ's face turns serious. "Try not to get your hopes up too much, Nessy."

"How come you never talk about her?" I scan TJ's eyes, searching for the truth.

"My mama never let me be around her like that. Said Uncle Daniel's wife had problems. Sure, I saw her a few times when I was a kid, but then one day you got real sick. And she just left, Nessy. My mama and the rest of the family—they seemed happy about it, and they never brought it up, especially around me. You know the saying—"

"Stay outta grown folks' business," I say, cutting TJ off.

His face returns to the wide smile I'm used to seeing. "All I'm saying is, no matter what happens, just know that you have a family who loves you. And Nessy, happy birthday."

TJ walks through the golden doors and disappears into the sea of hustlers.

I round the corner and head to Commerce Street. Commerce is lined with skyscrapers covered in navy blue mirrors, making me look crazy tall. My body grows larger with each step I take, every part of me feeling braver, like I know I done made the right decision.

Here I come, Mama. You ready for me, like I been ready for you all these years? I whisper to the winds. A ripple of wind, so cold, so sweet, sings back, *As ready as the sun rises and sets.*

A bus arrives every hour, and boy, it can't come soon enough. This cold is beating me up something awful! Instead of picking out something warm to wear, I was too busy trying to look cute today. My hat, scarf, and gloves are all sitting in my closet. A familiar voice invades my thoughts.

A smart singer always protects her instrument. Yeah, yeah, Mrs. Walton, I know.

When the bus arrives, I breathe a sigh of relief 'cause if I swallow one more drop of frozen air, my vocal cords might go into a state of hypothermia. The bus is almost empty, with two exceptions. One is an older black woman dressed in a maid's uniform. Her coat is propped against the window to make a pillow, and she's knocked out cold in the front seat of the bus. Midway along the aisle, a man who looks like he's in his twenties stares and then winks at me. He reeks of garbage and liquor and everything nasty in this world. And now I realize why Daddy doesn't want me taking public transportation alone. All kinds of riffraffs can be found in these places. I hurry to the back and take a seat. I place myself in the aisle seat and put my stuff on the seat by the window. Don't wanna give Creepy McStinky any invitation to come and sit with me.

The streets are lined with tall trees dressed in Christmas garlands. All the cars are covered in frost. Even though their wipers swipe away the icy layer, it returns as fast as it disappears. The clouds in the sky separate and release a scatter of flurries. It's the first snow of the season. But the flurries are light, almost dancing in the air, spiraling and gliding before they land on the ground to melt and evaporate their way back up to the sky again.

One by one the towns blend into each other. The bus strolls over a bridge where a river flows beneath us. We pass farms with rolling hills, frostbitten grasses, and plantation-style homes. Somewhere on a hill just like that, Mama is waiting for me. I just know it.

"Next stop, Route 513," the bus driver says into the intercom.

The maid in the front of the bus rises up at the same time I do, and we get off the bus. She hawks me up and down, like she trying to figure out why I'm here and not in school. "You best be careful out here all by yourself, little girl."

She makes a right and walks on down the road, probably off to one of those big, fancy houses I saw on the way up here.

As I stand in the cold with the snowflakes tickling my skin, I pull the crumpled envelope and directions from my pocket. I thought the house would be right there when I got off the bus, but, boy, was I wrong. The road stretches for miles and is long and windy. It twists and turns past bundles of trees with wet, snowy branches whipping at my face. Twenty-five minutes later, I finally arrive at the address. But it ain't the country home with yellow shutters and white picket fence that I pictured. Instead, extra-tall steel gates with spikes at the top surround the area. It looks almost like the Grafton Hill projects, except these brick buildings barely have any windows. And where there should be windows, tiny slits jut out of the bricks.

A man in a uniform calls out from behind the gate, scaring the living daylights out of me because I didn't see him at first. "Visiting hours start in ten minutes. Make sure you have ID!" His voice is throaty and heavy.

Visiting hours? Wait. What kind of place is this?

"Excuse me, sir. Am I at the right address? 30 County Route 513?" I hold up my crumpled envelope to show him.

"You've got it, sweetheart. You've reached the Edna Mahan Correctional Facility for Women."

I don't understand what any of that means. "Correctional Facility? Is this like a work program or something?"

The guard throws his head back and opens his mouth wide to release a hefty laugh. "Young lady, those ain't nothing but fancy words for prison."

Much, Much Too Late

This has got to be some kind of mistake. Mama wouldn't be here, right? At least not as a prisoner. My mind is on full speed. The snow is falling faster, piling up on the concrete.

"Seems like you're the only one here for visiting hours. How about I let you in early?" The guard unchains the gate and gestures for me to come inside.

Let me in? To a prison? Where there're murderers and criminals? What have I gotten myself into? Daddy is gonna kill me slowly when he finds this out. But I've come too far to run away from it all now.

"Yes, thank you," I mutter as I step forward into the chamber of doom.

The path to the prison entrance is long, and though no one is outside, I feel like I'm being watched. The hairs on the back of my neck stand at attention, and my fingers tremble, despite the fact that I have them buried in my coat pockets.

The guard leads me to a glass-enclosed booth with a lady seated inside. She's listening to music on her Walkman and chewing a large wad of bubble gum. When he knocks on the glass to get her attention, she keeps dancing and pays him no mind. Then he bangs on it so loudly that the glass shakes, and she yanks off her headphones.

"You got a visitor here. Do your job!" he shouts.

"Name?" Her voice is short, and she doesn't even look at my face.

"Um, Vanessa Martin." My voice is shaky and weak.

"Number?"

"My phone number?" I respond. I wonder why they need that.

She laughs for a second and says, "No, the inmate's ID number. Who are you here to see?" An oversized pink bubble emerges and makes its way toward the glass, then pops loudly and slurps back into her mouth.

"My mother . . . I think." My voice drifts off, and I already know the question that is coming next.

"What's her name?"

Well, clearly her name isn't Edna! I want to scream out that I don't remember my mother's name because she left me, apparently to do something stupid enough to land herself in this God-awful place.

"Take it easy on the young lady," the guard tells the woman behind the glass.

"You say your name is Vanessa Martin, right?" He places his hand on my shoulder, and the drumbeat inside of me slows down a bit.

I nod my head and bite the inside of my jaw, hoping that's enough to hold back my tears.

"LaToya, search the binder for inmates, last name Martin."

There are four women with the last name Martin in the Edna Mahan prison. Two of them are white, both in their early sixties, serving life sentences. One is a nineteen-year-old black woman who just arrived three weeks ago. And the final Martin is thirty-three years old, black, and set to be released June 1, 1984.

LaToya looks at the picture, looks at me, and then at the picture again. That's when her whole demeanor changes as she steps out of her glass-enclosed booth. Her eyes crease and slant upward as if they are smiling. She leans in to get a closer look.

"You're Tanya's little girl, Vanessa. Gosh, you look just like your mother. Darker, a little taller, but other than that, you guys could be twins." She takes a moment to scan me over.

Tanya. I say the name in my head one thousand times so that it remains stained in my memory.

Her name is Tanya Martin. My chest splits open, and all my organs spill out onto the floor. But somehow I'm still standing, feet like lead, knees like concrete. This is some sick joke or a dream. More like a nightmare. Tell me she works here as a guard or even in the cafeteria, serving up crappy lunches. I can deal with that. Tell me anything other than she's serving a prison sentence here. Because this is not the mother I pictured in my dreams. Not the one who sang lullabies to me and made me blueberry pancakes on Saturday mornings.

The prison rules are that visitors must be listed on the inmate's permission list. Visitors also have to be at least eighteen years old with a valid state-issued ID or be accompanied by someone fitting that description. I learn that Mama has had me, Pop Pop, and Daddy on her list for nine years. She's been locked away like some caged animal for more than half my life. I also learn that LaToya is friends with Mama, and so she breaks the rules and lets me in. She says her supervisor is off today, so "the man" isn't around to watch her every move.

I thank the kind prison guard, and he leaves the room.

"I have to do a search," LaToya informs me.

"Of what?" I ask.

LaToya scans her eyes up and down my body. Oh Lord.

I'm sure she tries to be delicate, but when she starts running her fingers over my arms, under my breasts, and down my thighs, all I feel are millions of fire ants invading my skin.

"Sorry, but it's procedure."

My teeth slice through the inner walls of my cheeks. I swallow the faintest taste of blood.

LaToya escorts me through a series of metal doors and finally leads me to an empty room that's cold, dull, and gray with white plastic tables and chairs.

"Nobody usually comes to visit when there's a storm on the way," LaToya says.

The whole time she is talking and explaining the procedures, the words melt and fizzle all together. I see her mouth moving and hear sounds coming out, but nothing sticks. My brain is flooded with my own thoughts, my own questions, my own fears. What in the world do you say to a mother you haven't seen in almost a decade? *Hey, Ma, how's life treating ya?*

Will she even recognize me? I'm sure that my baby-soft features have hardened over the years, thanks to her. Well, and Daddy. A sharp twinge travels from my head to my throat. An ugly reality surfaces. What if she doesn't want to see me at all?

LaToya leaves to get Mama, who she says is working the afternoon shift in the library. Minutes later she returns with a woman who stands—more like hides—behind her. LaToya reaches for Mama's frail hand and pulls her forward so she's standing just inches from my face. She sucks in a large breath and holds on to it for what feels like an eternity. It's okay because I breathe heavily enough for the both of us. Sips of breath both small and large, coupled with my booming heart, echo through the room.

"There she is, Tanya. It's your baby girl, Vanessa."

I do not know this woman. This ain't who checked for monsters under my bed before tucking me in at night. This ain't the vanilla-coated, freckle-faced beauty queen of a woman that I remember as my mother. This is some older, grayer, weaker, enslaved version of her. A shell of a woman formerly known as Mama. Dressed in prison rags and old, beat-up sneakers so dirty that not even the brand name shows. Hair matted so close to her scalp, it's obvious she hasn't seen a comb in a while. She used to have silky hair that hung past her shoulders. What happened to her?

We both stand there staring at each other. Me clutching onto Darlene with every bit of strength I got. Her staring at Darlene like she's more interested in the journal than she is in me.

Mama inches forward, eyes glued on Darlene, hands slowly extended like a moth to a flame. I tower over her weak frame, and I place Darlene behind me. She cowers to my largeness, taking two steps back.

LaToya speaks to break the silence in the room. "I'll give you a half hour. Even though the big boss ain't here, I can't break too many rules."

"Thank you, Toya."

Her voice. It hasn't changed after all this time. Syrupy sweet, each word sounding like the melodies I remember from many years of yesterdays.

My mother holds her stare, and her eyes begin to fill with tears. "Have a seat," she says.

The door slams, and we are left in this room of unspoken words, surrounded by the gray concrete walls. Alone. God, I wish Pop Pop were here right now. He'd think of something clever to say. Crack a joke or something to break up this awkwardness.

Mama's eyes are sad and covered in layers of folded skin. She suddenly unleashes a stream of thick tears. I sit there, not knowing what to feel. Sadness. Anger. Joy. Maybe a combination? Am I supposed to feel sorry for her? Sorry for me? Part of me wants to never let her go. I've prayed to have Mama back in my life every night, only to have my heart broken every Halloween, every Christmas, every motherless birthday. The other part of me wants to hit her one good time, straight across the face. Make the pain sting and settle right into the deepest parts of her soul. Make her feel what I've felt these nine long years.

"You finally came. And you brought the birthday gift I

made for you." She leans in to touch my hands. I lean back and throw them both on top of my lap, knocking Darlene onto the floor.

Mama is the one who gave me this journal? Year after year, Pop Pop would give me a new one, saying how special it is. How I should use it to lay out everything I got filling me up on the inside. Days have blended into weeks, weeks melted into months, months merging into empty, lonely years. And I had a piece of her with me all along?

My lips quiver as I pick Darlene up off the floor. I wanna hug Mama. I still wanna slap her too. I wanna know everything. Not the sugarcoated version. The full-out, unleashed truth. I've waited nine years for this. Page after page in my journals stained with my tears.

"What happened to our family? Everything was perfect, and then you left us. You left *me!*" The words spill out in panted breaths.

"Vanessa, I've written you letters for years explaining, begging for your forgiveness over and over again. I didn't mean for things to turn out this way."

Mama lays out everything. The gritty, dirty truth of it all. Seems me and Daddy were never a part of Mama's plan, though those weren't the exact words that came out of her mouth. Years ago she was on the fast track: modeling for *Jet* magazine, appearing in local television commercials, and competing in beauty pageants.

"I even won the very first Miss Newark Teen Pageant," Mama says, cracking a weak smile.

That was Mama's tiara locked away in Daddy's chamber of nothingness. Why didn't Pop Pop tell me? Why the secrets and the lies? Why did Daddy make it seem like pageants were such a bad thing, especially if Mama did them?

She was on her way to making it big. But you know how the old song goes: first came love, then came marriage, then came the lady with the baby carriage. And that rocked Mama's world something awful. I came in this world, screaming and kicking and jacking her body up. The modeling jobs stopped coming. Pageants were out of the question. Mama's superstar dreams were flushed away, all 'cause of me.

"I started doing drugs," Mama says, with her head sinking into her shoulders. "One night I got a new batch of heroin, and I wanted just a taste, that's all. You was so fussy that night. I had you ready for bed and then you threw up all over yourself. So I threw you in the tub and . . ."

Her words hit me like an uppercut. That nightmare. It was real. The memories, the dreams, all the night terrors blast back into my mind. For nine years, I suppressed it all. Tried to forget. My fear of looking at the bathtub, let alone going into it? That wasn't just some foolish kiddie phobia. It's real. I remember now.

"So *that's* what happened to me, Mama? You left me in a tub of running hot water? *Alone?*" My voice rises an octave with each word, each piece of the night terror flooding back to life.

"I was gone for just a second, baby girl. That's all!" Mama's crying all over again.

The air is being sucked right out of me, right out of this empty room. The pain. The white light. The sirens. The sound of Daddy crying. What happened in my nightmare—drifting, drowning, dying—that actually happened to me.

When Mama came back into the bathroom that night, I was facedown in the water. Who knows for how long? One thing's for sure, Mama didn't know or care. She was too busy shooting up, drifting off to another world where I didn't exist. No chains. No responsibilities. No me.

"The ambulance came, and they couldn't revive you." Mama's words come out in heavy, long sobs. "So you went into a . . . coma."

And then the police hauled Mama off to the deepest pits of hell. I look around the room—so sad, so dull, so lifeless. She deserves to be here, caged behind iron bars, trapped in her own jungle, left to stew in the memories.

"But I wrote you all the time, tried to explain myself. I begged for you and your father to forgive me. Begged him to bring you up here so I could see you. Pop still comes around every year, bragging 'bout how good you doing in school. You get that from me." Mama reaches for my cheek but then stops herself.

I suddenly become aware of my hands. My oversized, strong hands. Fingers curled up into a ball so tight, I swear that at any second I could snap. My mother, the woman who gave birth to me, the one who was supposed to love and protect me, almost killed me.

I wanna hit something so bad. And at that moment I realize

how close Mama is to me. The table feels shorter and shorter with each tick of the clock. All I can think about is wrapping my big, black hands around her scrawny, gray neck. Instead I stand up abruptly, knocking the chair onto the floor. Mama is shaken out of her tears.

A low boil stirs inside, works its way upward, and tumbles out of me. Loudly, I defy all notes in a chromatic scale. Mrs. Walton would be impressed.

"You ruined us! You ruined everything! No wonder Daddy didn't want me to know about you!" Now my voice turns baritone-deep and gravelly, laced with a level of anger I've never experienced in my life.

Back and forth, back and forth, I pace the room while Mama sits there, shaking like she needs a fix. Mama is a drug addict. Mama loved her drugs more than she ever loved me. Mama chose to shoot that crap in her veins and ruin any chance at a relationship with me. No one forced her to take drugs. Not Pop Pop. Not Daddy. And if she was that messed up from the changes in her body and in her career, she had other choices.

This whole time I thought Daddy was the monster. That he was the one who created all of these lies, all of the fears and the insecurities. Now I see the truth, clear as day. Daddy wasn't the only monster in my life. Mama was—is. With her drugs and her selfishness. She loved that poison more than she loved me. Loved her superstar life before me. The life where she was pretty and popular and a beauty queen. The same life that I was going after with my hopeless, starry-eyed

Miss America dreams. How could I be so stupid and shallow? No wonder Daddy doesn't want me to do the pageant. He wants to protect me from becoming like her. But he sure found the worst way possible to do it.

I came to this place thinking I'd find some big home in the country, with a mother who'd welcome me with open arms and rescue me from Daddy. What was I thinking? What I found was nothing but a druggie whose life went downhill. What I found was a mother who didn't want to be a mother at all. And in the end, what I discovered was that both of my parents are monsters.

I need to get out of here. Need to go home. Back to the jungle. To the projects. To the rhythms of my 'hood. Back to the people there who do love me.

"Well, I guess that's everything, then." I stop pacing and slowly make my way toward the door. There isn't much else to say. I wanted the truth. And that's what I got. Now I have to find a way to get past it.

I look at the clock on the wall. It's getting late, and the sky is already darkening. Through the window I can see black clouds gathering. The trip home will be long, and I'm supposed to meet TJ by six-thirty.

"Wait," Mama says. "Will you come back to visit me again? I get out of here in June. Maybe I can come see you graduate. We can start over. It's not too late for us."

For a second I think about throwing Darlene right at her. Shove those poems, those lyrics, those stupid dreams in her face. Make her read every page covered with me hoping and wishing and begging like some lovesick puppy. But then I look into her eyes. Those glazed-over, tear-filled gray eyes. She don't deserve one piece of me. So I wrap that book up in my arms, and I speak very slowly so that she can understand my every word.

"Tanya. It's much, much, much too late."

December 9, 1983

The End of the Beginning
Once upon a time, there lived a little girl
with a mom and a dad and sunshine and love.
Then one day,
the mom turned into the big bad wolf
and was locked in a cage far, far away,
taking the sun with her,
leaving her family behind in the wild.
And the little girl and the dad
lived happily never after.

Dear Darlene,

I changed my mind. Some fairy tales are real.

—Nessy

Me and My Stupid Miss America Dreams

I didn't expect to spend my fourteenth birthday in a prison, locked away in a concrete room, forced to face it all: my family's secrets; my foiled plans to find Mama and live happily ever after; my stupid, stupid Miss America dreams. My feet move like lead on the way back to the bus stop. Every step is painful. The crunch of the snow sends cold shocks up and down my body. The ride home is long and slow. Cars and trucks trudge through honey-thick roads, trying their best not to slide on the snow. Every few minutes I find myself turning to look at the seat next to me, foolishly wishing that Mama were sitting there. Pure. Clean. Beautiful. Wishing that what just happened were all in my head. That the woman back at the prison were a ghost, and the real Mama were here in the flesh. But there is no Mama to bring back home with me. There is no Mama to rescue me. Mama is in a cage.

After the bus drops me off at Commerce Street, I fight

through the snow to get to Penn Station, where I catch the number 13 bus home. It's almost seven, and I know TJ's gonna be mad at me for having to wait. As the bus pulls up in front of the bodega, I see a large crowd gathered at the top of the hill.

I walk toward the crowd and hear people shouting and see hands flying up and down in the air. There's a bunch of them. Guys and girls all huddled together in a sea of winter coats. Sometimes people in my neighborhood make huddles like this around two rappers when they're battling it out. Everybody knows that Raheem is the best rapper in Grafton Hill. Whoever's versing him right now is a brave soul.

I join the crowd, thinking maybe TJ is in here too. Maybe he was waiting for me to return and decided to listen to the rappers kick some fresh rhymes. The huddle is so thick I can't see any faces, and I can't make out who's in the center.

"I'm tired of this sissy prancing around my 'hood, putting on a front."

Junito. His voice is clear. Pissed.

"Front? What we have was no front, Juni. You promised that we could be together. That you didn't care about all of this!" I hear a familiar voice respond.

TJ no, TJ no. Shut up! Don't say another word! Walk away! What are you doing? Panic swells in my gut. My legs push me forward, lunging me straight into the belly of the crackling sounds of punching and wailing. But the crowd is huddled tight, blocking my every attempt to reach TJ.

I need to get to him. Need to pull him away. Rush him

past the hate, past the broken concrete, down the hill, and to the four walls of his own room.

Across the huddle I see Tanisha, with a front-row seat to the action. For a mere second our eyes meet. She's standing there chewing her bottom lip, left knee trembling like she knows exactly what's about to go down. On the inside, I know it too. This is how street fights go in Grafton.

"What's in the girly bag?" a voice yells out over the scuffle.

I stand on the tips of my toes, searching the crowd. It's Beatriz on the opposite side, holding up my garment bag. She rips it open and shows everyone what's inside.

Like a chorus, everyone goes, "*Ooh!*"

It's my dress for the pageant. My beautiful, perfectly finished, perfectly rhinestoned red dress for the pageant tomorrow.

"Stop! That's for Vanessa!" TJ cries out.

Beatriz notices me and throws me a cutting, triumphant smile. This is it. She's won. All it took was her slithering her way into my life, into my deepest fears and secrets, pretending to be my friend, only to destroy every piece of me I had left. She knows that TJ's gay. And deep down she knows her brother is too. But there was no way she was going to let all of Grafton in on her family secrets.

That is my dress in that bag. My Cinderella moment for the pageant in a bag. All along, Beatriz was looking for the perfect opportunity to make my dreams come tumbling down. Telling Daddy was the ticket.

The reality of her betrayal cuts me right down to the white meat.

"Yeah, right. Junito," Beatriz calls out to her brother, who's got a chokehold around TJ's neck. "This *maricón* likes to wear dresses. *Mira!*"

That's when the real beating begins. My screams don't matter at that point because everyone is chanting for Junito to kick TJ's behind. Beatriz and some other girls start to rip the dress apart right before my eyes. Next thing I know, Beatriz is coming at me with an iron fist. She swings, but I float like a butterfly and sting like Ali. She misses my face with that sorry hit, and it lands on my shoulder instead. But when you got extra meat on your bones, you don't feel a doggone thing. Just as I'm ready to body-slam this chick, Tanisha rushes through the crowd and pushes Beatriz straight to the ground. Beatriz's crew tries to step our way, but the crowd grows thicker, and Beatriz runs back to her brother.

The snow is coming down hard now. TJ is fighting back the best he can, but his flailing arms are no match for Junito's boxer-like skills. Junito's boys join in, and Beatriz spits at TJ and throws the torn red fabric at him like confetti. And no one dares stop them. Everyone stands there enjoying the show. Blood is spilling in multiple directions on the pillow-white snow. TJ hunches over, then stands up straight as a nail with each uppercut.

And all this time I'm screaming, "Somebody *help* him!"

I'm begging everyone around me to do something. Anything. Everything's moving in slow motion. The sounds of kicking, moaning, punching, and blood splatter swirl around me while everyone stands there.

Every time I rush toward Junito to pull him away, a few people in the crowd pull me back and throw me to the ground.

"You're gonna kill him. *Stop!*" My voice is raised and high pitched, but Junito and his gang don't back down. TJ's on the ground now. They growl as they kick him in the ribs with their combat boots.

TJ lies on the snow, lifeless with a pool of blood slowly growing around his face. The blood pours out red, then freezes.

"Yo, five-o coming. Roll out!" one of the Latin Diablos screams over the scuffle. No one cared to hear my screams, but they sure hear his.

Sirens echo through the neighborhood, and the crowd instantly thins out, with people scattering everywhere. One by one, the lights inside the surrounding apartments turn off. This is the norm when the police come to Grafton Hill. Nobody ain't heard nothing. They ain't seen nothing either. But I witnessed every single moment.

I crawl to TJ's bloody body. My red dress lies near him, torn to shreds. Rhinestone pieces, spread across the snow, glisten in the glare of the streetlight.

Everything around me becomes muted. I don't even hear when the paramedics tell me to get in the ambulance. I only see them place TJ on the gurney, his fingers curled into a tight ball, then releasing to a motionless limp. And I let out a scream that might shake all of Newark to its core.

TJ is dead. Dead because he could never be free from the secret of who he wanted to be. Dead because of me. Me and my crazy plans. Me and my stupid Miss America dreams.

Dreams Tell Lies Too

The waiting room at the Clara Maass hospital is surrounded by glass walls, and I am all alone. Pacing back and forth, back and forth, each step like a long, never-ending dance. Shaking all over, every vein throbbing in rhythm with my steps. I pace. I sit. I stand. It's like an angry symphony of three different songs.

My body refuses to remain still in the chair, mouth drinking desperate sips of air.

What are the doctors doing to TJ? If it's taking this long, he must not be dead after all. Did they stop the bleeding? The questions rush into my head like a raging river.

No one is telling me anything. The nurses are busy; the doctors are nowhere to be found. As soon as I arrived, a nurse called Daddy and Pop Pop to tell them to get here as soon as possible, but apparently they already knew. Tanisha and her mom had rushed to the eighth floor to get Pop Pop and also Daddy, who happened to have come home early from work.

Seconds feel like hours, minutes like days. What do I say when they get here? TJ got beat up, and it's my fault. I included him in my plan. Had I gotten to the top of the hill on time, we would have gone home together like we'd planned. Nobody would have noticed him or the dress because I would've been carrying it.

"Where's my nephew?" Daddy's voice booms as the double doors at the entrance slide open.

I stand up at once, see him through the glass windows. He's talking with the nurse, and Pop Pop, Tanisha, and Mrs. Bennet aren't far behind. The nurse gestures toward me. Though I can barely hear her soft whispers, I know she's trying to calm my father down. He catches sight of me and stands there for a second.

His wiry, tar-black hair stands at attention. Shoulders seem wider than the four walls caving in around us. All these years being around my father, I've learned to be present and invisible at the same time. Present for when he needs something. Like a glass of water or the Sunday paper. Invisible for moments like this, where the whole world erupts before us and all he can do is look for someone to blame.

The tenor of Daddy's voice flashes me right back to the street. The blood circling TJ's face. The sound of cracking bones. TJ motionless in the snow.

Daddy falls slowly into the chair across from me and massages his fingers in his temples. I remain standing. "Your school called because you didn't show up today. Do you have any idea how worried we were? Where the hell were you? And now this?"

Pop Pop throws me a look that urges me to tell the truth

because "God don't like liars." Mrs. Bennet and Tanisha slow-walk to the chairs behind me.

"I went . . . to see Mama." The truth slips out before I can stop it.

"*You did what?*" Daddy bolts up so quickly, the chair falls backward and slams onto the floor.

Pop Pop looks relieved, as though finally the burden of secrets can be lifted off his shoulders. The skin around Daddy's mouth tightens, and he looks at me with bloodshot eyes.

The endless pause between us is filled with words. All the negative words that ever existed in the English language. In this moment, I am every single one of them. Stupid. Careless. Impulsive. Irresponsible. Secretive. Sneaky. But you know what? He is those words too. His eyes glue to mine as I sink lower and lower into the shell of myself. His tired, worried, angry eyes are like acid on my skin.

Daddy sets his hands out in front of him, breathes himself calm, and then walks toward me. I stiffen from the soles of my feet to the crown of my head. At this point I'm too terrified to make one move because if I do, I think my whole body might shatter like broken glass.

"What did she tell you?" His face is real close to mine. The heat of his breath torches my nose, and I don't inhale one bit.

"Everything." I don't dare look at him for fear of turning into a pillar of salt. I stare at the floor really, really hard.

Two cops enter the waiting room just as I'm about to spontaneously combust. "Mr. Martin, we need to ask your daughter a few questions."

The number one rule in the 'hood is that snitching ain't allowed. Snitches don't belong in Grafton. A snitch is a punk. A snitch is nothing but the policeman's slave. Well, call me a snitch and throw me on a plantation because I tell the cops everything I saw. From Junito harassing my cousin and trying to cover up the fact that the two of them had a thing going, to Beatriz being the ringleader during the fight and hyping up the situation. Tanisha warned me not to trust that girl, and I should have listened. I told Beatriz about keeping the pageant a secret from Daddy. I told her about my dress. That heifer knew TJ was making it. She knew what the dress would look like, from the color to the rhinestone detail, to the very last stitch. Her "friendship" was nothing more than a performance. Nothing more than a weapon to hurt me and TJ to the bone. Mission accomplished.

The doctor walks in just as I'm finishing up answering questions for the police officers. "TJ will be fine. He's bruised up pretty badly. He has a broken nose and a couple of broken ribs. He'll need to stay here for a few days, but he should be good enough to go home soon. I'm prescribing some medication to ease the pain, and lots of bed rest," she announces. She leaves the room along with the cops.

Tanisha squeezes my hand tight, and I can finally breathe again. TJ isn't dead.

"Daddy, I'm sorry for going behind your back." I turn around to look my ex–best friend in her eyes. "Tanisha, I'm sorry too for not believing you when you warned me so many times."

By now the tears are gushing out, and there ain't a thing I can do to stop them.

"We'll figure things out later, Nessy," Tanisha whispers softly.

But Daddy's face is empty. There are no words left.

"I understand now. I understand everything. I just wanted to know the truth, Daddy." I say all of this through tears and snot running down my mouth. Mrs. Bennet grabs a tissue from her purse and wipes my face.

"Take her home. I'll stay," Daddy whispers, and shoos us all away.

By this point I'm sobbing, but my father doesn't care. He sits there with his face buried in his hands, probably crying his own tears.

I want to scream out to him how I feel. Tell him how much I hate him. Tell him that I love and hate him at the same time with every breath I take. That his secrets and his lies broke me. That even after all of this, I will never, ever turn out like her.

Pop Pop and Mrs. Bennet usher us out of the room and back to Grafton. Before I can even think of going to sleep, I rip up those stupid prayers from my journal, toss the rhinestone crown pin I bought on the boardwalk in the garbage, flush the Sol-Glo down the toilet, and tear down every single Miss America poster taped to my wall. This dream is all a lie. This dream was never meant for someone like me.

Truth Swells

🌾 I once read a line in a Countee Cullen poem that said something about not being made to eternally weep. But my entire night was spent crying. My dreams had no chance to surface. No dreams of Mama. No dreams of drowning. Just a sea of blackness surrounded by the tears that continued to fall even as I slept. No dreams of me foolishly thinking that I too could be like Miss America. Escape this jungle and mend the broken pieces of my family. By the morning, my face is salted dry.

When I wake up, two faces hover over me like night and day. Pop Pop and Mrs. Walton, both with deep creases around their eyes. I'm used to seeing what Pop Pop looks like in the morning, but Mrs. Walton looks crazy with a capital *C*. She's got her reading glasses propped at the tip of her nose and no makeup on, and her mass of blonde hair is piled in a bun on top of her head. Behind her is a duffel bag, stuffed to the rim, sitting on top of a suitcase.

"What are you doing here?" I sit up.

"Your grandfather called me early this morning and told me

what happened last night. I know about your mother, Vanessa. Why didn't you feel like you could talk to me about it?"

I stare at her blankly because, quite honestly, I got nothing to say. I should've gone to her. Of all the people in my life, she knows what it feels like to run on empty. But still, the embarrassment of it all was too deep. Mrs. Walton's mother left, but at least she didn't go to jail. My mother robbed me of any chance at good memories. And even the ones I do have are probably all a lie.

"I wish I could change everything, Mrs. Walton." On the inside I'm still crying, even though my tear supply has dried out.

She pulls me to her and holds me so tight that all my broken pieces slowly start to mend back together. "I heard about TJ and the fight and your pageant dress being ruined. All on your birthday too. I'm so, so sorry, Vanessa."

My arms, weary and lifeless, fold around her.

"I think you need to be getting ready, Nessy. We got a pageant to win tonight," Pop Pop says.

Pageant? How can I even think about doing a pageant after everything that happened?

"Pop Pop, I'm not doing it. Daddy doesn't want me to, and I don't even want to anymore. This pageant has done nothing but ruin my life. I already lost Tanisha as a best friend. Almost lost TJ last night."

Pop Pop throws his long, thick finger in my face. "Now looka here, Nessy. I'll deal with your father and slap some good sense into him. You worked real hard for this, and dang it, you gonna go for it, or you'll regret it. Plus, TJ would want you to still do the pageant after all the time he spent helping you."

"But I'm not ready. TJ was supposed to do my hair today, give me my first relaxer, do my makeup. And what about my escort? He was supposed to do that too! But he can't, and it's all my fault. I have no one now."

And the tears start all over again. Pop Pop rubs my hands. So delicate. So attentive.

"Now, now. TJ is a strong boy. He'll be just fine. You have me here for you. I love you, baby girl. So I'll be your escort. I'll even wear my good suit."

Through the tears, I bust out a belly-deep laugh. Pop Pop's idea of his good suit is his 1972, mauve-colored, bell-bottom ensemble with a tie-dye, butterfly-collar shirt. Not really sure if that qualifies as "good." But even in my worst times, that man always finds a way to turn my day bright.

"Sure, Pop Pop," I reluctantly agree.

"And I can help you with your hair and makeup," Mrs. Walton chimes in.

I wanna ask, *What in the world do you know about doing black hair, white lady?* Instead I nibble the corner of my mouth and let out a doubtful groan.

"What? You think I don't know how to do your hair?" Mrs. Walton snaps her fingers. "You'd be surprised."

She reaches into her purse, pulls out a picture, and hands it to me. The image staring back at me is a gorgeous little bronze-skinned black girl dressed in a pretty-in-pink outfit, with her hair styled in two soft afro puffs with pink bows.

"Who's this?" I ask.

"My number-one hair client. My daughter, Sasha."

"Your *what*?"

Mrs. Walton smiles and folds her arms. Pop Pop stands there clapping his hands at her like she just preached a sermon at church. "See, I know a lot more than you think I do. I know how to press and curl, cornrow, pin curl, French roll. I can do it all. I've had lots of practice on my daughter's hair."

That Mrs. Walton is full of surprises. All this time, I knew she was married and had a daughter, but she never mentioned that her daughter was black. Well, half black. I guess the both of us have spent these past few months acting like turtles, slowly revealing our own truths. But like Old Man Lee said, the truth is the one thing you can't hide from.

"I'm 'a leave you two young ladies to do your little girly makeover while I go on in the kitchen to make y'all some food. Any requests?" Pop Pop asks.

Thank God it's the beginning of the month. There's actually a good amount of food in the fridge to offer Mrs. Walton. I just hope Pop Pop sprays so the roaches don't come out.

"Oh, I'm easy. Whatever you whip up, I'm sure it'll be just fine."

"She likes grits, Pop Pop!"

"Coming right up!" Pop Pop closes my door and leaves Mrs. Walton and me alone in my room.

"Okay, little lady! Here's your robe, toiletries, and this pretty flowery book. How about you go take a nice, hot bath while I get everything set up?"

I stand there, clutching onto Darlene, feeling something hurling from my stomach and racing toward my mouth. Words. Bare. Exposed. Fearless.

"You're right, Mrs. Walton. A bath is just what I need."

December 10, 1983

I Am More
I am more than my fears,
trapped deep inside for years.
I laugh in your face.
Fear, you have no place.
I'll wave good-bye. Go away.
Fearless Me is here to stay.

Dear Darlene,

    The pageant starts in eight hours, and I'm gonna be on that stage. And somehow I lie here unafraid. The truth swells larger than the tub walls can hold, cleanses me more than the water and bubbles ever can. I signed up for this pageant to be like Mama. To be like Miss America. When all along what I really needed was to find a way to be like . . . me. Like Vanessa.

        —Nessy

This Is for Me Now

I've waited all my life to get a perm. Every time I'd see a commercial for Dark & Lovely with those gorgeous black models and their swinging, straight, shoulder-length hair, I'd beg for Pop Pop to give me the money to get a perm. But he never allowed me to.

"I ain't giving you money to put some creamy crack on your scalp and burn the mess out of it! You better work with what the good Lord gave you!" Every time I'd ask, that was his reaction.

Today was supposed to be special, because TJ had learned how to do perms at school, and he was going to give me one as a birthday present. But today that wasn't going to happen, not if Mrs. Walton had anything to do with it.

"Your hair is beautiful the way it is. I don't see why you need to put any chemicals in it anyway." Mrs. Walton parts my carpet-thick hair into four sections.

Easy enough for her to say. She's got that white-girl hair. I'm sure she doesn't have any problems getting a comb through it.

"I'm going to give you the same deep condition treatment

that I give my daughter. She has thick, curly hair like yours. I make the conditioner myself."

"What's in it?" I ask. Now I'm worried.

"Some honey, egg, avocado, mayonnaise, and a few other things."

Sounds more like breakfast than a hair product. "I've tried mayo on my hair before, but I don't know about those other things. Are you sure, Mrs. Walton?"

"Oh, it works. You just wait and see."

We make our way to the kitchen sink to wash my hair. First Mrs. Walton lathers my hair with a vanilla-almond scented shampoo. She works up a nice amount of suds in each section and rinses twice. I have to admit that it smells amazing, especially mixed with the smell of the breakfast Pop Pop's got cooking on the stove. Next she sits me down at the kitchen table and applies her homemade conditioner. She uses a wide-tooth comb to comb it through to my ends. My curls loosen and stretch past my neck. I've never seen them stretch that long before, and they spring back up again into a spiral pattern when Mrs. Walton lets them go. She sweeps my hair up into a high bun and clips it tight with a banana clip. Next she places a plastic cap on my head and sits me under her portable hair dryer. This lady has turned my kitchen into a full-service hair salon.

"You have to let that sit for a half hour."

While the conditioner works its magic, we eat the breakfast feast Pop Pop prepared: T-bone steaks, cheese eggs, grits, coffee, and orange juice. I know he is still trying to impress

Mrs. Walton, and I so want to tell the old man he doesn't stand a chance.

After the half hour is up, Mrs. Walton rinses out the conditioner and combs some jojoba oil into my hair from the root to the tip. "When I'm done with your hair, you're going to wish you'd never even thought about putting those chemicals in it."

She twists my hair into tiny double strands all around my head. "Now these have to dry for a couple of hours. Then I'll take them out, and you will have a full head of gorgeous, shiny curls."

While my twists are clipped and drying, Mrs. Walton has me try on the ivory princess gown we got from Bamberger's. Pop Pop waits in the living room for the big reveal. I never even tried the dress on. What if it doesn't fit? What if it's too high-water on me? What if the ivory color is too much of a contrast with my skin? I make a vow to myself that if there is a single thing wrong, there's no way I'm going through with the pageant. I'll stay home, locked away in my room, staring at all my Miss America posters crumpled in the trash can, and telling Vanessa Williams, *Listen, girlfriend, I tried!*

Mrs. Walton carefully unzips the dress and has me step into it. I'm waiting for the moment when she slides the dress up and my hips fight to get through the lining. But instead the dress goes up with ease. When she zips it up, I don't even have to suck in my gut. The boning of the waistline cinches me in all the right places and lies flat.

"There, it's perfect." Mrs. Walton turns me around to look

in the mirror. The image I see staring back at me is a complete stranger. I don't even know who this person is. But I think I like her.

Mrs. Walton fluffs the crinoline slip under my dress and puts on my glasslike Cinderella-style slippers. Then she takes out my rhinestone jewelry set and helps me put it on. The dress was gorgeous alone, but that jewelry adds a whole new level of sparkle and shine.

"Let's go show your grandfather."

When we walk into the living room, Pop Pop is watching the news. But then he catches a glimpse of me and immediately hobbles up to turn the television off.

"Wow, Nessy. You look . . . you look . . . stunning." And then I see my grandfather do something I ain't never seen him do before. He starts to cry. The oversized teddy bear who's always telling jokes actually has a soft side. He reaches for me, but Mrs. Walton stops him short.

"Save the hugs and the tears for later, sir. We don't want Vanessa to mess up her dress."

Pop Pop doesn't even argue back. Instead he takes a seat and claps thunderously loud. And in that moment, that's all I need. Standing in my very own living room, I feel like I've just won the pageant.

When we go to my room and take off the dress, Mrs. Walton says the next step is to get a manicure and pedicure. She digs in her oversized duffel bag and pulls out a bunch of equipment. She has five different colors of nail polish and all kinds of surgical-looking instruments. I do recognize the scissors and the pair of tweezers, but the rest of the stuff looks like an assortment of small knives and swords. I've always wanted my nails done, but looking at these weapons has me thinking twice.

Mrs. Walton examines my hands and feet. I curl my toes, one on top of the other, to hide the dried-up, crusty skin surrounding each nail. Effort failed.

"Ooh, your cuticles need a lot of help. And your nails are all different sizes!"

She seats me in the chair at my desk and then goes in her bag of tricks and pulls out a large bowl and a small bowl, some bottles of oils, and a bag of rocks. Before I can even ask her what she plans on doing with those rocks, she's in the bathroom, filling the bowls with water. When she returns, she places the small bowl on my desk and the large one on the floor. The rocks go in the bowls, along with a few drops of the oils she brought: lavender, lemon, and rose. She places my crusty feet in the large bowl and instructs me to place my hands in the small bowl.

The warmth of the water instantly soothes my skin, while the oils start to work their scented magic.

Mrs. Walton returns to her bag (did she pack her whole house?) and pulls out a tape player, some jars of cream, a cucumber, and a knife. This is all just getting weirder by the minute.

"What's all that for?"

"Be patient, my child. You'll see."

When she pops the tape in the player, classical music pours out of the speakers. The violins pluck over the booming chords of a piano. The music is like air—light, flowing, and giving me life. It's *The Four Seasons*, by Vivaldi, she explains.

"Now close your eyes, Vanessa, and forget about everything. Don't worry about your mother. Don't worry about TJ. He's fine and will be home soon. Be thankful for that. Now picture yourself onstage tonight, being the best that you can be. Picture yourself shining brighter than the stars in the sky."

I do as I am told. When I used to imagine myself on the pageant stage, the girl I saw was the spitting image of Vanessa Williams or the spitting image of Mama. That girl shined in all of her beauty, or at least what I thought was the definition of beauty. But this new girl in my vision is me. My fearless, talented, black self.

My eyes are still closed as I hear her slicing the cucumbers. The smell is everywhere, seeping into my skin. She places them, cold and sticky, on my eyes.

"All princesses need a facial before the big show," Mrs. Walton says, and I can practically feel her warm smile.

Next she covers my face in a minty-scented cream that hardens into a mask, and I sit there picturing how crazy I look with my eyes covered in vegetables and my face like a ghost's. But on the inside I'm smiling just as wide as I'm sure Mrs. Walton is. I've never done anything like this before. This is what it must feel like to have a mother to do girly stuff with. And somewhere deep down inside, even though it may seem hopeless now, I know I'll still long for a day when Mama and I could do pedicures and facials and manicures together. A day when she could do my hair and give me a perm. Maybe there is still hope. But for now, I ain't ready.

I doze off and on through the whole makeover. That classical music stuff makes you drift off worse than NyQuil, then fires you awake soon as the violins get to screaming. When Mrs. Walton taps me on my shoulder, my hands and feet are perfectly manicured. My nails shimmer with a clear coat of polish and a small white line drawn at each nail tip. It's a French manicure, Mrs. Walton explains.

She's cleaned the cucumbers and cream off my face, and my skin is pimple-free and as smooth as silk.

Mrs. Walton turns to my makeup. The nutmeg blush complements the hint-of-pink lip gloss. Each eyelash gets mascaraed in long, lush layers. My jojoba-scented hair cascades to my shoulders in Z-patterned waves.

As I stand motionless in front of the mirror, Mrs. Walton holds the dress up to my shoulders. I do not recognize the girl staring back at me. She is pretty. As in beautiful. As in gorgeous. And not pretty even though she's dark, but pretty *because* she is dark. This skin. Unique, unbleached, rich, the color of the finest materials on earth: oil, coal, volcanic sand. And in that moment I'm glad that the Sol-Glo never worked on me.

The sound of the phone ringing echoes throughout the house.

"Nessy, phone's for you!" Pop Pop screams from the living room.

When I pick up the phone in my room, TJ is on the line.

"Break a leg, little cuz!" His voice is raspy, weak.

I'm painfully reminded of yesterday. Guilt settles in, presses heavy on my shoulders. "I didn't want to go through with the pageant today, TJ, I swear." Now I'm feeling guilty because he should be here with me instead of Mrs. Walton.

"Why on earth would you have even considered dropping out? Because of last night? Don't let that stop you, Nessy." His voice is laced in pain.

"I'm sorry about everything. It was all my fault."

I can hear his whimper through the phone, soft, wispy, begging to be hidden. The air between us is deathly silent. "Nessy, you better not be crying too!"

"I'm not." The lie forces me to stop.

TJ sniffs away his last tear. "I thought what I had with Junito was real, but I was wrong. He was never going to truly be with me, never was a real friend. But you are, Nessy. And that's why you gotta do it big tonight. I'll be there in spirit. Everyone's rooting for you. Even Uncle Daniel."

"Wait, what do you mean? Daddy's the one who didn't want me to do the pageant in the first place."

"Well, I don't think he actually meant it. You two have a lot to talk about when he gets around to it."

"Well, where is he? Is he there now? Can I talk to him?" My skin is tingling with excitement. Daddy is okay with me doing the pageant. Maybe he'll come see me onstage tonight.

But my hopes are shot when TJ replies, "He's not here today, but he stayed with me last night, and we talked about everything. From Junito to the pageant. No more lies or secrets."

Knowing Daddy, he went to work to get away from us. To get away from the shame. The phone line is so quiet, all that's left is the sound of my staggered breath. Then TJ opens up that tenor voice of his and starts to sing this song he wrote for me many moons ago.

My Vanessa, pretty as the sun above.
My Vanessa, you fill my heart with love.
My Vanessa, pretty little queen, I love you so.
I don't ever think that you will know,
that you're the only girl I need.

"And, honey chile, you know that's the truth!" TJ says in the middle of the song.

I just die laughing. "You're too much, TJ."

I can feel his warmth through the phone. He finishes the song, and the way he sings is like a big ole hug sent all the way from the hospital to my room here in the projects.

"Now I want you to repeat these words after me: I, Vanessa Martin, am about to compete in my very first pageant. Miss King Middle School, here I come!"

And I do exactly as I am told.

Daddy steps into the house just as Mrs. Walton and I are leaving. His tread into the living room is long and slow. No vibrating walls. No earthquaking cupboards.

And there I am, standing with all my bags for the pageant, waiting for him to shoot me down.

Mrs. Walton takes my things from me, forces out an

uncomfortable cough, and says she'll meet me outside. Pop Pop hobbles to the television and turns it off so he can return to the couch and watch the real show.

"You go on and do that pageant, Nessy."

I can see that it pains Daddy to say these words. I step forward and wrap my arms around him, though he doesn't return my embrace. He stands there, frozen, as though questioning if he's making the right decision. But it's okay. I squeeze hard enough for the both of us.

I look up at his face to meet his eyes. Those earthy, onyx-rich eyes outlined in weary, teary folds of skin. "You don't have to worry, Daddy. I'm doing this for me now. Not for her."

Jell-O Knees and All

The parking lot of King Middle is packed when we pull up. Even though I'm inside Mrs. Walton's car, I can feel people's eyes piercing me. Today's at-home spa session made me forget about yesterday, but now I feel like telling Mrs. Walton to turn the car around and drop me back home.

Police officers surround every corner of the building, and there are even a few cruisers at both entrances to the parking lot. Never in my life have I seen this many cops in my 'hood. Cops usually come around after a crime, but never for anything like a school event.

When we walk inside King Middle, the line for the show is super long. Tanisha and Mrs. Bennet wave at me and throw me a good-luck hand signal. People are pointing and staring and whispering in my direction as Mrs. Walton wraps her arm around my shoulders and pushes me past the crowd.

"Snitch!" a voice whispers from the line.

But when I turn around to see who it is, all I see are crowds of people and cameras flashing and blinding me.

"Are the police here because of me ratting out Junito

yesterday? Oh my God, is Beatriz here? What about the Latin Diablos?" I whisper to Mrs. Walton. A surge of fear weighs down on me. Will they do to me what they did to TJ?

"They're only here for security for the night, Vanessa. This is a high-profile event, you know. The first of its kind for Newark schools. The newspaper is here to cover the pageant too. And don't worry about Beatriz. She's been disqualified from the pageant."

I want to believe Mrs. Walton, but I can feel Beatriz's ghostly presence hovering over me, waiting for me to fail. Those cops are here to make sure that I don't get jumped by the Latin Diablos. Though I'm sure in gang life, that's not how it's done. The Diablos probably get their girls, the Latin Diablas, to beat up on other females. And I'm pretty sure, after last night's incident, that Beatriz is a member. Probably the leader.

Mrs. Walton opens the door of the dressing room, and I can hear the chaos inside. The energy level is on high. All the contestants are talking, doing their hair, and laughing, but as soon as everyone catches sight of me, the room falls uncomfortably silent. Like they all heard what happened and are wondering why I even decided to show up.

Mrs. Ruiz claps her hands twice. "Okay, ladies, listen up. It's time to take a vote." She struts around the room in her white pumps and gives us the ballots to vote for Miss Congeniality.

"Vote for the girl who has been the friendliest throughout

the time we've prepared for this competition," Mrs. Moore announces.

In the far corner of the room, I see Stephanie Bowles looking at the ballot real hard, like she wants to rip it up or something. Truth be told, some of the girls weren't that nice to her. Not even me. The teasing. The accusations. When all along she was just trying to make friends with me, with all the girls. She didn't push me in that pool. I'm certain of it now. A sickly feeling crawls way down to the soles of my feet.

My gaze is magnetic. Stephanie looks up to meet my eyes, but only for a second. She scribbles a name—not mine, I imagine—and hands the ballot back to Mrs. Moore. Just as I prepare myself to go talk to her, the teachers hurry us to change into our opening-number outfit. Each contestant is given a "Miss King Middle School Pageant" T-shirt to wear with our own jeans and sneakers. I throw the shirt on with my Guess jeans that Mrs. Walton got me from Bamberger's.

As I'm looking around the room, I see Mrs. Walton, Mrs. Moore, and Mrs. Ruiz doing everything they can to make all of us feel special for tonight. They're applying lip gloss, fluffing up curls, tying sneaker laces. I even see Principal Carlisle backstage helping out. And for once she ain't lugging her bullhorn around. But I don't see Mrs. Caldwell.

"Mrs. Walton?" I ask. "Where's Mrs. Caldwell?"

Mrs. Walton's putting on one final coat of lip gloss when she says, "We won't be needing her help, or her criticisms, tonight."

Then she winks at me. The twinkle in her eye says it all. Mrs. Caldwell put a little too much effort into trying to shoot me down, when she should've been trying to lift me up. I'm kinda glad her raggedy ole behind ain't here.

Adrenaline hovers like a storm cloud in the dressing room, and I can tell that my heart is not the only one racing. I look around to be sure that Beatriz isn't here, and I see that Maricela and Julicza are. They were there last night too. Egging the whole fight on. I didn't see them touch my dress, but their laughter was enough to make them guilty by association in my book. While they're changing into their outfits, they're staring at me hard and whispering about me in Spanish. But I act like I'm not sweating it. I stare at them right back with my eyes cold and unflinching.

"Focus, Vanessa!" Mrs. Walton snaps me out of my stare.

From the dressing room, we can all hear the doors of the auditorium open. People flood in to take their seats. Our school auditorium is massive, probably able to fit at least six hundred people. Only three of those seats will be filled for me: Pop Pop, Tanisha, and her mom. I guess three is better than none.

The house lights dim low as Mrs. Moore and Mrs. Ruiz tell us to line up backstage. I reach for Stephanie's hand as she heads to her place in line.

"I owe you an apology." I try to grab her other hand, but she places it behind her back like I got a contagious disease.

Stephanie's hand grows clammy as her eyes start to water up. She kind of stands there for a second, shaking her head.

"This whole time, all I wanted was to be cool with you. You were the girl who ripped up the stage during auditions. The girl who fell but got back up again and *still* made the cut. It was like you had this kind of magic. Black-girl magic, and I wanted that. To be like you."

Her words take me by surprise. No one's ever wanted to be like me. Heck, until very recently, I didn't even want to be like me.

"But then you started hanging out with Beatriz, and you changed. I didn't push you into the pool. That was all—"

"I know," I cut her off. "I know now that it was Beatriz. And I'm an idiot for not believing you when you tried to tell me at the restaurant."

The audience begins a chant. "Start the show! Start the show!"

"Let's try this from the beginning," I say. I hold out my hand to shake hers. "I'm Vanessa Martin. Nice to meet you."

Stephanie returns with a firm grip. "Right back at ya."

"Friends?" I say.

"Only if I can sit with you at the eighth-grade table during lunch next week."

"Hold your horses, girl. Baby steps, Stephanie, baby steps."

Then we both bust out laughing.

Our emcee for the night is Takia Johnson, Miss Black New Jersey USA. Even in the dim light, her silver evening gown and large crown sparkle through the darkness. From backstage, the music begins and blasts through the speakers, and the audience creates a rumbling applause.

Mrs. Walton choreographed our opening number to "Dreamgirls," a song from the Broadway show. When she taught it to us, she said we needed to learn other styles of music outside of rap. Most of the girls don't like the opening song, but they force a smile through it for the judges. The trumpets blare, the bright lights flash on, and we make our way onstage single file, like a chorus line. From the stage, I can barely make out anyone in the audience. The lights are blinding, and I can't tell where my people are sitting.

In the middle of our choreography, we split into two groups to make a path for our emcee to walk down and grace the audience with her beauty.

The crowd is going so crazy that I can barely hear her say, "Welcome, ladies and gentlemen, to the inaugural Miss King Middle School pageant! Tonight one deserving young lady will make history by winning the title of Miss King Middle! Let's hear it for the stars of the show—your Miss King Middle pageant contestants!"

One by one, each of us steps to the microphone to state our name, grade, and ambition in life. Stephanie has the largest cheering section. When she says her introduction, it seems like a hundred people stand up and shout her name.

"Next up, help me welcome contestant number eight!"

Oh Lord. That's me. My intestines are all bundled up inside of me, and a slew of thoughts run through my head. My knees feel like they're wobbling. Are they? Can anyone see? Does it matter if I'm wearing jeans? God, I wish I had on a long skirt right now because at least then I'd be able to hide the shakes. My mouth is dry. Did I forget to put Vaseline on my teeth like Mrs. Walton showed me?

"Let's hear it for contestant number eight!" the emcee announces for a second time.

A hush falls over the audience. Jell-O knees and all, I step to the microphone and see the smiling panel of judges beneath me. *Remember your coaching, Vanessa. Channel your inner pageant girl.*

"Good evening, ladies, gentlemen, and distinguished judges. I am an eighth grader on the high honor roll here at King Middle School, with dreams of studying music when I attend college. I will one day grace the Miss America stage. I am fourteen-year-old Vanessa Martin."

There. I said it, with the pause between my age and my name too. And I didn't make one mistake. Thank you, baby Jesus!

The audience cheers, and there are a few people screaming at the top of their lungs, "Go, Vanessa!" It sounds like more people than just Pop Pop, Tanisha, and Mrs. Bennet.

When the introductions are over, the curtains close and the teachers rush us to the dressing room to get changed for the next segment of competition: talent. Mrs. Walton helps me get dressed in my angel costume and has me review my vocal techniques. Spit flies out of my mouth as I do my lip trills, but Mrs. Walton tells me not to worry. The trills will help me relax my mouth for when it's time to sing.

Julicza and Maricela are tucked in the corner, already dressed for talent. Julicza is reciting the Puerto Rican national anthem, "La Borinqueña." Maricela is doing a magic trick. Really? In my book, their talents don't require much practice—or nerves, for that matter. Because if they did, they'd be doing just that—practicing. Instead, they're all up in my business, whispering to each other, looking like they're ready to start something.

From backstage, I hear the emcee call my name. There's no time to focus on them. I've got a song to sing. My feet push me past those haters, toward the microphone, and plant themselves center stage. Mrs. Walton takes her place at the grand piano below and plays a single B flat. She nods my way for me to begin the melody. My mouth opens and begins the song a cappella. No music. Just me and this Mahalia Jackson voice of mine. Midway through the first verse, Mrs. Walton joins in with her thunderous piano playing, and the auditorium is instantly transformed into Cotton Temple.

People are standing up, hands clapping. Someone cries out, "You better *saaaaang*, girl!"

The lyrics of the song couldn't be more true. I was blind for so very long. But now I can see. I can see the real meaning of beauty, and it ain't got nothing to do with having light skin and a little waist. All these years of watching the Miss America pageant, and I ain't never seen a girl who looked like me. And all I ever wanted was to live up to that American definition of beauty. I did everything I could to fit the description: prayed to God to change the color of my skin; used that Sol-Glo, hoping it would make a difference. But I can see now. You can't buy beauty or pray for it to come in the form of what you see on the television screen. Beauty is just something you gotta be.

Every lyric of "Amazing Grace" is consuming me, opening my eyes real wide. I am beautiful. I am free. I am whole. My little cheering section in the back, in the darkest corner of the auditorium, is going nuts. In this moment, this is all I need to make me feel whole again.

After I belt out that final note, I take a bow and walk off-stage—gracefully, of course. The contestants are clapping and congratulating me. Everyone except for Julicza and Maricela.

I don't even stay behind to see how they do for their talent. A poem and a magic trick performed by two hateful groupies just ain't worth my time.

Next up is the onstage interview. Mrs. Walton helps me change into my interview outfit. "Now, Vanessa, don't forget. Speak as though you are reading one of those beautiful books of yours or writing one of your poems that would make Toni Morrison jealous. Be yourself: charming, witty, intelligent," Mrs. Walton reminds me.

"Word, yo!" I respond, and Mrs. Walton slaps me on the shoulder.

I let out a throaty laugh. "I'm kidding, Mrs. Walton. Don't worry. I will be *smoooth*."

A smile dances across Mrs. Walton's face. "Exactly. That's more like it."

For this segment of the competition, the emcee makes the contestants pick a number out of a bowl, and the corresponding judge asks the question.

The emcee announces my name, and I walk out onstage. The audience is sickeningly quiet. Maybe they're feeling the same vomit-inducing nervousness that I feel. This is the one part of the competition that I didn't look forward to, even though I practiced every night with TJ and Pop Pop for months. I slowly pull a card out of the fishbowl. My card is for judge number five. Here goes nothing.

She asks me, "What is the most valuable lesson you've learned from participating in this pageant?"

I pause for a moment, carefully crafting the words in my head. I'd practiced a similar question with Mrs. Walton. *Just speak from the heart.*

"Every year since I was a little girl, I've watched the Miss America pageant with my grandfather. I'm always amazed by the glamour of it all, the gorgeous dresses and the beautiful women giving it all they have on the Miss America stage. Deep down, I've always wanted to grow up and be right up there with them. The problem was no girl on the Miss America stage ever looked like me. Dark skin, coily hair, big boned. Because of that, I never had the confidence to say my dream out loud. That I too want to become Miss America. Even when my teacher and family encouraged me to do this pageant, I was afraid. But here I am. Facing my fears. Breaking stereotypes. In the end, I can say that tonight's results aren't all that important. I've got my real friends and my family here, and that's all I need to make me feel like a winner already."

Yes, I, Vanessa Martin, the student who used to hide in the back of class in order to avoid talking, said all of that! For a moment the audience is quiet, but then they go wild, standing up, screaming. I hear "That's right, girlfriend!" and "Speak the truth, my sista!"

My smile is cheesy, spreading from ear to ear.

After the interviews there's a fifteen-minute intermission. The teachers tell us to put on our gowns because we'll move into the final segment of competition once intermission is over. After Mrs. Walton zips me into my dress, she turns me around and exhales a long breath.

"You look so beautiful."

She stands me in front of the mirror so I can see the final result. Every piece of the puzzle is almost perfect, but something is missing. I reach into my bag and pull out the brooch I auditioned with—Mama's brooch. A symbol of when Mama was whole, complete, and living her dreams. It's my turn now to do the same.

"Will you pin this to my dress?" I ask Mrs. Walton.

Her eyes light up at how pretty the star pin is. "You should wear this pin close to your heart. Because more than anyone here, you are destined to be a star. I have no doubt that you'll be on that Miss America stage one day."

Mrs. Walton throws me a wink and walks away to take her place in the front row of the audience because, according to her, she wants to be front and center to watch me win my award.

It's five minutes before show time. Where is Pop Pop? We need to go over the evening-wear walk. I can't have him messing this up with his wobbly leg. Backstage, I pace back and forth, waiting for him to come and meet me. The first two segments of competition weren't that bad, but I don't know how this one's gonna turn out. I didn't even get a chance to practice walking with Pop Pop. Did he bring his cane? Or will he try to walk without it? What side should he hold it on so he doesn't trip me in my gown? And what is he wearing? Oh Lord! He better not be wearing that 1972 played-out suit. He was joking, right? I should've checked his outfit before I left the house.

The door to the dressing room cracks open a little. Mrs. Moore sticks her head in and says, "Vanessa, your escort is here."

Finally. I have all of three minutes to show Pop Pop what to do. I step outside into the hallway. My grandfather isn't standing there, though. It's Daddy. Tall, blue-black dark, and dressed in cargo pants, paint-stained boots, and a tattered brown sweater. All of the other dads and escorts are dressed in dark suits and tuxedos, but my father is the most handsome of them all.

This Stranger Named Daddy

"Wait, what are you doing here, Daddy?"

I want to hug him, hold him tight, and feel the sky fill up with a million stars. But I'm also still mad. I want to feel all the good memories rush back. The pleasant days when he was happy and Mama was around. When he took me to the park and rode his bike alongside mine. I remember the not-so-good times too. But he used to feel and smell like everything that is right in this world. Daddy used to feel like . . . love. Will we ever return to that place again?

Daddy showed up. He came to see me. But he just stands there, motionless, like sealed concrete.

"Nessy, we got a lot to talk about. And now's not really the time. I just wanted to show up for a quick second and wish you good luck."

Pieces of my heart spill out of every part of my body and land straight on the floor. "That's it? Just good luck?"

Daddy starts to walk away. I lunge forward, yank his hand into mine, and force him to look at me. We stand face to face. His six-foot-five frame towering over my five-foot-nine one.

"All these years have gone by, and we don't even know each

other. You could have shown me a little bit of love, made me feel like I wasn't invisible. Like I mattered to you. But most of all, you should've trusted me enough to tell me, Daddy. I'm not a little girl anymore." I say it all in a long-winded breath. Tears will destroy every layer of makeup I have on, but I don't care.

He nods his head slowly, as though he's digested every word.

Pain and truth hover over us. Each moment of deafening silence speaks louder than words could. I was never destined to turn out the way Mama did. As drunk as Pop Pop is during the week, he gets me to church every weekend and makes sure I study hard to make straight As. There's just no other choice. I'm constantly reminded of the meaning of hard work. Drugs were never in my future, even if I had a mother who shot up that poison like her life depended on it.

"Thirty seconds to show time!" Mrs. Ruiz calls out to the contestants, who are now lining up with their escorts. "This is it, ladies! It's the final segment of competition. Good luck!"

Mrs. Walton rushes toward us with tissues and touch-up makeup in her hands.

"Jeez, Vanessa, what did you do?" she says as she starts reapplying my makeup.

"Mr. Martin, glad you made it. You make a perfect escort," Mrs. Walton says, not even noticing what Daddy's wearing.

"Wait, I was just about to—"

Leave. He doesn't need to say the final word. It's the one I know all too well.

Next thing I know, Mrs. Walton's pushing the two of us backstage, and there ain't no turning back now.

The Best Prize of the Night

I've often heard that when people die, their body draws closer and closer to a white light. Heaven's gates open, and you are finally set free. Free from the hurt. Free from the pain. God takes you as you are: black, white, tall, short, skinny, or fat. In his eyes you are perfection. Well, that's exactly how it feels when the emcee announces my name for evening wear, and Daddy and I walk on that stage as though we're gliding on clouds. We didn't even practice together. It's like we are both living in the moment, already knowing what to do.

Daddy is shaking as he walks me to the center spotlight. Then he releases my hand for me to model my belle-of-the-ball gown. I don't even care about what Daddy's wearing anymore. Effortlessly, I hit every mark onstage. TJ's voice floods inside my head as I'm doing the pivot turn: *Right foot step, left foot step, turn, bring it back into the model's T.* The nerves have disappeared, my Jell-O knees are gone, and there I stand, strong and poised.

I'm on that stage soaking up my every moment. And though I can't see Daddy's face behind my back, I sing a prayer on the inside that for once there's a twinkle in his eyes too. That for once I am the star in his universe, even if for only this moment.

The stage lights flicker colors of red, blue, and yellow, and my rhinestones shine from wall to wall. The judges are smiling back at me. And as soon as I begin to exit the stage, I see them scribbling away on their score sheets.

When we're backstage again, he releases my grip on his elbow. Only two words exit his mouth. "Good job."

It's the best I could hope for between us, among the tension and the secrets that we've drowned in for all these years.

Daddy starts to walk away with the other escorts, who will return to their seats in the audience. I can't help but wonder if he will stay. Or will he do what he does best? Leave.

The emcee calls all the contestants back onstage, where she announces: "Our prize package for the overall winner of the Miss King Middle School pageant is quite extensive. She will win a two-hundred-fifty-dollar cash award sponsored by the Newark Municipal Council, an all-expenses-paid trip to the Miss New Jersey pageant in Cherry Hill, a one-hundred-dollar gift certificate to Brick City Books, a chance to audition for a four-year scholarship to attend the Crest Lake Academy of the Arts, and of course, the Miss King Middle crown, banner, rose bouquet, and trophy."

As the emcee is saying all this, we contestants are wide-eyed and mouthing, "Oh my God!" to each other. We weren't told that there'd be such a long list of prizes. I thought every contestant would get a little trophy, and the winner would get a crown and the money. But a trip to Cherry Hill? My family hasn't been on a trip in, well—never, really. The farthest we go as a family is taking the car service to church. And a scholarship to attend Crest Lake? That's an all-girls boarding school way upstate. The guidance department always has their flyers posted, but I ain't never heard of anyone actually going there for high school. Somewhere out there, there's a world to see outside of Grafton Hill—a place with meadows filled with real sunflowers. I never knew until this very moment that I want this title more than anything. It's not Miss America, but like Mrs. Walton said, it sure is a good place to start.

"We begin with the academic-achievement award winner. She will receive a fifty-dollar gift card to Brick City Books and a custom bronze plaque sponsored by Royal Crown Trophies. And the winner is . . ."

The drumbeat blares. "Vanessa Martin!"

The audience claps, but not loud enough to cover up my grandfather hollering, "That's right, girl! You make them straight As, Nessy!" Followed by a husky-toned, "Good job, Vanessa!" That's Daddy. He's here. He stayed. My cheeks blush pink as I step forward to receive my award.

"The next award goes to the most popular girl in the Miss King Middle pageant. The Miss Congeniality winner was selected by our pageant contestants."

I know I'm not winning this one. In fact, if Beatriz hadn't been so busy being hateful and getting disqualified from the pageant, she probably would have won that award hands down.

"The winner is Stephanie Bowles!"

Stephanie steps forward, cheesin' in her lilac dress covered in pearls and soft ruffles. When Stephanie receives her award and joins us back in the contestant line, she hugs each and every one of us. I'm glad that I voted for Stephanie. She deserves it more than any other girl in the pageant.

The next award is for talent. "And the winner is . . . Vanessa Martin."

Needles of excitement prick up and down my skin. Once again, my little cheering squad darts up out of their seats, screaming at the top of their lungs.

Three awards down, but there're more still up for grabs. My name's been called twice already. I'm not sure if I can be so lucky to be called again.

"And the next award is our evening-wear winner. She will receive a trophy courtesy of Royal Crown Trophies and a fifty-dollar cash award sponsored by the Newark Municipal Council. And the winner is . . . Stephanie Bowles!"

By this point I'm thinking that Stephanie might win the pageant. Maybe I'll be first runner-up. Coming in second isn't so bad for a first-time pageant girl, I guess. I could always come back next year and try again. Wait, I won't be here next year. This is my last year in middle school. Will they have anything like this in high school? And even if they do, I'm not sure if I can go through all this again.

"The next award is given to the highest score in the onstage-interview competition. And surprisingly, we have a tie! The winners will each receive a fifty-dollar cash award sponsored by Bamberger's."

I suck in a long breath and prepare to hear the names of the winners. Interviewing was never my strong suit.

"And the winners are Lanetta Gainer and Vanessa Martin!"

My eyes widen, and the next thing I know, Lanetta is grabbing my hand and yanking me with her to center stage.

There's a smell on that stage, thick and reeking of tension something awful. Julicza and Maricela are cutting their eyes at me real hard as I take my place back in the lineup. I wasn't the girl who was supposed to win awards. I wasn't the pretty, popular girl here at King Middle, and the fact that I'm being recognized is eating away at their flesh.

"Ladies and gentlemen, now the moment you've all been waiting for. May I have the final decision from the judges?"

I look down at the bodice of my dress, and I see my heart thumping out of my chest. All the practices, all the drama—was it worth it? Could I be the girl who could take it all? I look at the judges for a sign. Any sign. Tell me that I still stand a chance. But they're not even looking at me. Instead it seems like they are staring at everyone else but me. Maybe they allowed me to win a few awards so when the final results are announced, my feelings won't be hurt. I guess I shouldn't feel so bad. At least I won a few awards. I could still give the money I won to Daddy to help with the rent.

The drumbeats roll in with each announcement of the runners-up.

"The fourth runner-up is Kayla Knight!"

"Your third runner-up is Brianna Banks!"

"The second runner-up is Lanetta Gainer!"

By this point I'm accepting the fact that maybe I lost the pageant. When this is all over, I'm going to run off this stage and straight into the arms of Pop Pop and Daddy. For me, the fact that they're both here is all the winning I need. But part of me wants to run straight through the stage door and home to bury myself in my room. Mrs. Walton says that part of being in a pageant is being a good sport and congratulating the girls who did make it to the top five even though you worked as hard as they did. Right about now my emotions are like a big pan of scrambled eggs. Exhaustion takes over, and my knees soften. I could fall over any second.

"The first runner-up is Stephanie Bowles!"

Stephanie jumps up and down and claps her hands like she just won the lottery. Shouldn't she be upset? She was the front-runner. But before stepping forward to receive her award, Stephanie hugs me and whispers in my ear, "I think you did it, Vanessa. That crown is yours!"

"But what about . . ." I respond. My jaws sink low to my shoulders.

"Don't worry about me. I can compete again next year. You got this, girlfriend!"

Then she smiles at me, braces shining like the moon. Like she really means what she said. I look down the line at the rest of the girls. They are all dressed to the nines. And even though I've changed a bit, they're all prettier, better dressed, and more girly than I could ever be. With Maricela and Julicza still standing, I can't help but wonder if one of them will be called as the winner.

The drums are screaming now. My arms break out in a million goose bumps. My hands get all clammy. And honestly, at this point I don't even think I can hold my bladder anymore. To settle my nerves, I close my eyes and transport myself to a place where anxiety doesn't exist. Church. The organ is playing, and sunlight is pouring in through the stained-glass windows. And suddenly it doesn't matter if I've won or lost. I've already gotten the best prize of the night.

June 20, 1984

It's Okay

It's okay to be me.
It's okay if you're gay.
It's okay to be free.
It's okay if you walk away.
It's okay to be dark.
It's okay to be light.
It's okay to have heart.
It's okay to make it right.
It's okay to be poor.
It's okay to make do.
It's okay to want more.
It's okay to be YOU . . .

Dear Darlene,

I get it now.

—Nessy

The Stuff Dreams Are Made Of

Once upon a time, there was a little girl who had big dreams. She dreamed of becoming Miss America. She dreamed that her mama would come home. She dreamed that her daddy would find his way back to happy and that she'd be the one to help him get there. She dreamed that her grandfather would quit drinking. That her cousin would be able to live his life freely, with people no longer judging him for who he chooses to love but instead appreciating him for who he is on the inside. And for this little girl, some of those dreams did indeed come true.

Time waits for no one. Six months have passed. Beethoven's "Für Elise" is blasting through my headphones as I'm putting on my cap and gown for today's graduation ceremony. The melody is sweet and thunderous and intoxicating all at once. I'm getting used to this classical stuff. Mrs. Walton got me a bunch of different classical, Broadway, and jazz music tapes. She says that I will study all types of music and art when I go to Crest Lake this September. Yes, that Crest Lake. The number-one boarding school for girls in upstate New York.

The school with a selection committee who dropped their jaws when I auditioned with Puccini's "Vissi d'arte" last Saturday. *We certainly didn't expect that, Ms. Martin . . . in Italian, no less.* The school that's granting me a four-year scholarship. A school where in a sea of faces, I'm sure mine will be the only dark one.

When I think back to the night of the pageant, it seems like it was a lifetime ago. The memories are blurry yet blissful. I don't even remember the emcee announcing my name. I'm pretty sure I was suffocating by that point.

"And the winner of the first-ever Miss King Middle pageant is . . . *Vanessa Martin!*"

Stevie Wonder's "Isn't She Lovely" blasted through the speakers. I remember that. At first I was unable to move. Then my knees dropped to the floor. I lifted my head to the sky and mouthed, "Thank you, Jesus!" And everyone was clapping. The audience, the judges, Daddy, Pop Pop, and Mrs. Walton too. Next thing I knew, the contestants rushed up to me, giving me one big group hug and saying congratulations. Well, all the girls except Maricela and Julicza.

I stood up and stepped forward to accept my award. The emcee draped me in the Miss King Middle banner. The crown was almost an exact replica of the Miss America one, with its four points dripping with sparkly rhinestones. She put the trophy in front of me. And lastly she placed the bouquet of flowers in my arms.

"Take your walk," the emcee whispered in my ear.

After all these years of watching Miss America, I should

have known what to do, but I was so excited, my mind drew a blank. All pageant queens have to take their first walk and wave to the audience. Me. A pageant queen. Like Vanessa Williams and each Miss America I see crowned year after year on television.

After I took my walk, the house lights came up. As soon as they did, I saw Daddy, Tanisha, and her mom rushing to the foot of the stage, with Pop Pop wobbling behind them.

The tears flowed because this was the way I had always imagined it.

Mrs. Walton came up to me on the stage and squeezed me tight. "I have someone who's been dying to meet you and get your autograph."

A little girl came running up to me, screaming, "Look, Mommy, it's Miss America! Will you sign my autograph book?"

Mrs. Walton's daughter, Sasha, handed me her empty pink-and-purple book. I was the very first person to sign it. I scooped the little beauty up in my arms and held her tight. She called me Miss America. She thought I was famous! Not quite, little princess, but I sure was on my way.

That night was perfection, seeing my pageant dreams and my family come together like that. And ever since then, I've still been living a dream. My happily-ever-after. Well, almost. Daddy's now the manager at his job. All those long days and nights of working finally paid off. He saved enough money to buy a car—a 1976 Monte Carlo. Daddy drives us to church every Sunday now. We still can't get him to stay for service, but we ain't lost hope yet. He talks to me more these days.

And not only one-word responses. I can happily report that he's up to at least five words per sentence. Hey, it's a start.

Pop Pop is still the same. Cracking jokes, drinking Monday to Friday, though a little less now, and walking the poison out to make it in time to worship the good Lord on Sunday.

Things are a little better between Tanisha and me, though I know it'll never be the same. We each had our moment where we put another friend first, and at times it's still a stain that's hard to get rid of. Pop Pop calls it growing pains. Says that time and miles of distance will be the true test of our friendship. If it's meant to be, we'll find our way back to normal.

TJ left Grafton for San Francisco as soon as he was discharged from the hospital. His caged bird was set free—free to live in a place where loving "differently" is the norm, unshielded and unwavering. I never cried so hard in my life as the day TJ left. But I knew it was for the best. No longer did he have to wear a mask to cover the shame, to cover the truth that on the inside he was crumbling, weakened by his secrets.

And though I miss my cousin, I'm happy that he can live his life unchained.

As for me, my own caged bird is soon to be released. That moment will begin when I walk across that stage today, diploma in hand, ready to start my new life at Crest Lake surrounded by meadows of sunflowers and rhythms of peace. At the same time, a part of me is scared of the new road that lies ahead. Will I fit in? Will I make friends? Will there ever be another Mrs. Walton?

266

There's a loud knock at my bedroom door.

"Nessy, we gotta go now. You're going to be late."

That's Daddy. He's gonna be there for my big day. And all is right in the world.

Half Full, Half Empty

The auditorium is packed for today's graduation. From wall to wall, there are balloons and decorations everywhere.

As the students line up in alphabetical order, I turn and see Beatriz take her place two people behind me. Spirit gone. Quiet. Withdrawn. Not the Beatriz I've known all these years. Things haven't gone so well for her or her family since the night of the fight. A few months ago, Junito was killed in a drive-by shooting. A piece of Beatriz died the same day that bullet took Junito's life. A piece of Mrs. Mendez died too. I see it every time I walk past the bodega and see her sitting on the stoop. Mrs. Mendez ain't got no soul now, probably ain't got one tear left to spare. I used to think that karma would taste sweet, but the bitterness it leaves on the inside ain't sweet at all.

The graduation march begins, and cameras are flashing, blinding me to the point where I almost miss Mama sitting in the last row. The line is moving so fast, I only see her for a split second. It's the old Mama I remember from my good dreams. The one with the buttery voice, the one with sparkling eyes, the one who used to love me. Not the shell of a mother I remember from my night terrors or from my prison visit.

When I turn around to look again, she's not there. It was just a silly figment of my imagination. The memory of her ghost haunts me, makes me realize that the pain, the longing, the wanting, never goes away.

As the class valedictorian, I have special front-row seats for my family. Four tickets, to be exact. That fourth ticket could've been for Mama. She got out of prison a few weeks ago. She hasn't called. Hasn't written. Hasn't even tried to check on me, but I'll be just fine. My mood changes when I see Pop Pop, Daddy, and Mrs. Walton sitting front and center, smiling from ear to ear. I got all the family I need right here in this auditorium.

In a lot of ways, graduation is like a pageant. There's music, bright lights, people cheering, and awards. Tanisha cleans house in the visual-arts and athletic awards. Every time she comes off that stage, she throws me a smile and a high five. I love that girl. But I can't help worrying about what will happen to our friendship when I leave Newark. While I'm off to boarding school, Tanisha's headed to Saint Anthony's to play basketball. Her and Amaryllis Rodriguez. In the end Tanisha got her scholarship, her way out. And I guess I did too. Will things be awkward when I come home for holidays? In her heart, does she truly forgive me for choosing Beatriz's sham of a friendship over her?

When the principal, Mrs. Carlisle, announces it's time for me to give my valedictorian speech, the pageant nerves return.

You'd think I'd be used to being put on display by now, but my stomach still backflips every time I hear my name called to step up to a microphone.

For weeks I thought about what I'd say. What message did I have to give? Just like in the days of my pageant training, Mrs. Walton always reminds me to speak from my heart. Don't be afraid to tell my own truth and talk about the journey that led me to where I am right now.

I clear my throat before the words come out. The stares coming from the audience pierce right through me, but the one I can't deny is Mama. Her ghost is back, eyes glued on me, holding on to my every word.

"I spent my entire life feeling like I lived in a jungle. I wanted to be anywhere but here. So I escaped through the words of Maya Angelou and Toni Morrison and Richard Wright, hoping to feel something greater than what I had in this place called home.

"But when I researched the word *jungle*, a whole new world opened up for me. In the jungle, there is life. There is beauty. There is abundance. There is family. There is love. As we each move on to the next stop in our individual journeys, we should never forget where we came from. Because no matter how perfect things seem on the other side, there is no place like home. As I move on to a high school that seems stars and galaxies away from here, I will miss the rhythms of our neighborhood, the laughter that fills homeroom every morning, the people who work so hard to make sure we are the very best versions of ourselves. I encourage the graduating class to move forward in their journey throughout high school and even college . . ."

I direct my eyes straight at Beatriz and then at Tanisha.

". . . and forgive those who may have done you wrong, and find a way to forgive yourself for friendships you may have broken along the way. But most of all, never forget the times and memories made here at King Middle."

For a moment there is silence, and as I look into the audience, I see teary eyes and hear noses sniffling. Even Curtis is sitting there boohooing like a dang fool! And then one by one, the entire eighth grade is standing up, clapping and hugging each other. Next thing I know, the whole audience is on their feet.

I stand there taking it all in, shoulders growing ten feet tall. Thinking about everything that happened to me this year. The memories, sweet and sour. The growth. The loss. The journey back to happy. Everything I've ever wanted is right in front of me, right now. The men in my life, my best friend, and my favorite teacher. I look toward the back of the audience, and the ghost of Mama is nowhere to be seen. I'm not sure how much longer I can hold on to her memory. Still, I can't help but wonder if somewhere out there she's wanting what I want, feeling what I feel. Half full or half empty?

August 31, 1984

The Beginning of the Beginning

The close of summer brings forth autumn winds,
sweeping away memories of long-ago sins,
of gray ghosts crawling the deepest parts of me,
of shields blinding my ability to see.
Of sad hellos, even sadder good-byes,
of half truths told in the belly of lies.
Pouring in oceans of light, promises of forever,
love, beauty, family, together.

Dear Darlene,

My beaten, tattered Darlene. What a beautiful image of my
unraveling! A year in my life that I won't soon forget. A year full of
mistakes, but we all make them, right? Mama, Daddy, Pop Pop, TJ,
Tanisha, me . . . and even Vanessa Williams, it turns out. One thing I
know for sure, mistakes will never, ever be the definition of who we
truly are.

—Nessy

I Remember

At the front door of our apartment, my suitcases are ready. I take a look at my nearly empty bedroom and breathe in the memories that I made here. My bare walls were once covered with Miss America posters from floor to ceiling. Mrs. Walton got me new ones to replace the ones I threw away. Those are now packed so I can display them in my dorm room at Crest Lake.

So many memories were made in this room. I remember my makeover with Mrs. Walton like it was yesterday. The day where I came to accept my natural beauty. I never did get that perm in my hair, and I don't think I ever will. I remember the many nights of being lulled to sleep by the hypnotizing rhythms of hip-hop and salsa hovering over Grafton Hill. I remember dreaming of Mama, of days of songs and long embraces and love. But I have that now. Finally found it on the inside.

Daddy cracks my bedroom door open. "Everyone's in the car, Nessy. Crest Lake is waiting."

"You're right, Daddy. On my way."

I step out of my room, out the front door, down the eight

flights of steps. Outside, the sun hangs low in the horizon, refusing to give way to the entrance of the moon coming from a world away.

Daddy places my suitcases in the trunk while Pop Pop, Tanisha, and I wait in the car.

"You think you gonna miss this raggedy ole place?" Pop Pop asks.

Tanisha locks her fingers in mine, and I feel the warmth of ten thousand suns.

"I miss it already."

Daddy revs up the engine of the Monte Carlo and speeds off, past Grafton, past the alleys, past the thumping, pumping neighborhood beats, past the memories caramel-sweet and lemon-lime bitter, and off toward my new journey of fear and hope and possibilities. Will the sun shine in this new place that waits for me? Maybe, but never like it does here on the edge of my town, among the concrete and the sunflowers of the place I will forever call home.

The History Behind Vanessa Williams's Miss America Win

Today, many people would call Vanessa Williams an icon, but her path to stardom wasn't easy. In 1983 she made history by becoming the first black woman to win the title of Miss America. In today's multicultural society, this may not seem out of the norm. But back then it was a *big* deal.

The Miss America pageant has been around since 1921. Some of the pageant's earliest rules stipulated that women of color weren't allowed to enter the contest. Many believed that this was because women of color were not seen as beautiful. In fact, the earliest Miss America shows cast African Americans as slaves in some dance productions.

So when Vanessa Williams was announced as the winner, many people, especially people of color, rejoiced. Finally Americans would bear witness to the notion that ideal beauty is not only white. It is black and brown and every beautiful shade in between.

The job of Miss America was (and still is) about more than swimsuits and lipstick. Vanessa Williams would get to travel more than twenty thousand miles a month to do volunteer work and act as an ambassador for charitable causes.

In the beginning she received tons of fan mail congratulating her on her historic win. But her reign soon turned into a time of terror when she began to get mail with messages such as:

You're black scum!
You're dead!
You're a liar—you're not really black!
You'll never be our Miss America!

This is only a small sample of the hate mail and death threats she received.

The FBI became involved. Armed guards held watch outside her hotel room. Sharpshooters hid atop roofs when she visited towns where the Ku Klux Klan was still very much active. All these actions were put into place to protect her.

This is the America that existed not too long ago. And in many ways, this is the America that still exists today.

But then on July 23, 1984, Vanessa Williams made a speech that would serve as a historic footnote for the rest of her life. In that speech, she relinquished her Miss America title.

Here's why: A year prior to winning Miss America, Vanessa Williams had worked for a photographer as a receptionist and makeup artist. As described in her biography, *You Have No Idea*, in the summer of 1982 Vanessa Williams was nineteen years old and in college. Though Ms. Williams earned partial college scholarships and her parents covered tuition, she still wanted to work to earn her own money. Her parents instilled a work ethic in her at an early age. So, Ms. Williams scoured the PennySaver Classifieds and came across an ad entitled, "Models Wanted." The job sounded easy enough, and it was better than spending the summer flipping burgers. Little did she know, though, that this job would turn into the biggest scam of her life.

Her new boss, a photographer, asked Ms. Williams to pose nude for professional photos. He promised it would be very "artsy." The photos would mainly show silhouettes and not clear nudity, he said. She would be unidentifiable and the photos would never leave his studio. By this point, Vanessa had met his wife and children. He was a respectful boss who always paid her on time. They were friends. She trusted him.

After Vanessa Williams gained national fame, the photographer sold the photos to a magazine without her consent. Perhaps he wanted money, or maybe he wanted fame, too—we can't know for sure. But word got around to the Miss America board of directors, and Vanessa Williams was forced to resign. Just like that. No one offered to fight on her behalf, even though she'd faced racism and bullying as Miss America. Even though she'd technically done nothing wrong. But some people felt as though she wasn't a good role model as Miss America because these photos existed.

In the midst of scandal, in the midst of hate, bullying, and death threats, she chose to rise. Her spirit and faith were unshakeable. Never once did she give up on pursuing her dream of becoming an entertainer. She went on to sell millions of albums, star in movies and on television, develop a fashion line, write a book, and reclaim the pride that her fans had in her all along.

Thirty-two years after resigning, Vanessa Williams was invited back to the Miss America stage in 2015, where she finally received a public apology on the pageant's behalf. They had decided that what she'd done and how they'd punished her didn't match up.

As you read *Like Vanessa*, I hope you remember this: In life, everyone experiences setbacks, but those moments don't have to create the path for how your life will turn out. Like Vanessa in the story, and the real Vanessa Williams, you can emerge wiser and stronger. Life is an arrow. Sometimes you get pulled back only to be launched into something beautiful.

How I'm Like Vanessa

Watching the Miss America pageant was a tradition in my family. As a little girl, I dreamed of seeing myself on that stage. For me, the dream was possible because of Vanessa Williams.

Beginning in 1921, with a revival in 1933, Miss America crowned the "ideal" all-American beauty each year. None of the winners ever looked like me. That all changed in 1983. Vanessa Williams made history by becoming the first African American woman to win the title and the fame, travel, and college scholarships that went with it. Because of Vanessa, girls like me had a chance.

I started competing in pageants at the age of thirteen. Pageants opened many doors for me and taught me lifelong skills that I am thankful for today. Above all, pageants were my pathway to a college education. Because of my academic record, community service, and pageant history, I earned a full scholarship to the College of Saint Elizabeth. And while I never made it to the Miss America stage, I won three preliminary titles for Miss New Jersey America. More important, I gained a sisterhood of women who are still my close friends today.

Many of the characters in *Like Vanessa* were inspired by people in my life who helped me achieve my pageant dreams. My own "Pop Pop," may he rest in peace, was a gentle soul who planted the seed early on that I could achieve anything I'd dreamed of. TJ is based on George Diaz and Fidel Garcia, my local Miss America directors, who were dedicated to my Miss America journey and who always made sure I had the best competition wardrobe. Mrs. Walton is based on two people: Janet Gregg, an African American woman who ran the Lucky Kids USA Scholarship pageant, and Kimberly Renee, an Italian American woman who directed the Miss New Jersey American Teen pageant. Janet was my very first Miss America coach. She taught me opera and took me on a trip to Atlantic City to see the Miss America pageant live. I will never forget her kindness and unwavering faith in me. Kimberly saw something in me that at times I didn't see in myself. Unlike Vanessa Martin in the book, I had what many would call a "white picket fence" upbringing. With two loving and supportive parents, I had all the resources I needed to succeed in pageantry. Kimberly Renee knew that, but she wanted to be a part of my journey, standing right next to my parents, beaming with pride. Kimberly helped me prepare for Miss America by opening her home to me and hiring professional coaches to work with me on talent and interviewing skills. In the novel, I blended personality traits of both Janet and Kimberly to create Mrs. Walton. The only difference is that I chose to make Mrs. Walton Portuguese American in order to best reflect the culture represented in the Ironbound neighborhood of Newark.

I was born in and went to school in Newark, although I'm a little younger than Vanessa Martin. Almost all of the references to music, books, products, television shows, and other cultural references in this story are historically true for 1983—I remember them well from childhood. (I called Grafton, or Grafton Ave., Grafton Hill because the hill felt big to me then.) There's one notable exception: the Edna Mahan Correctional Facility for Women was called the Clinton Correctional Facility until 1987. I took the liberty of time traveling just a little bit with this fact for the sake of my plot.

When I penned the final lines of *Like Vanessa*, a surge of questions flooded through me.

I wondered if Vanessa Williams knew the impact she had on many young girls' lives. Did she know there was a young girl from Newark watching her win? And that her historic moment would help set my life's path? Did Vanessa know that despite her struggles, she has remained a beacon of hope for many girls like me? And that, like wings, hope takes flight, even in the darkest of skies? *Like Vanessa* was born with these questions in mind.

In the years that have passed since Vanessa Williams's crowning, much has changed. Several women of color have gone on to win the Miss America title. Nine as of 2016, in fact. Our country elected its first African American president. That only took 220 years. But at the same time, a lot hasn't changed. Race, beauty, and representation are issues that impact many people every day. As you read this book, I hope you see yourself in it, no matter your background. Let your inner Vanessa shine through. Deep down, I hope you understand that you are beautiful and powerful and significant, even on days when it doesn't seem like it. Seek to carve your own path like Vanessa Williams did so many years ago.

Because Vanessa Williams did, we all can.

And the Crown Goes To . . .

Many people played a role in helping me take this project from concept to bookshelf.

I thank God for his many blessings. Thank you to my parents, Jennifer and Robert Peters, and my brother, Tony. Thank you for your love, your daily inspiration, and for always offering to watch Sebas so I have time to write.

Nasser Charles, my husband and best friend. The minute I understood the meaning of love, I began my search for you. I was unaware that this was not my path to seek, for it was HE who knew all along that we were meant to be.

Christopher Sebastian Charles, you bring me joy and

laughter, and I am honored to be your mommy. I love you more than Daddy, but don't tell him. (He won't survive.)

My loving extended family, the Peters, Carlisle, and Velazquez families; and to my in-laws, the Charles, Dumont, Dorleans, Marcel, and Tucker families: *Mwen renmen nou ak tout ke'm. Los quiero mucho.*

My supportive community of readers and writers, many of whom read *Like Vanessa* at various stages and provided tough-as-nails feedback: Deborah Amadei, Katie Bartlett, Sasha Baynes, Sherry Berrett, Kelly Calabrese, Gwen Charles, Candice Davenport, Christine Duval, Vivian Fransen, Joan Heleine, Stephanie Jones, Beatriz Velazquez, Pat Weissner, Susan Willett, and Lynda Wronski.

SCBWI, Westfield Children's Critique Group, and Women Who Write for providing the resources I needed to jumpstart my writing career.

Mary Kole for your editorial guidance in the early stages of agent submissions.

Lara Perkins, my amazing, thoughtful, and supportive agent, for seeing the light in Vanessa and pulling out the best in me. I'm still wondering when you'll figure out that I have no clue what I'm doing. In the meantime I'll keep enjoying this crazy ride.

My editor, Karen Boss, for saying "Yes!" I didn't think anyone could believe in Vanessa as much as Lara and I did, but then we found you. A down-to-earth, thought-provoking advocate who inspired me to reach deeper than I ever knew possible. Let's make some more books together.

Vanessa Brantley-Newton for the inspiring and gorgeous cover. You are a beacon of light!

Janet Gregg, Kimberly Renee, George Diaz, Fidel Garcia, Chris Wilshire, Michelle Anderson, and Sue Dougherty. Your lessons extended way beyond the pageant stage.

Luisa Da Silva for never complaining when I sought advice about all things Ironbound/Portuguese. *Obrigado por tudo!*

My incredible teachers at University High School: Marie Gironda, Darnell Davis, Quetzy Rivera, and Juanda Boxley. You lit a fire in me that still burns today.

Brian Edwards, my personal wish granter. Vanessa L. Williams, my forever "Miss America." It's been an honor to pay tribute to you.

Lastly I thank *you* for reading this book. You could have picked up any book from the shelf, but you chose this one. And for that I am forever grateful.

Turn the page
for a sneak peek at
Tami Charles's next book.

"Redemption is a heartbeat away."
-GUADALUPE GARCIA MCCALL, AUTHOR OF THE PURA BELPRE AWARD-WINNER UNDER THE MESQUITE

BECOMING BEATRIZ

TAMI CHARLES

READ ON FOR
EXCERPT FROM

BECOMING
BEATRIZ

COMPANION TITLE TO
LIKE VANESSA

ON SALE SEPTEMBER 17, 2019

FiRST TO DaNCE

BY THE TiME THE BUS pulls up and stops around the block from the Newark Community School of the Arts, I'm already more than a half hour late.

The music hits me before I even get to the door. I feel it vibrating against the sidewalk. For a moment I hesitate and ask myself what the hell I'm doing here.

Through the glass windows, I see Nasser standing among the rows and rows of dancers, dressed in the type of clothes that make him look like he's serious about his art. White tank top showing off muscles I didn't know he had. Black dance pants, loose where they should be and tight where it matters most. And here I am in my baggy sweatshirt, stirrup pants, and red Reeboks. My hair is at least five inches too long, begging to be cut, combed, relaxed—something.

In the corner, a drummer beats his drum. In the center of the floor, a dance teacher twirls like there's no tomorrow. Even the tips of her fingers have perfect rhythm. She's short like me, but you wouldn't know it from the way she's moving, like her legs can touch the sky if she tried.

I can't go in there. What was I thinking? Just as I get ready to turn and head straight back to the bus stop, Nasser catches sight of me standing outside the glass door. He runs outside.

"Glad you made it. I was starting to think you weren't coming. You're gonna love it. Señorita Amaro is amazing!" He's got starlight gleaming in his eyes.

I chew on my bottom lip and try to come up with my best excuse. *I'm not prepared. I'll look wack like that. Everybody else clearly knows what they're doing.*

"Look, I can't stay. I got a lot going on back home. I just came to tell you that."

Nasser doesn't care. He just grabs me by the wrist and pulls me inside.

The teacher sees me and cuts off the music. "Why, hello there . . . you're late."

Rows and rows of dancers dart their eyes at me, hawking me up and down, probably wondering why I even bothered to come, since class is basically over. No worries, 'cause I'm thinking the same thing.

"On your feet! Miguelito, from the top!" Señorita Amaro screams.

The drummer attacks the drum like a fire is burning inside of him.

"Try and keep up." She cuts her eyes at me and yells, "A five, six, seven, eight!"

The class begins the routine. Yeah, the one I would have learned had I showed up on time. They're kicking and jumping and spinning and soaring through the roof. And there I am, mimicking every other move, wishing I could spin the earth backward. They go left, I go right; they go up, I go down. The awkwardness of how rusty I am hangs in the space between me and Señorita Amaro, and all the while I catch her looking at me—too much.

She throws her hand in the air, a signal to cut the music. "Good work today, everyone. Same time next week! Class is dismissed."

And just like that my whole world crashes. The room empties out, and I'm ready to follow right behind everyone as they exit. But Nasser won't hear of it. He makes me stand right alongside him.

He waits for the teacher to come over. "This is the girl I was telling you about, Señorita Amaro."

I stand there, begging my body not to burst out into a cold sweat.

"Nasser tells me you dance. That it's in your blood—in your name, even," she says.

"I used to dance. . . . I took classes for a while at Maria Priadka's. . . . And my mom taught me the dances of Puerto Rico. Almost competed in a pageant once. . . . but it didn't work out."

Every word is dressed in fear. I want to escape. I want to stay. I want to run. I want to feel that music again and get it right this time.

"Well, that's too bad. I think the pageant world could use some spicing up with a good dancer. So you like competitions, huh?" She takes a sip from her bottle of water.

"I haven't danced in a long time."

"What happened?"

I hesitate before speaking. "One day I just lost the music is all."

"Well, we just have to help you find it again. Miguelito!"

Señorita Amaro sticks her thumb and index finger in her mouth and whistles loudly. "Música, por favor!"

Next thing I know, the drummer starts to play a beat, a different one this time. Slow at first, then climbing and climbing to a pace that my heart can barely keep up with.

"You feel that? That's the rhythm of Africa. Spain wasn't your motherland. Africa was." She points to Nasser. "And yours." She points to me. "And mine. It's where we come from. We are no different, you and I. Haiti, Puerto Rico, Cuba . . . one people connected to Africa, our motherland."

Haiti? Nasser is from Haiti?

I don't have time to ask because Miguelito is pounding the timbales now. I feel a tingle in my toes. It begs the rest of my body to move, but I fight the urge. I don't want to be here. I tell myself that over and over again. This is not where I belong. But then that beat sinks in so deep, I forget I have knees. By this point, Nasser is flailing his arms and kicking his feet. And it looks like he is kicking away whatever pain he's got locked up inside him too. My back arches, my hands take flight, and it's like I'm flying through the roof.

The rhythm quickens. Lion. Tiger. I am a hunter searching for its next meal. All three of us are moving, releasing, connecting to the rhythm that bleeds from Miguelito's fingers to the skin of the timbales. Nasser clasps his hands into mine, and Señorita Amaro takes a step back. Together we soar. My hands lock in his, like everything and nothing at the same time. He spins me round the globe, and my legs flick straight and back with precision.

When Miguelito taps out a final pam pam, my body goes limp, and I collapse to the floor.

Señorita Amaro claps wildly. "Now that's what I'm talking 'bout!"

But Nasser is scared out of his mind. "Beatriz, are you okay? Say something." His hands graze my sweaty face.

"She's fine, Nasser. I know exactly what she's feeling. When you're a true dancer here in the corazón"—she points to her heart—"you can't escape it. And when you ignore that desire, that passion, even for a day, it can exhaust you once you finally revisit it."

Nasser helps me stand on my two feet. Señorita Amaro walks to the far end of the studio to chat with some of the other staff members. We're putting our regular shoes on when she walks back over to us.

"You two make a nice couple," Señorita Amaro says.

Nasser and I look at each other and smile weakly.

"He's not my—"

Señorita Amaro cuts me off. "Well, I don't mean in that way! I mean the dancing. The chemistry. I saw a fire in both of you tonight. Now Beatriz, you need some more work, though, on your feet and hand positioning, especially if you're auditioning for Fame."

"I know." I chew on my bottom lip.

"Of course, we can get you some proper training. Two weeks isn't enough time, but we can at least straighten out your lines, work on your form in time for the big day."

"But I'm not a student—"

"Yet," Nasser jumps in. "She's registering for classes . . . *today*."

"I am?" I cough the words out, but I'm no idiota.

Nasser purses his lips and gives me a shut-yo-mouth-

and-play-along look. And on the inside, half of me is screaming at the other half. *You knew exactly what you were doing when you packed your stash.*

Okay, I guess I'm enrolling in dance classes. Money ain't the issue. Time is. I don't have time to dance, be in a gang, and take care of Mami.

Señorita Amaro hands me the paperwork with the requirements and fees, which I fill out before pulling out a wad of cash and forking over the tuition like it's nothing.

Both she and Nasser look at me with the same question painted on their faces: *Where the heck did you get all that money?*

"Oh, this?" I point to it and quickly start up my lie. "I work at my mom's bodega and today was payday."

Señorita Amaro puckers her lips, almost like Abuela does, and throws in a stern, "See you next week ... *on time.*"

It's almost nine o'clock when we leave the dance studio. Buses are running less often by then.

"I can drive you home," Nasser says.

It is a little cold. And I'm exhausted as all get-out. Maybe I can take just this one ride. "Okay, cool."

We walk to his car, and I realize it's not a car. It's a yellow taxi. "Umm, Nasser?"

"Yeah, I know. I'll tell you all about it. Hop in."

Nasser revs up the engine and pulls off under a full moon. I'm not sure why, but when he asks me for directions, I give him all the wrong ones that take us the extra-long way. I have him drive me all through Branch Brook Park. The trees are especially pretty in the moonlight. His super-white teeth gleam as he smiles while talking.

"You sure you live in Newark?" Nasser asks. "Because I

don't think it takes forty minutes to get around the city . . . not that I'm complaining or anything."

I just smile at him, and then he turns up the music on the radio. New Edition's "Cool It Now" comes on.

"What's your story, Beatriz?"

"I don't have one," I respond.

"Everyone has a story."

"Okay, so then tell me yours, Mr. Taxi Man."

Nasser Moreau speaks three languages—English, French, and Creole (and is learning Spanish)—and is damn near perfect at math and dancing and reading and basically breathing. But he doesn't actually say that last part. I already knew that from watching him at school.

"My parents left Léogâne in Haiti to come to the States so my sister and I could make something of ourselves. The taxi belongs to my dad, and my mom is a home health aide. They bust their butts so I can have a shot at this thing called the American dream."

"Why didn't you tell me you're Haitian?" I scan his face, not really sure what I'm looking for. Something familiar? But I come up empty.

Out of nowhere a cat bolts across the street, making him swerve the car a bit. It distracts him, I guess, because he never answers my question. So I try another one.

"When did you say you moved to Newark?" I ask.

"I finished out my sophomore year in Miami, and then we came here over the summer."

So he wasn't here in April. Could he still be connected to the Macoutes somehow?

"I didn't realize that introducing myself as Haitian was

a necessity around these parts. Where'd you think I was from? Don't tell me—"

"Jamaica," I blurt. Laughter spills out of his mouth like a rushing waterfall.

"And let me guess the other one: Africa?"

I nod shyly and feel like my intelligence level lowers five points.

"That's like saying Puerto Ricans and Dominicans are the same."

"Two different places, idiota!" I slap Nasser one good time on the shoulder.

"Bingo!"

Ahead the light turns yellow, and he slows the car and stops by the time the red light appears. He turns his face to mine, the rows of street lamps glittering in the darkness of his eyes.

"Is it a problem that I'm Haitian?" he asks.

I try to stop the oversize lump lodging itself in my throat. Try to block out the words I'd heard Abuela say over and over back in Aguadilla: mejora la raza. Translation: Don't even think about getting with someone with dark skin. Life is hard enough when you're dark. So why make it harder? I never understood that backward thinking, especially since Abuela is dark herself.

"No, I don't care where you're from. Far as I'm concerned, you're my Caribbean brother." I hold my hand up for a high five, and Nasser's smile spans the perimeter of his whole head.

I change the convo real quick. "So what you wanna do, like after you leave Barringer?"

"That's the problem. There's so much I want to do. I thought about being a lawyer because I love history—"

"And words," I add.

He starts laughing. "Yeah, that too! I like the arts—dancing, poetry, singing, guitar. And I already told you how I go to town in the kitchen."

"What's your specialty?"

"Oh, I make rice and beans like you wouldn't believe!" He grins and those teeth gleam.

"And what do you sing?"

"Anything."

"Then sing a song for me."

He shakes his head, puts the signal on, and turns onto Broadway. As we draw closer to home, I know my time is almost up. I point to Grafton Ave and ask him to turn there because I know for a fact that if any of the guys are standing in front of the bodega, this scene won't play out too well. I can just picture it now, the Diablos threatening Nasser to stay away from me, even though there's nothing going on between the two of us. I think.

"One day I will sing a song for you, Beatriz Ayita Mendez." The smile in Nasser's eyes glows.

We sit parked in the taxi at the bottom of the hill near the train tracks. Random people knocking on the window asking for rides. He turns every one of them down. The saxophone intro for "Caribbean Queen" rolls in through the radio speakers.

I'm sitting there trying to think of what to say next. *Err, see you at school. Umm, thanks for the ride.*

But all I can do is stare at the halo of moonlight that

frames his face. Julicza and Maricela were right. Damn, this boy is fine. Make that *foyne*.

The memory of us standing at my locker comes flooding back. Him saying I was a vision of pulchritude, which, it turns out, is derived from Latin, meaning "beautiful." *Thank you, Merriam-Webster dictionary!*

But I also remember him floating away and what happened when I opened my locker.

"Hey, I've been meaning to show you something." I pull out the Polaroid picture from my bag.

Nasser turns on the light in the car to get a better look. "Whoa! Who took this photo?" He looks at me, puzzled.

"I think I'm the one who should be asking you that. My friends think maybe it's for the yearbook or something."

He shrugs his shoulders.

"Any idea what it says? You're the one with the international vocabulary."

"Kisa ou vle. It's written in my native language, Haitian Creole. It says 'what you want.'" Nasser's voice rises above Billy Ocean's soulful melody.

"What I want? You mean, like, what do I want?"

"No, this is a declarative, not an interrogative," he explains.

"You're killing me, bro."

"The words are telling you *this is what you want*. And judging by the picture, I'm guessing whoever wrote it is trying to say you want . . . me?" His voice turns soft.

I snatch the picture out of his hand. Why is this note written in Creole, Nasser's language—the same language of the Macoutes?

"But I don't want you." And as soon as I say that, my shoulders cave in. "What I mean to say is, I don't want anything."

Except for my life and my mom and my brother back.

"Whoever took the picture must think I like you or something," I blurt out loud.

Nasser's mouth spreads wider than the Passaic River behind the projects. "Well . . . do you?"

If there was a way to disappear into thin air, now would be the time.

"You're different, Beatriz."

"How so?"

"I can't put my finger on it, but I just know you're not like any girl I've ever met. For starters, you're not one of those wannabe gangsta girls starting drama—"

The ball growing in my throat feels too big, too unmanageable.

"And your face . . ." His voice drifts off.

I pull my hair forward to cover what others say is no longer there, though to me, it remains as clear as the day it was bashed in.

"It's unique. Like a piece of art."

You mean the abstract kind, where colors and lines are thrown together and nothing makes sense?

"I, um, had an accident a few months ago. Before that, my face was different . . . better." And that's all I'm sharing.

"Well, I'm glad I met you with the face you have now." He smiles, and I swear I want to hear him say that a hundred more times.

"So about me and you?" Nasser leans in a little closer to my shoulder.

I peep those eyes, that neck, that chin once more, looking for a reason to run away. There's no tattoos, no battle scars, not a single thing that screams, "I'm in a gang."

I know what's coming next. *Please don't ask me out. Please don't ask me out.* But this little voice inside says, *Please do.*

"Are we going to audition for Fame or what? Those casting directors won't know what hit them."

My belly becomes a pit of relief and disappointment. "Yeah. Audition. Um, sure, but let me talk it over with my mom first."

"Do you think your father will be okay with all of this? I can talk to him if you'd like, so he won't have a cow."

"My dad is back in Puerto Rico."

Saying those words reminds me that he is anywhere but here. And in that moment the memory of his face appears. A reminder of what love and hate looks like, all wrapped in one.

"Oh. Well, now you have to audition and make it in, so he can see you on TV!" Nasser's all hyped up again.

My skin turns hot, and suddenly I'm ready to go. What if I do make it on Fame and Papi sees? Will he come running back, apologize, and make everything right? And as for Nasser, can I even trust this guy? I mean he's nice and all, but everybody's got a hidden side.

"I'll let you know. But right now, I gotta go." I slam the door behind me and pretend I live in the projects, walking farther down the hill, past the train tracks. The last thing I need is for him to see me at the bodega surrounded by a bunch of Diablos. Especially if it turns out that he's a Macoute after all.

Tami Charles is a former teacher who now writes for children and young adults. She has competed in pageants, just like Vanessa. Tami lives in New Jersey with her husband and son. *Like Vanessa* is her debut novel.

www.tamiwrites.com